Miss Not So Fine

Tea DeLuca

Copyright© 2017 M. Bisciaio

All rights reserved.

No part of this book may be reprinted or distributed without the written consent of the author. All characters and events are fictional and any resemblance to anyone living or dead is accidental.

ISBN-10: 1548187135

ISBN-13: 978-1548187132

Melanie

Thank you for all your expertise and skills, but especially for your constant support and encouragement.

You never know when love will find you.

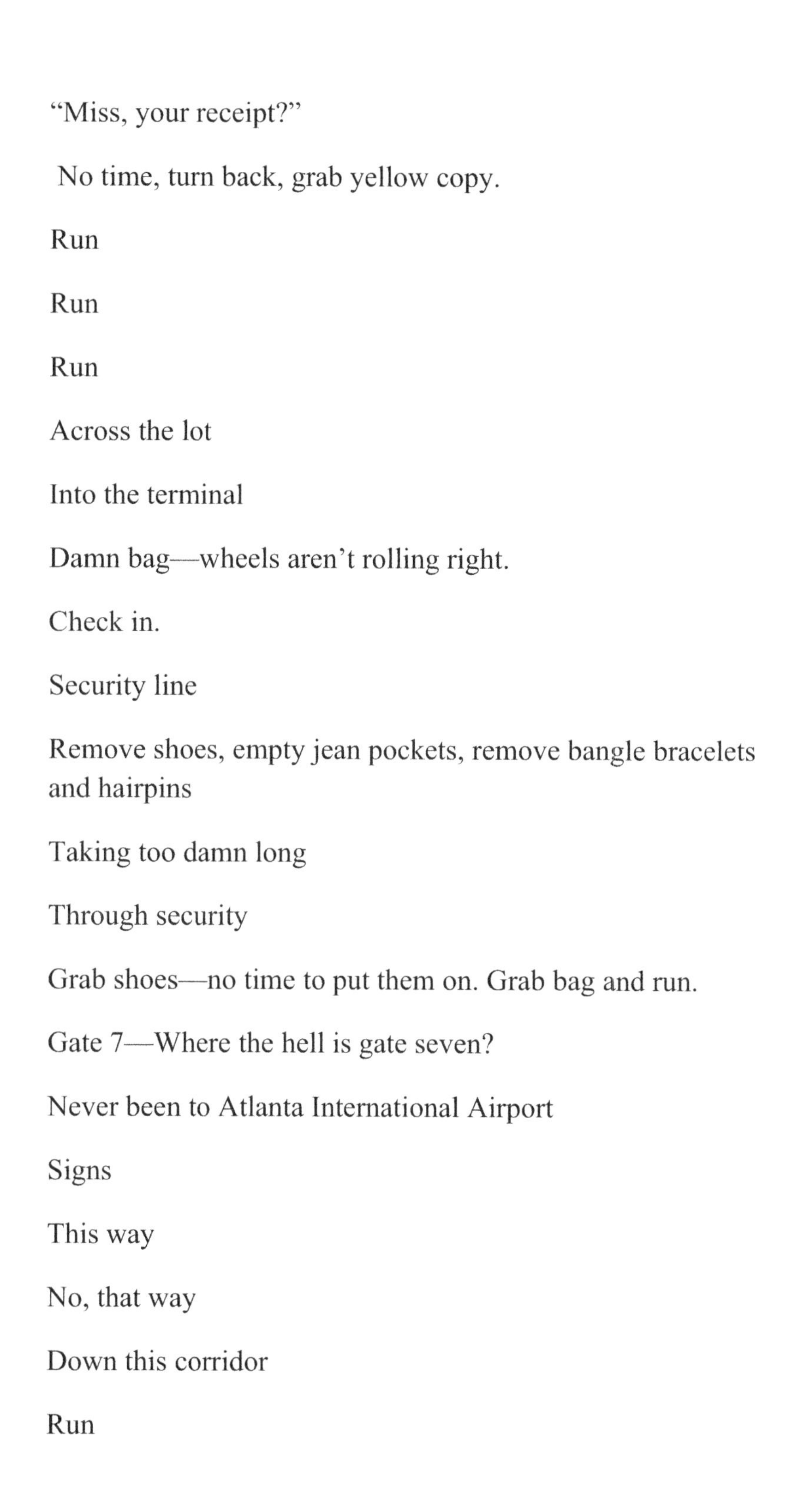

"Miss, your receipt?"

No time, turn back, grab yellow copy.

Run

Run

Run

Across the lot

Into the terminal

Damn bag—wheels aren't rolling right.

Check in.

Security line

Remove shoes, empty jean pockets, remove bangle bracelets and hairpins

Taking too damn long

Through security

Grab shoes—no time to put them on. Grab bag and run.

Gate 7—Where the hell is gate seven?

Never been to Atlanta International Airport

Signs

This way

No, that way

Down this corridor

Run

Coffee—Kill for coffee. No time.

Stop. Shoes. Put them on.

Line to board is short. They are calling final boarding. She exhales slowly. Three hundred miles and five hours in a rental car to catch her plane. She made it.

Chapter One

She lifted her carry-on over her head and stuffed it into the overhead compartment. Two hands and all the strength she had, the lock snapped. She moved into her window seat and did what she always did—yanked down the window shade. The last thing she wanted to see were the clouds to remind her of the ridiculous altitude this plane would climb. She searched her tote for her survival kit—book, headphones, MP3 player, and small sleep pillow, and if these weren't enough to distract her, there was always alcohol. The plane was filling quickly, but the seat beside her remained empty. A little extra space would be nice, but the universe would probably fill it with a doting grandmother with ten babies who would talk about them continuously for the next eight hours. She scanned the aisle and saw there were only a handful of seats left. Oh, God. Following a sweet little old lady was a Greek god. Jet black hair neatly trimmed but long enough in the back to spill over his collar, dark caramel eyes, bronze skin, t-shirt threatening to rip across his solid muscular chest and arms, and she shamelessly stared at his tight ass as he leaned over and hoisted his carry-on into the storage compartment. Grandma kept walking as Mr. Gorgeous settled into his seat beside her. He ignored her as he checked his cell phone and pulled a newspaper from his satchel. It was expensive leather, the kind that left a faint scent in the air; it was manly, soft and supple beneath his very large hands. Mr. Gorgeous caught her staring, and she sensed he was about to acknowledge her. Making conversation would definitely act as an unexpected and pleasant distraction from the pilot's insistent drone over the speakers. She tried to calm her thundering heart as this thoroughly magnificent male creature turned his attention to her.

"Your bag?" He stared with complete disgust. "Your bag is in my way."

"My tote? Oh, my God, I'm sorry." She pounded on it with her fists to flatten it enough to get it under the seat. She looked up at caramel eyes gone cold. Of course, the universe would seat him beside her to torture her. He could never be interested in her.

Chapter Two

Damn, he was tired. He had been away from home too long. He was pleasantly surprised that the seat next to him wasn't occupied by a grandmother with her brag book, but the young woman next to him wasn't much better. She was pretty in a simple sort of way. Long brown hair wrapped and stuck in a messy mass on her head. Soft olive skin missing the tan of a California girl. She wasn't going home; she was leaving home behind. What was extraordinary about her were her crystal blue eyes—a blue he couldn't define. Caribbean blue but less green. Lavender blue but less purple. Azure like the sky, but closer to the ocean with flakes of amber like his favorite bourbon, but she had no backbone. She had winced and complied much too rapidly when he barked at her to move her bag. Not his type—no one was his type for anything serious, but she wasn't his type for his usual fling. He liked strong, independent, confident women in the bedroom and everywhere else. It made moving on easier.

The plane taxied out to the runway, and she forgot Gorgeous sitting beside her. All she heard was the roar of the engines and that horrible rumble that reminded her brain to dredge up the pictures of the numerous plane crashes she had investigated. A well-meaning friend had suggested if she studied plane crashes, she'd be less fearful. Knowledge was power. Bullshit, knowledge had made her this quivering mass of womanhood. She could explain every crash in US history in the last ten years. Most often pilot error was to blame, and less frequently, equipment malfunction or weather conditions. If that was supposed to make her feel better, it didn't.

She squeezed her eyes tightly and gripped the arm rest in a white-knuckled grip. Slowly, the plane taxied and gradually picked up speed. As it lifted and started to climb, big hands pried her hand off the chair and cradled it between his. Gorgeous stroked her palm and flexed her fingers and just held on. "Relax," he said quietly. "You're safe. Flying is safe."

The pilot made some insane comment about flying at 30,000 feet like he was cruising along at 60 mph on the freeway. Safe wasn't even a possibility. The plane leveled off, and he replaced her hand on the seat. No backbone—no guts—probably no damn life experiences, and he concluded again, definitely not his type. Though, her hand had been warm and soft and pleasant to hold. He waved the stewardess over and stole a glance at her. She set down two little bottles of alcohol and two plastic cups. Pushing down her tray, he set one bottle and cup on it.

"Oh, no, thank you, I'm fine."

"You're not fine," he said briskly. "It'll steady your nerves. We still have to land." He unscrewed the top, poured a little, and handed her the drink. "Sip," he ordered. "You don't strike me as much of a drinker. You might drink enough not to care if you are on the plane, but you'll probably have to be carried off."

She turned the little bottle to see the label. "Whiskey, warms my mouth. It's not bad." She tried not to wrinkle her nose. She sipped slowly, hugging the cup in her hands. He turned his attention back to his newspaper, and she took that as her cue to leave him alone. Pulling a stack of papers from her tote, she dug for a pen.

"Manuscript?" he asked, trying to disguise his interest. "You write?"

"I edit," she answered. "I work for a small publishing company in Charleston. We publish a lot of first time authors and a small magazine which features writers and writing tips."

"Minelli Publishing?" he asked.

"You've heard of us?"

Oh, yes, he had heard of them, and he knew Peter Minelli well. He contacted him, at least, once a month requesting an interview for his magazine. He didn't do interviews; far too easy to trample his privacy and misquote his words.

"You know what they say?" He changed the subject. "Editors are frustrated writers."

She reached for her drink and sipped quickly.

"Are you a writer?"

"No, that requires talent. I edit."

He didn't believe her. He recognized that writer's soul that hadn't found a voice and never would unless she attacked life instead of just ambling through it. She'd never hone the skills to be a published writer. The stewardess left a plate of cheese and crackers, and he slid them over to her tray. "Share."

Her eyes met his for a moment. Everything he said sounded like an order. She tried to appear unfazed by his presence, but he was gorgeous, financially secure, and confident, and the universe was definitely laughing at her. She chewed a piece of cheese and turned her attention back to the manuscript. Without looking up, she reached for a cracker at the same time as Gorgeous, and her fingers tangled with his. "Sorry."

He sat there contemplating her more than he wanted, but details tended to bother him, and right now, he had a nagging suspicion. "So, you live and work in Charleston, right?"

She nodded suspiciously. Why was he asking?

"But you're on this flight to San Diego from Atlanta. Were you visiting friends or family or…?" He watched her eyes—darkening, guarded, maybe embarrassed.

"No, I don't know anyone in Atlanta. Never even been there till today." She nervously reshuffled her papers and tried to ignore the look of interest on Gorgeous' face.

"So, why didn't you fly out from Charleston?" he asked. He was enjoying dissecting this woman and her obvious discomfort. He'd wait her out, because he knew she would eventually feel obligated to answer.

She finally exhaled. "It isn't a mystery. It's just…Charleston doesn't fly direct to California." She swallowed hard at the amusement in his eyes. "Some international airport—no international flights and no non-stop flights west."

"Let me get this straight. You drove about three hundred miles to avoid ascending and descending more than once on a plane?"

That feeling of dread slithered up her spine. It was exactly the reaction Pete had when she told him she wouldn't fly if it wasn't without stops. He had booked her on a flight out of Atlanta and informed her that it was her problem how she got there. "It wasn't a big deal." She stole a glance at him.

"You're a coward," he said softly.

And then the bottom fell out of the plane. It dropped like a marionette with its strings cut. The table trays flew up, but she moved quickly enough to catch her half-filled drink before it sailed in the air. The plane pitched tossing her sideways, and the drink flew out of her hands. A muffled cry escaped her, but a steady hand caught her shoulder. She leaped for him, and if the arm rest hadn't been between them, she would have crawled into his lap. She gripped two fists of his shirt and buried her face in his chest, and then she...inhaled deeply. Damn, he smelled so good. If she was going to die, at least, the universe gave her a slice of heaven as a preview. God, he was rock hard and muscular, warm, and...just breathe. She felt his hands making small circles in the center of her back. The pilot regained control, and the plane leveled off. She was still going to die only now it would be from complete embarrassment. Her cheeks burned as she pushed back to look at him. "What was that?" she whispered, a breath away from full inviting lips. He tipped her chin to meet his eyes.

"Pilot just explained. Maybe you missed it."

She nodded slowly, releasing her grip on his shirt. She ran her palms over the fabric to smooth out the wrinkles and realized her drink had caught him squarely in the face. "Oh, God," she cried, looking for a napkin. "I am so sorry." She knelt on the seat, wiping haphazardly at his cheek with some of the napkin and more of her palm. "You are probably so sorry you sat next to me. I tried to save it from spilling." Her brain gave up as she wiped across his lips, and appropriate was lost on her. In an effort to catch the bead of whiskey that was sliding down his cheek, she swiped at it with her tongue. Oh, God, what was happening to her?

The poor man grabbed her hand. "Stop! I'm fine."

She carefully eased back in her seat.

"Do you want me to tell you what just happened?" he asked.

Was he going to try and explain her errant tongue? She needed to deflect the conversation. "Turbulence?"

"Yes, change in wind direction or speed like hitting a pot hole on the highway." He wiped his hand over his brow.

"You don't drop out of the sky on the road," she said in her defense. She was feeling exceptionally stupid, and his eyes seemed to agree.

"We only dropped a few hundred feet—not much at 30,000 feet." The caramel eyes melted a bit and softened.

"I'm sorry again," she whispered, till she noticed her manuscript was scattered all around her. "Damn." By the time, she had recollected the papers, she wanted to sky dive out of the plane. Before she could embarrass herself further, she switched to headphones and closed her eyes. God, the universe was still laughing only hysterically—as she could still smell his scent, and she had licked his face. She turned away from him, hoping she could sleep. She didn't notice Mr. Gorgeous staring at her.

He should be angry, but he wasn't. He should be concerned for his safety; she was crazy, but he wasn't. Maybe she was prettier than he originally thought. He'd very much like to pull the rest of the pins from her hair and watch it cascade over her shoulders. He wouldn't have minded too much if she had cleared the arm rest and landed in his lap. At least, he got a better look at her. Nice rack, perky nipples, sleek contour where her back met her ass, studs on her jeans to draw the eye, and she smelled of vanilla, not surprising, warm and homey and so damn good. She had clung to him like a life preserver. He couldn't even think about her soft wet tongue on his cheek. Maybe she had a backbone. No, she wasn't fooling him. Miss not so fine was horrified at her behavior and was hiding inside her headphones, hoping he'd go away. He closed his eyes, a grin threatening to escape his lips. He drifted a little and slept till the pilot ordered seat belts on for landing. He felt her tense up before he looked over. She had her hands pressed together in her lap to prevent any further leaping, and she chewed fervently on her lower lip. It looked damn tasty.

"This is ridiculous," he finally said with annoyance. "Why are you even on this flight?"

"Work."

Pete had sent her. The tears were on stand-by as she braced herself in her seat. He reached over and snatched up the shade.

"No!"

"Yes! We are coming down. Live a little. Embrace your fear. You might get passed it."

She glared at him then turned toward the window. Holding her shoulders as the plane slowly descended, he ordered, "Open your eyes, damn it, and breathe."

She watched as things came into focus—till she could see the city, houses, street signs, and the airport. His breath was warm against her ear as he whispered, "The pilot is bringing this massive bird down with the gentleness of a mother with her child." She sighed as the plane touched and leaned back against him.

As the plane taxied back, she scrambled to refill her tote. She wanted off the plane, but she was reluctant to say good-bye to Mr. Gorgeous, pain in the ass. He waited till most of the passengers fought through the aisle, grabbing their bags. Then he pulled down his own black bag with ease. "Purple bag yours?" he asked with amusement.

"Yes." Why was she embarrassed as he pulled it down and set it on his seat? She rose to follow, but he didn't move and held her gaze. He pressed his hand gently against her cheek and rubbed the pad of his thumb over her lower lip. She didn't move—might have even stopped breathing, but the flexes in her eyes darkened against the blue and held his. He stroked the softness and wondered how she'd taste. Then he moved closer and braced her shoulders.

"Miss not so fine," he said softly. "Get that stick out of your ass, and go experience life. Get a backbone." He straightened up and walked away down the aisle.

♥♥

Chapter Three

He kept a steady pace and didn't look back as he moved through the airport to the cabby stands. The hotel was too nice; Jenny always got him the best, spending extravagantly with his money, but he loved Jenny. She had been his agent from the very beginning when no one else would read his books or take a chance on him. And Jenny would not like Miss not so fine. Why the hell hadn't he asked her name? He knew the answer. Something even that simple could be misconstrued as interest, and Jenny would frown on him showing interest in someone as vulnerable and inexperienced as that woman on the plane. She knew about Victoria and had no problem with her. Vic was sophisticated, didn't care about his career, and was his Chicago hook up. They had been friends with benefits for years; he cared about her, but it hadn't gone beyond that. Jenny appreciated Vic wouldn't get in the way, wouldn't get upset especially in public, and behaved. But she had warned him many times to stay away from the newbies and the wannabees as she called them. The women, in particular, that wanted to publish their first book or were self-publishing and were sure they were now in his league. They tended to be demanding and latched on for dear life. He reminded himself he didn't do relationships, and the mess on the plane clearly needed more help than he could give her. You couldn't give someone a backbone.

Restless, he left his hotel room and wandered down main street to a small Italian restaurant. The smells of warm bread and pasta reminded him of his mother's kitchen where he learned the art of cooking with love. Pulled in, he quickly was seated and ordered a bottle of his favorite red wine. A bottle, because it was going to be a lonely night. The dimly lit restaurant had seating in tables for two—for lovers celebrating an anniversary, an engagement, a moment just between them. As he glanced over the menu, the prices were steep, hence, the absence of families, but off to one side was a smaller dining room just for pizza. Rather smart from a business point of view. Pizza and children, in and out, and keep the price down, while lovers spent leisurely time over a fine wine and paid for it. The room made him sad, though he wasn't sure why. He liked his life. At 35 he had two books currently on the best sellers list in New York, and with 18 books to his credit, he was financially sound. He traveled the country doing book signings and giving seminars on writing techniques and how to sell a book. He was even going to be a guest on a talk show in a couple of weeks, promoting his latest book. So, what the hell was bothering him? The waitress refilled his glass, settled his eggplant parmesan in front of him, and ran her hand lightly over his. It certainly wasn't about women. In addition to Victoria, women were always throwing themselves at him. Strong, vivacious, confident women looking for a push up the ladder of success or others that hoped to rob him of his single status. He'd love them and leave them without a second thought. They knew it was a risk, but he didn't make bullshit promises. So, he earned his reputation of sleeping with every woman he met except one. Miss not so fine's amazing blue eyes caught him by surprise. He wasn't thinking of her, or was he? His waitress brought him a very large piece of Tiramisu that he hadn't ordered, but that wasn't unusual, either. He'd have her number before he left, and he wouldn't have to ask for it. Across the room at a table in the back, a man toasted the beautiful woman he was with, and then kissed those wine soaked lips in a hot deep kiss. His insides hurt. He thought about a frightened woman clinging to his shirt and breathing him in. Oh, yes, he noticed, and so did his libido. It was the sexiest thing he had ever seen and so was she. Surprised she was still in his thoughts, he finished the last of his wine and paid his check.

Outside he crossed the street and ducked into a bookstore. He loved books, always had. Probably the only boy in the seventh grade who'd rather read a book than play baseball. That's when he knew he wanted to write—wanted his books on display for people to buy.

By the time he returned to his hotel, the city was draped in darkness, and he had a long day ahead of him tomorrow. He was the key speaker presenting three seminars at the local university, and he needed some sleep. Instead, he sat on his balcony and wondered why he was still thinking about the woman on the plane.

♥♥

Chapter Four

Samantha sat down at the last empty table in the university dining room and looked at the schedule of workshops. She checked off two on editing that she was obligated to attend since Pete had paid for her trip, but she was looking forward to several others.

"Hi, can I sit here? There aren't any more tables."

He was cute, probably younger, maybe a student, but had a genuine infectious smile. "Samantha," she said, extending her hand. "Are you here for the workshops?"

"Absolutely," Jeff grinned, diving into his breakfast, "doesn't everyone want to be a writer?"

"Maybe, which are you interested in?" she asked.

"Workshop on point of view, on writing fantasy and sci-fi, and the one I'm looking forward to the most is Steven Corso's presentation. Damn, his murder mysteries are amazing. I've read all of his books, and I saw a seminar he gave last year in Florida."

"I'm going to that one, too. I love his books; once I start one, I can't put it down. He has a workshop starting in ten minutes." She started to rise.

"Don't waste your time. They closed that one an hour ago. If you want to get in, you have to get there early and wait till the auditorium opens. Once it's full, they lock the doors."

"Maybe I should go to one of these other presentations first." She glanced through the list again.

"Want some unsolicited advice? By the time you go to another one, and come all the way back, you will have missed your window of opportunity."

"I won't get in?"

"Probably not."

"I'm going to be here a couple of days. I guess if I only see Mr. Corso today, that's enough. I can see some of the others later."

Jeff laughed. "Or you might want to sit in his others as well. He doesn't use notes or anything. He just talks, and people ask questions, and he talks some more. The words just…" He stopped. "He's pretty impressive."

She finished her coffee and invited Jeff to sit with her. It felt a little strange, but it wasn't a date. He was funny and lived here and, yes, he was a student, and, at twenty-nine, she was too old for him. By the time the auditorium emptied, a huge crowd milled outside waiting to get in for the next presentation that wouldn't even begin for another hour. Usually, she sat hidden in the back, but Jeff was not having it. He grabbed her arm as the auditorium quickly filled and found two seats in the middle of the third row just to the left of the podium and table. After his presentation, Mr. Corso would sell and sign his newest book. She had read it in the brochure.

"This is really close," she whispered to Jeff.

"Isn't it great?" he grinned.

Sometimes presenters elicited audience participation. She would die if this amazing author looked at her much less expected her to answer a question intelligently. She shifted in her seat and pulled out her notebook and pen. She was certain she'd want to write down his every word. When the back door opened, and Mr. Gorgeous came out, Samantha's brain struggled to make sense of it. He was Steven—Steven Corso, and she had inhaled him. Oh, my God. She slumped down in her seat. He couldn't possibly see anyone in this mass of people. He looked around briefly and took a copy of his new book off the table. He held it against him as he gazed into the eager faces of the people who had come to worship him.

"Do I have aspiring authors in the audience?" he asked. "Please don't be shy. Raise your hands."

She couldn't. He was doing it to her again. She was mesmerized by him in a well-made suit, probably Italian, that hugged his body like it was made for him, probably was.

"Do you wonder," he continued, "if you should quit your job and just write? Do you think you might have talent, but you're not sure, because no one has ever told you, you have talent? Do you spend time around your work schedule, around school, around family obligations, around your time with your friends writing? Do you dabble in writing?" The auditorium was eerie quiet. "You can stop wondering," he said directly. "You are not a writer. Don't quit your day job."

A hand went up immediately, and he took it head on. "But," the young man said, "you have to make a living—pay the bills."

"So, do it," Steven said with a note of finality, "but writing should never be second. If you have to ask what you should do, you aren't a writer. If you need validation from others on the quality of your books, you aren't a writer."

Another hand shot up. Pretty, college girl, maybe a little older. "When you sell your books, aren't you being validated?"

He smiled the most seductive smile as he glanced over his audience. "I would write even if my books didn't sell. I'm glad they do, but I write because the voice inside me won't still. I write, because everywhere I go and everything I see has potential to be my next story. If I go to the beach, I am thinking of a murder on the beach. If I visit my favorite bookstore, I am writing the story of a murder in a bookstore, the murder of a librarian, the librarian who turns out to be a murderer, or the key to solving a murder is found in a bookstore. I have written hundreds of books here." He pressed his finger to his temple. "And only sold 18. I flew in for this conference from Atlanta where I had a book signing. There were lots of potential characters for my next book on that plane. For example." He moved to the left of the podium and walked slowly and deliberately scanning the audience. She slid deeper into her seat and willed herself to invisibility, and, yet, she couldn't take her eyes off him. "A beautiful woman, beautiful blue eyes, soft brown hair, lips that a man would walk over coals for. This jewel was an emotional wreck, but, as a result, she was funny, entertaining, and the sexiest damn thing I've ever met." The audience laughed and cheered. "There is a story and inspiration everywhere."

He couldn't possibly know she was here. He couldn't possibly have found her among all these people.

"The question I get most is how do I get a good idea for a story? Where do ideas come from?" Steven moved back across the auditorium and took several steps up into the crowd. "Where do ideas come from?" The auditorium grew quiet again. Who in their right mind would tell Steven Corso where to get an idea? “No one knows where ideas come from?”

Her heart was pounding; she felt like she did when she was twelve with the right answer, and she could be the smart one right now in front of all these people. He had growled the answer at her as he left her on the plane yesterday. But what if she was wrong? She’d be so damn embarrassed. She didn’t notice him walk back; didn’t notice the book sail from his hand till it landed on her lap. Then her eyes met his. “Well, Miss not so fine, where do ideas come from?”

She swallowed the nausea that threatened to bring up the contents of her stomach. Her face turned bright red as she cleared her throat. “Ideas come from life experiences.”

“Louder,” he ordered.

Her face grew redder, and she gripped his book tighter. Damn, she had thought all night about what he had said. “Ideas come from life experiences,” she said steadily. “A writer writes about what he knows.”

He stared at her long and hard with that scientist studying a specimen under a microscope look. “Very good,” he said softly. “Ideas come from life experiences. If you have no ideas, go experience life. Go to the beach, jump out of an airplane, take a cruise in Alaska, make love to a woman till she screams your name and won’t let you go.”

Her heart stopped beating again. The universe took this specific moment to kill her, because the celebrated author, Steven Corso, had acknowledged her before this auditorium of people. This had to be heaven.

Jeff leaned in. “He tosses one book every session; he’ll sign it for you at the end.”

But she wasn’t listening to Jeff. Steven had her wrapped around his spirit, his joy in his art, and his overwhelming masculinity—and it was overwhelming and powerful. He continued, “You can’t write what you haven’t experienced.”

A voice called out without raising a hand, and Steven turned to the beautiful woman rising to her feet. She was older, probably closer to his age, confident, defiant, and obviously more interested in the man than his art. "People write sci-fi and fantasy. If I wanted to write a story about living on the moon, there would be little chance I could experience it. Yet, many people write wonderful books and have made millions without the personal experience. Can you explain that, Mr. Corso?"

Samantha saw Steven register every inch of the sultry blond, and he wasn't the least bit subtle. His penetrating stare screamed sleep with me, probably his next conquest. If only a man looked at her that way.

"Sci-fi, fantasy, vampires, shifters are born of a writer's imagination. A good writer of these genres has to convince the reader the world he's created is real. You still need life experiences to play off of to create something different yet, something that the reader is familiar with and can identify with. In any kind of writing the story must be carefully constructed to draw in the reader, and your language supports what you create. Take someone skydiving. You can write how they step to the edge of the open door, how they are frightened as they take the step out, how they fall to earth quickly till the chute opens. But…" His smile broadened, and his voice deepened. "If you had gone skydiving, you'd know the anxiety as the plane climbs to some crazy elevation, the rush and terror as you stare out at the clouds, the wind trying to steal the very breath you can't catch, the moment you step out into nothing, the fall—fast, twirling, catching colors, then the fumbling for the rip cord, and you pull. The chute yanks you back up into the clouds. You expect it, but it still shocks you, and finally you glide as the chute brings you down to earth." The auditorium was still. "How do you want to write?" He stared long and hard at the blond.

Jeff raised his hand to ask a question, and Samantha cringed. He was coming her way again.

"Last question. Make it a good one, young man."

"Love," Jeff said calmly like he had rehearsed his question. "Your characters seem to find love; your details hint at an attraction or maybe just an interest, but it doesn't go anywhere. I know you don't write romance novels, but have you ever considered giving your readers more?"

The question seemed to hit a nerve, and Samantha straightened up in her seat. He looked uncomfortable. "If you've been listening to anything I've said today, you should be able to answer that question. Roger, two books ago obviously has an interest in his partner, Julie, but it is secondary to the story. I don't write love stories, because ..." He moved to the table and sat. "I've never been in love." An audible hum moved quickly through the auditorium. His shoulders suddenly relaxed, and he waited for quiet. "I know my reputation, and I have known some incredible woman—beautiful, charming, independent, giving, and sexy. I like women, in general; God created exquisite creatures, but I've never been 'in love,' so I can't do it justice in my books."

He moved behind his table and poised his pen ready to sign. He was signaling the session was over, and many people moved to buy his new book from the woman who had been waiting patiently for this moment. As the line formed, Jeff left to get his book and signature, but Samantha remained rooted in her seat. Mr. Gorgeous, confident, money, abrupt, considerate at times, a legend in the publishing world, a man of contradictions, and vulnerable. She waited for the line to disappear and finally waited in front of the podium as the last person took his book. Then he stared with an unapologetic sneer. "Learn anything, Miss not so fine?" He reached for her book, but she took a step back.

"How did you know I was here?"

He shrugged. "Knew when I stepped out the door."

"And how did you find me amid all these people?"

He let out his breath impatiently. "Not a big secret. I just looked for a woman slouched down in her seat hiding from life."

She shoved her book at him. "I do bring out the best in you, don't I?"

He signed slowly then slammed the book shut, and her startled look reinforced his resolve to steer clear of her. First impression—solid. Definitely not his type.

"Thanks for the book," she said over her shoulder, heading for the stairs.

"Wait. I'm entitled to your name," Steven said, expecting compliance.

"Entitled?" Meeting his eyes, her back straightened.

"Yes, entitled. You did grab me on the plane with both hands and buried your head in my defenseless shoulder. That does seem a bit intimate, doesn't it?"

She climbed higher to the back of the auditorium and finally shrugged. "Samantha Westerly. Everyone calls me Sam." And she was gone.

♥♥

Chapter Five

Steven looked up to an empty auditorium as he signed the last book after his last presentation. He tried to appear busy as Jenny made her way to him. He knew she had something on her mind. She had been staring at him through the entire last session.

"You seem a little out of sorts," she observed, "and if you like, I can pinpoint for you exactly when it started."

"I don't know what you are talking about," he said evasively. "I'm just tired. I'm thinking of getting away to the cabin for a few days."

She shook her head. "You have a few more signings scheduled promoting the new book and the talk show after that."

"I know, maybe later."

"I know you well, Steven, what's wrong?"

"Nothing—it went well today, didn't it?"

"It did. Who was the woman you called out in the second session? She seemed terrified of you."

He laughed softly. "No one. Just a woman I met on the plane from Atlanta."

"I see. And your interest in her?" She looked at him disapprovingly. Nothing escaped Jenny's attention or her nose for trouble.

"No interest. She's exactly the kind of woman I avoid. Definitely not my type."

She nodded. "I have a thought. Maybe Victoria could help. You're going to be here a few days. Why don't you invite her here? I'm sure she'd come, and it would do wonders for your spirit."

She probably would come, but whether it would help him Steven had his doubts. "No, when I leave here, next stop is Chicago. I'll catch up to her there. I can use the time on my own."

She kissed his cheek at the door before leaving him and paused thoughtfully. “I’ll get you some down time in a few weeks.”

“Thanks, Jen. That’ll work.”

Steven moved slowly bothered by the note he had written in Samantha’s book. What had possessed him to goad her—push her, and why was he worried? She’d never respond, and he’d never see her again. Maybe Jenny was right. Maybe he’d call Victoria tonight and see if she could meet him here. The crowd thickened as he reached the door. It was raining hard, and lightening flashed across the sky. Damn. He had spent a lot of time in New York and knew how to hail a cab. These people would be here all day. The key was to forget about being polite and be aggressive. He pushed his way through the crowd into the pouring rain. Stepping off the curb, he set his sights straight down the street to a parked yellow cab. Raising an authoritative hand, the cab driver lunged in his direction and stopped. He didn’t see her till her hand landed on his on the door handle of the cab. “Mine,” he growled, stepping toward her. She had the same ‘deer in the headlights’ look from the airplane except the cold rain soaking her t-shirt had her uncontrollably shivering. “Get out of the rain, and take the next one.”

She wasn’t looking at him but at their hands still together over the handle of the cab. She suddenly stepped back almost apologetically. “Don’t you dare.” He grabbed her wrist and fought for control. “Are you really going to let me just take it from you?”

“Your hand was there first,” she stuttered. “I didn’t see you with the rain.”

“Damn it.” He yanked on the door, shoved her inside, and followed her in. He gave the driver his hotel and told him he could drop her off after.

“I’m on the way,” she interrupted and gave the cab driver the address.

He was livid—spineless. How could she go through life a passive, pathetic…? She wiggled uncomfortably in her seat. “What’s wrong?” he asked. Her clothes were soaked through, her shirt clinging to her wet skin.

"I just wanted to protect it from the rain." The color rose in her cheeks as she pulled up her shirt and removed his book from the waistband of her jeans.

His jaw dropped. He coughed and tried to ignore the lacy pink bra and the soft wet skin. Over and over his brain repeated—not your type, not now, not ever. "Did you read what I signed in your book?"

"Not yet." Water dripped from her thick hair, and she quickly pulled the pins, and let it fall across her shoulders.

Steven knew better. He wasn't sure why he did it, but he slid across the seat and moved her against his chest. She didn't say anything, but her eyes registered her surprise and waited for an explanation. "You looked cold, and we're both wet. All I can offer you is body heat."

The cab driver turned off the main highway into a residential neighborhood. It suddenly occurred to Steven that she wasn't staying in a hotel. The houses were small and all relatively the same. Quaint, adequate, with a touch of brick, but not his taste. When the cab pulled to the curb, she fumbled with her wallet.

"Forget it. I'll take care of it," he said, pushing her hand aside.

"No, I've got it," she insisted, throwing the money at the cab driver. "Thanks for sharing." She was out of the cab before he could respond.

He watched her run for the door and fumble with her keys till the door flew open and a handsome young man filled the doorway. He wrapped his arms tightly around her and kissed the top of her head. She looked up at him adoringly and moved in as he closed the door behind her.

Steven felt an uncomfortable sensation in his chest. Probably just hunger, but he rubbed at the ache in his chest that physically hurt. He was even more sorry he had written his challenge in her book, but he was sure she'd laugh and dismiss him. It didn't matter, because he'd never see her again.

♥♥

Chapter Six

Samantha wrapped a soft fluffy towel around her as she got out of the shower. She was still chilled from the rain, but the shower and hot tea had worked wonders. Steven's caramel eyes invaded her thoughts. The man was a royal pain in the ass. Rude, abrupt, and even condescending, but sometimes he was sweet. She laughed, knowing how much he would hate her for even thinking that. What was wrong with him? How did he find her in that auditorium? When he called on her, did he expect her to know the answer? And when he told the audience about the woman on the plane, was he really describing her as a hot mess? Why didn't that offend her? Probably because she hadn't behaved like an intelligent, sophisticated, enticing woman like the women he knew intimately. Maybe he was with that stupid blond from the workshop this afternoon. And why did that make her stomach roll and her fists clench? God, if he looked at her like he looked at the blond with heat and lust, she'd melt at his feet. Odds were she'd never see him again. Tomorrow, after the workshops, she'd be on a late flight back home. She groaned out loud. Back on that wretched airplane and heading as far from San Diego as possible. She wrapped herself in her robe and curled up in bed with his damn book. This was as close as she would ever be to him again. Her mind wandered. 'Never been in love.' Then her eyes fell on his note, and she gasped.

Miss Not So Fine,

I am issuing a challenge to broaden your life experiences. Let me know, which one you will try.

A. Sky diving
B. Scuba diving
C. Have dinner with me

Steven

Her fingers traced the words as she tried to unravel their hidden meaning. Did he really think she was crazy enough to jump out of a plane? Or did he really think the allure of the ocean bottom would drive her to him? Both frightening and unrealistic goals, but the most frightening of her choices was the third. How she would love to sit across from him and have an intimate dinner for two. Soft music, a rich wine, heavenly smells, and his eyes lustfully glued to her. She shuddered as she thought of Steven Corso in all his overwhelming and overbearing maleness wanting her and only her. God, she needed to wake up from this dream. He was offering her an experience, and she couldn't take any of them. She needed to explain before he assumed she was the coward he truly believed her to be. It was late, but maybe he was done with the blond. He said to call, and if it went to voice mail, all the better. She would explain briefly and be done. She dialed carefully and held her breath.

Steven saw the number, didn't recognize it, and didn't answer. He poured another bourbon and settled in a comfortable recliner. He hadn't expected a guy when he dropped off Miss not so fine. Maybe he had underestimated her. He had just assumed, but why did it even matter? He registered a voice mail and listened till he recognized her voice. If she was going to make excuses, she'd have to make them to him. He returned her call and waited impatiently till she answered the phone.

"I knew you wouldn't take my challenge."

"I knew you would think that," she countered, "but it's not like that. Didn't you listen to my message?"

"You're a coward, sweetheart. Tell me now if you can manage a little courage," he sneered.

God, he could be such an ass. "Choice number one is too ridiculous to explain," she said defiantly. "You know how much I hate being in a plane so you want me to step out of one into nothingness?"

"You can't imagine the rush."

"You've done it—jumped out of a plane?"

"Many times."

"Of course, many times. Show off."

He laughed despite wanting to smack her. "If you were with me, you would jump."

"You are talking to the woman who molested you when we hit a little turbulence. I wouldn't jump."

"It's all about trust. Give me two months, and I'll have you jumping out of planes and loving it."

"No!"

"All right, what's wrong with choice number two? You are safely back on earth," he said sarcastically.

"I have a major problem with scuba diving."

"It's amazing," he declared with exasperation. "I can take you to the clearest water so you can see sea life that you can't see on the surface. You would love it."

"I'm sure I would. I've always wanted to swim with the dolphins."

"That was great, too."

"You've done that, too?"

"Honey, each thing is a life experience. I like being open to new things, and if you weren't so damn closed minded, you might …"

"It's not that."

"Then what the hell is it?"

She cringed. She didn't want to tell him. He'd never understand. "You'll laugh."

"Try me."

God, he sounded warm and beautiful, and the words finally slipped out of her mouth. "I don't know how to swim."

He laughed so hard, he dropped the phone.

"Damn it, I knew you'd laugh."

"You live in Charleston, for God's sake. How can you not know how to swim?"

"I wasn't born in Charleston. I'm originally from Detroit."

Quiet followed till he broke the silence. "My geography skills might be a bit rusty, but I believe there is water in Michigan—lots of lakes, five of them great."

"Shut up, I was traumatized as a child."

"How?"

"Choice number three," she continued, ignoring his question, "dinner."

"Oh, this should be good. What's your excuse? Allergic to food? Nothing to wear? Or do I upset your stomach so much that you couldn't possibly eat?"

"You are impossible; a real ass sometimes."

He laughed again. Maybe he could provoke her into standing up for herself. "Or is there something I'm missing? Is there a man in your life, Miss not so fine? A boyfriend, maybe right here in San Diego?"

What the hell was he talking about? "No boyfriend, Steven, here or anywhere else. Why would you think that?"

"Who was the man at the house when I dropped you off earlier? You know, the one that hugged and kissed you."

"Ray?" she asked. "Ray is not my boyfriend, and what kiss? Did he kiss me?"

"On your head," he growled impatiently. "Rather benign and, I guess, intimate."

"Do you kiss your lady lovers on the head?" she shot back angrily. "How about the blond from the workshop this afternoon? Kiss the top of her head before you screwed her?"

He gritted his teeth. She did have a spark and some fire. "No, not usually, but, at least, when I kiss a woman, she knows she's been kissed." He cleared his throat. "So, if he isn't your boyfriend, who is he?"

"My brother," she said quietly. "He lives out here, and we don't see much of each other."

"I see." He thought he should probably apologize, but it wasn't his strong suit; he wasn't sure how to do it. "So, why don't you want to have dinner with me?"

"I'd love to have dinner with you, but Pete has me booked on a flight home tomorrow. By the time you finish your workshop, I'll be at the airport."

The silence lingered. "Do you have a little black dress? That all occasion dress women wear?"

"What? Yes, my just-in-case-I-have-to-go-somewhere dress. Why?"

"Heels?"

"To go with the dress? Of course."

"I'll let you know where dinner is tomorrow. Keep your phone handy for my call."

"Steven, what are you going to do? I've got to be on that flight, or Pete is going to kill me."

"Wait for my call," he repeated insistently.

"Do you always get what you want?"

"What do you think?"

He seemed so damn confident; she decided to play along. "Hair up or down?"

He didn't miss a beat. "Definitely down."

"If I don't hear from you, I'll go to the airport. I've enjoyed meeting you and…"

"Don't say good-bye," he interrupted. "Wait for my call."

"All right, Steven. Good-night."

"And, Samantha."

Her breath caught. He had never called her by name.

"The woman from the workshop? I wasn't interested. She left her number on the table, and I threw it away. That happens all the time. Good-night."

♥♥

Chapter Seven

By lunch Samantha knew she was headed home. She hadn't heard from Steven, and she needed to collect her bags and start for the airport. She had to admit she was disappointed. She was hoping for dinner with the incredible man, but…She looked at her phone, disappointment grew, and answered her boss.

"I hope you're enjoying sunny California," came Pete's unusually cheerful greeting.

"Between rain showers."

"You aren't going to believe this, Sam." His voice got higher and more excited. "You are never in a million years going to guess who called me."

She didn't care. "You're right; I can't. Who?"

"I couldn't believe it was him calling me for a change."

"Who, Pete?"

"Corso—Steven Corso. Can you believe it?" He was downright giddy.

"What did he want?" she asked casually.

"I have called him every month for almost a year asking if he would do an interview for the featured writers section of our magazine, and every month he flatly refuses. Then out of the blue he called me and asked if I was still interested in interviewing him. Is he kidding? Do you know what a boost this will be for us?"

Samantha smiled. "I'm sure you'll sell a lot more magazines."

"That's why I am calling you. Everything sort of depends on you. His first condition was that you were to do the interview. No offense, but I tried to tell him I had more experienced writers, but he said he met you at one of his seminars, and he was impressed. That he'd only give the interview to you."

Her smile widened. "He said that? He has more faith in me than you."

"His second condition was he has the time now. He's spending the next few days in San Diego, and he wants to do the interview with you this week. So, of course, I changed your ticket. You're staying till Sunday. I'll text you the new flight information."

"You're letting me stay here almost a week?"

"This is important, honey, and you saved me a bundle staying with your brother. He had one more condition."

"What else did he want?" Her face hurt with the intensity of the grin that stretched from ear to ear.

"He wants me to give you a raise. Don't get your hopes up now. I told him it would depend on how well you did the interview, but come home without it, and I'll fire you. That you can be sure of." He laughed, but Samantha was sure he meant it. "Make sure you get the dirt—the good stuff. I'll call you in a couple of days."

She looked at the time and knew Steven's next session hadn't started yet. She texted quickly; her fingers barely skimming the keys. **Just heard from Pete. What time is dinner?**

He came back a split second later. **Sending a car for you at 6:30. Don't keep the driver waiting. No lipstick especially that clear greasy stuff.**

She laughed out loud, and several students turned in her direction. **It's called gloss. Anything else you want?**

She could see his smile as she waited for his response. **Warm bread, a good bottle of wine, and you.**

She planned on one more session; one that Pete recommended. Instead, she found herself outside the auditorium alone except for one gritty security guard. "Am I too late? I wanted to see Mr. Corso before I head back to Charleston." She batted her eyes, hoping she didn't look as foolish as she felt.

"It's filled," he said, barely looking at her.

"One seat? There must be one seat. I don't take up much room." She smiled comfortably. At least, she could do that right. "Please. Maybe I could stand in the back?"

"Mr. Corso doesn't allow unseated guests." His gaze made her uncomfortable like he was studying her, trying to reach a decision. "But there is a folding chair in the back. It's my seat, but I wasn't planning on using it. I'll get you in."

He barely opened the door, but she squeezed in, and he pointed to the end. The lights flickered just as she sat down. And when he came out, he stole her breath. He dressed down for the last session—more casual, more California. Light khaki slacks and a blue button down shirt with the sleeves rolled up to the elbow. She could never look at him again without thinking of the risky and exciting things he did. He was talking and walking, and too late Samantha realized he was climbing the stairs to the back of the auditorium. There was no escape. She slid lower in her chair and prayed for a huge sinkhole to swallow her up.

"Ladies and gentlemen, excuse me for just a minute as an error has been made." Smoothly, he reached the top and headed in her direction. The audience had turned and followed his every movement. "I insist when my public comes to see me that they are seated comfortably. That is why I don't have standing room or wooden chairs." He stopped in front of her and gave her a wicked smile. She couldn't look at him and continued to stare at her hands in her lap. Reaching for her hand, he pulled her to her feet.

"Steven, no," she whispered as heat and color did a dance on her face.

But he wasn't listening. Holding firmly to her hand, she trailed behind him as he led her back to the main floor. She was going to kill him.

"What is your name, honey?" he asked thoroughly pleased with himself.

"Samantha," she whispered, deciding she'd poison him at dinner.

"Where shall we find a seat for Samantha?" he asked, looking around the auditorium.

Samantha could see people shuffling around to free a seat to accommodate Steven and his hostage.

"I know," he said like he had just thought of the idea. "You will sit here." He pulled her to his chair behind the table that he used for book signings. It was a nice desk chair, but damn it, it faced the audience. She was far too embarrassed, at this point, to look anyone in the eye. She slid into the chair and set her notebook on the table as an excuse to continue staring anywhere but at the crowded auditorium. "Are you comfortable?" he asked.

"Yes, thank you." He tipped up her chin and smiled, and her heart skipped several beats. She wanted to be angry with him, but he was charming her and his presentation, different again from his other, expanded her ideas and made her anxious to get back to her own writing. The time flew by.

"All right," he said as he neared the end of his presentation. "Let's see what you've learned. You've been sitting in this auditorium for the last two hours watching me interact with people. Are you creating characters? Maybe there's a plot running through your head? If you're a writer, did your experience here give you any ideas?"

"An auditorium would be a great place for a murder," someone yelled out. "Easy in and easy out."

"Good," Steven encouraged. "What else?"

"Not everyone writes murder mysteries," one indignant young lady piped up. "I was thinking two strangers make eye contact across the auditorium, and when they reach for their books, their hands touch."

Steven took a step back. "Keep writing, and thank you for reading." The applause resonated through the room and died slowly as people moved to get their books.

Samantha got up as he approached. "Thanks for the chair. I'll kill you later."

He didn't touch her, but his eyes were strangely like a touch—warm, embracing, sexy. "You were too far away, and I wanted you closer to me."

"I should go, Steven." She hesitated and paused directly in front of him. "Do you know just how inspiring you are?"

"Don't be late," he said abruptly, more than a little embarrassed.

She turned and looked back half way up the stairs. How did he know she was in the auditorium? She didn't tell him she was attending. She didn't know till she actually showed up minutes before it started. So, how did he know? And why was the woman selling the books still staring angrily at her? ♥♥

Chapter Eight

Steven poured a little wine into his glass and swirled it around. He rearranged his silverware three times and moved the centerpiece out of the way. He was never nervous around women; he was in control so there was no need to be nervous. Samantha was different—not his usual type of woman, but why couldn't he still have what he usually had with a woman? He was generous with his time, his money, and his compliments with his jewel of the moment. He'd buy her little gifts, take her dancing or to the theatre, and rock her world in bed till they were both satisfied. When he walked away, he knew he had treated her well, and neither could complain. Why not Samantha? She could probably benefit from the experience he could give her. But as his rational mind tried to justify it, his heart knew he couldn't play with Samantha. She had called him inspiring. Her eyes gave away too much—her heart and her soul. She would get her heart broken, and he would be responsible. Maybe that was what Jenny was worried about. He had seen her scowling at him through the entire last session, and he bolted like a coward from the auditorium to avoid her questions. This could just be a business meeting tonight to discuss the article for the magazine. Lord knows, Samantha would try to turn it into one. He could enjoy her company, answer her questions, and send her on her way tonight. In the morning he'd fly to Chicago, find Vic, and take out his pent-up frustrations on her. That was the plan until she walked into the restaurant.

Simple black dress of a soft willowy fabric that loosely hugged her curves, a tiny gold cross on a delicate chain, hair that fell in gentle waves and moved with her across her shoulders, and rather large hoop earrings that peeked out through her hair. Steven swallowed a large sip of wine. She came around the table to his left, and his eyes went straight to her feet. His pants tightened as he tried to look anywhere but at the black open toe, open heel shoes that laced up her foot with ribbons that swirled delicately around her ankle and calf. God. He rose as she reached the table and pulled out her chair.

"Am I…"

"You're beautiful," he whispered, pushing her in. He noted the pad she placed strategically beside her plate. "You want to start the interview?"

"I have to get this done," she said firmly. "Pete is expecting the moon from me, and I want to do the article justice."

He poured her wine and sat back in his chair. "Fair enough, but, I assume, you're not opposed to enjoying tonight as well?"

"I've been looking forward to this since I left you earlier."

"Good. I'm ordering for us tonight. That all right with you?"

"Fine. The wine was a good choice."

"And you like Italian?"

"My favorite. Oh, the bread smells like heaven." She tore a piece of the hot loaf and coated it with butter.

"Since you are not a risk taker, you've probably stuck to the old favorites. So, you're in for a treat tonight, because I'm going to dazzle you."

She cocked her head to the side and dove into his caramel pools. "How did you know I was in the auditorium?"

He shrugged. "I just knew the minute I came through those doors."

"And you couldn't see me from the floor, but you zeroed right in."

"Is strange, isn't it?"

"I'm never coming to one of your seminars again. I can't believe you brought me down to the main floor."

He reached for her hand. "Samantha, you should always be center stage, not hiding in the rafters."

Her hand moved unconsciously through his, threading their fingers. The waiter stepped up, and Steven quickly dismissed him, ordering an appetizer. Then he refilled the wine glasses.

"Can I ask you some questions for the article?"

"Ground rules first," he sat up straighter.

"I agree," she interrupted. "The first rule is you have to answer all of my questions."

"No."

"Yes, every last one. Can't pass, can't say no, and can't give me one word answers."

"No, there are things I don't want to see in print," he said angrily.

She cradled her glass lovingly and nodded. "All right, you have to answer all of them, but you can tell me if you don't want it in the article."

"And I can trust you not to print it?"

"Of course, Steven, and I will email you a copy of the article to examine before it goes to print. Do we agree?"

Damn, if she kept looking at him like that, he'd likely agree to anything. "Almost, for every question you ask, I ask one."

"Are you writing an article about me?" she laughed.

"I want to know more about you."

"All right. Deal. I get the first question." She opened her notepad and wrote quickly. "Rumor has it you've slept with enough women to fill the state of Texas. True or False?"

"You don't waste any time, do you?" he snickered.

"Is that a true or a false?"

"An exaggeration—more like the state of Nebraska." The waiter brought a very large plate and set it between them. "I know a lot of women; professionally I meet with publishers, book cover designers, other authors, and personally I have family, friends, neighbors. I don't sleep with all of them, but the press seems to think I do." He stabbed a morsel from the plate and held it to her mouth.

"Mm, garlic and oil and kind of a chewy texture. Good." She stabbed another and chewed slowly. "What is it?"

"Something you would never order," he replied. "My turn, boyfriends?"

"Is that a question? What do you want to know?"

He tore off a piece of the bread and dipped it in the oil. "Taste." His finger brushed passed her lips as she took the bread, and she lowered her eyes self-consciously to her plate. "Tell me about your last boyfriend."

"We were together a year. He loved to travel. He'd wake up in the morning and decide he was going to Brazil or Italy or on a safari. He'd take off and be gone for two, three, even four weeks at a time." She sipped the wine quicker.

"You didn't go with him?"

"You already asked your question. My turn."

"No, that was only half an answer, and you'd be all over my ass if I tried that. Tell me why you broke up, and that wasn't a question so it is still my turn." He took the last bite on the plate and offered it to her.

"I didn't go with him, because somebody had to be a grown up and pay the bills. He was in grad school, and his dad was giving him a huge allowance so he could just pick up and go. We broke up, because …" She twisted her napkin in her lap.

"Just say it," he prodded curiously.

"I wouldn't sleep with him," she said with exasperation. "And don't you dare say it. The relationship had no purpose. It wasn't going anywhere, and I don't do one-night stands. I guess he got tired of waiting." She finished her wine and reached for the bottle. Cheeks flaming, she nearly knocked over the glass as she tried to pour.

"Calm down," he said, taking the bottle. "If he wasn't the right person for you, then you did the right thing." Why did that please him?

"My turn, what's the first thing you notice about a woman?" She turned a little and stretched, and the sexy shoe peeked out from under the table.

"You're stuck on this topic, aren't you? First thing is different depending on the woman. Maybe it's her hair or her long legs or her tight ass. Depends."

"Not her tote bag? Or her fear of flying?" There was her heart, and Steven saw how clearly he had been right.

"Do you want to know what I noticed first about you?"

"Not my turn."

The waiter interrupted again, and Steven ordered dinner.

"I'll give you this one—your eyes. Bothers me, too. I'm a writer, and I can't define the color." He stared her down till she set aside her pen.

"Just ordinary blue."

"Steven!" Jenny's voice shattered the cocoon; they were no longer alone. "I'm surprised to see you here. If I'd have known you wanted Italian, you could have joined Ben and I."

"Jenny," Steven said through clenched teeth. "This is Samantha from Charleston."

"Oh, I've seen you in the workshops," Jenny said, turning to her. "What is your interest in my client?"

Steven could usually control his anger, but he was surprised at Jenny's rudeness. Samantha, though, seemed unfazed and smiled over her wine glass. "My interest is purely professional, Jenny, is it? I'm writing an article on Mr. Corso for the magazine I work for."

She glared accusingly at Steven. "You agreed to this without running it passed me? I've been setting up these kinds of things for you for years."

"Jenny, you're my agent not my mother." He would never hurt Jenny normally, but he could make his own decisions, and she was embarrassing him.

"I wanted to talk to you, but you left the auditorium in such a rush. Now, I see why. I will be calling you later tonight." She left with the gentleman who nodded apologetically at Steven.

"Jenny's my agent, and Ben is another one of her clients. He writes non-fiction, mostly travel documentaries."

"You're angry. Because she doesn't like me? Doesn't think I'm good enough for you?"

"Samantha, she doesn't think that."

"Yes, she does, and since I've seen the kind of women you're usually with, I guess I can't blame her."

"Damn it. That pisses me off. Where were you when they passed out backbones? Doesn't anything make you angry? Maybe I'm not good enough for you." The waiter placed two plates of food between them, and Steven ordered another bottle of wine, but the mood had shifted.

"Are we done?" she asked quietly. "Do you want to end this dinner?"

"No," Steven said firmly, "I want to rewind to before Jenny came in. Do you?"

She smiled slowly. "I think I'd love a little more wine. What was the appetizer?"

"*Calamari*—squid, a cousin to the octopus." He couldn't help smiling at her shocked expression. "Are you mad?"

"Why would I be? I'm surprised, but it was wonderful. What are these dishes?"

"Just eat off both. One is chicken with spinach and mushrooms in a white wine sauce and the other is veal with prosciutto and mozzarella in a lemon sauce. I think you'll like them."

"Oh, God, Steven, these are incredible. I like the veal the best." She finished her wine and held out her glass.

"Getting a tad drunk, Miss not so fine?" he smiled. God, she was so beautiful. What would it feel like to hold her, to press her flush against the growing ache, and feel her let go—give in?

"Steven? Where did you go?" She was staring at him, amusement written all over her face. "You were lost in thought and smiling."

"Sorry." He coughed nonchalantly. "I was just thinking about you drinking on the plane."

"My turn," she said, savoring another piece of veal. "Serious question. I've heard you say over and over in the last couple of days to write what you know. Go have life experiences." She rolled her eyes. "So, what life experiences have helped you to write your murder and crime books? Have you killed someone or been to prison?"

She burst into laughter that Steven suspected had more to do with the wine than the joke, but mostly he noticed her joy, and he smiled back at her. “I’m cutting you off, sweetheart, before I have to carry you out of here.”

“I’m fine, and the question was serious. Just research? Your books are very detailed and accurate.”

He pushed the chicken around his plate. “I have a brother who’s a cop. He’s a wealth of information. He’s been able to get me permission to ride around with him some nights as an observer. Some you can pick up hanging around open courtrooms. That sort of thing. Not as adventurous as jumping out of an airplane, but information I needed to grasp to write my books.”

“Steven, I’m glad I came tonight.”

He folded her hand in his. “I’m glad you did, too. Ready for dessert?”

“I’m stuffed, but I’d love dessert if we’re still sharing. Tiramisu?”

“Too traditional. I’m treating you to *limone tartufo*.”

“If I promise I’m sober, can I have a little more wine while we wait for dessert?”

“I think we need to finish the bottle,” he agreed. “I think the next question is mine.” His thumb rubbed against her knuckles till she slid her hand deeper into his. “Will you come back to my hotel room when we leave here, Samantha?”

She sipped the wine slowly and paled at his suggestion. “Steven, I don’t think…”

“You shouldn’t think, honey, you should feel.” He kissed gently her palm and read the indecision on her face. The waiter picked that moment to bring dessert. Cold, icy, the lemon ice cream with whip cream and lemon pudding centers was the perfect light treat after the heavy meal. Her tongue rolled deliciously over her lips, and he fought to remain seated or tug her over the table. “Coffee?”

“I really can’t.”

He nodded, secured the waiter, and paid the tab. Outside the night air was cool, but the glow of the wine kept out the chill. He spun her around and pulled her close. “Come back to my hotel room, Samantha,” he whispered in her ear.

She shook her head, but he persisted. "We can work on the article or watch television if you want." He cupped her chin in his warm hand. "I promise you nothing will happen that you don't want to happen."

She punched him hard in the chest. "I hate it when guys say that."

"Say what? You pack quite a punch."

"You say nothing will happen unless I want it to like I have some sort of control. You dim the lights, pour the wine, get us both hot and bothered, then expect me to be the one to keep control and cool things down."

He chuckled softly. Was the alcohol talking, or was this her real take on the situation? "Honey, all I meant was I want to spend more time with you." His hands were still on her hips, and the fabric was truly like silk.

"We have a few days, and I had a wonderful night. I'm going to go."

He sighed. Maybe she was right. Before she walked in, he had intended to leave her after tonight. She was slipping away as a cab pulled up to the curb. "Good night, Steven, and thank you."

He let her go. Happy and smiling and more than a little drunk, he let her go. The cab drove only a few feet then slammed to a stop. She hopped out and ran back to him. Grinning like she had some marvelous secret, she pressed her cool lips to his cheek, letting her tongue catch an imaginary bead of whiskey. As she turned to go, he caught her arm. "Not so fast," he murmured, backing her against the wall of the restaurant. Fully flushed against her body, he saw only her piercing blue eyes for a long minute before his hand cupped the side of her face, and his thumb felt her pulse pounding at the base of her throat. He moved his fingers lightly over her cheek till one brushed gently over her lips. She was a magnet, drawing him in, and he watched her reaction. Her eyes widened as he lowered his head, capturing the corner of her mouth with his and journeying to the opposite corner. He felt every soft quiver of her nearly motionless body as he grazed her lip with his teeth. Then he moved his hands to the wall on either side of her head and captured her mouth in a soft tentative kiss. He jerked against her when her tongue, sweet with his favorite wine, timidly slipped between her parted lips seeking his. He wanted her closer, off the wall, and snaked his arm around her waist and hips. His other hand slid into the silky threads of her hair, holding her head while his tongue explored the warm corners of her mouth. He sucked in her air, breathe in her scent, and finally broke the kiss. He was shaking as her hands slid around his waist, and she leaned unsteadily against him. "*Cara mia. Ti voglio,*" he mumbled, pressing the small of her back to bring her in closer contact with him. He couldn't get her close enough.

"Steven," she whispered. "That was…you are amazing."

"*Bellissima.*" He wouldn't, couldn't let her go, and she didn't try to move away either.

"Steven." He watched as her eyes fluttered. "I'm sorry." And she passed out in his arms.

♥♥

Chapter Nine

Steven held her in the cab and decided to take her back to his hotel. His only other option was to take her home, and he had no intention of facing her brother for the first time with his sister drunk and passed out in his arms. It was her own fault for pushing her limit on the wine. He also had no choice but to carry her through the hotel lobby to the elevator and to hold her on the ride up to the sixth floor. She stirred murmuring his name, but she seemed unaware of her surroundings. In his room he laid her on the sofa and placed a cool damp cloth on her forehead. She would have a hell of a hangover tomorrow. He made himself some coffee and heated some water in case she preferred tea. “Samantha, are you all right, honey?”

She opened her eyes slowly and groaned. The last thing she remembered was everything going black. The universe was laughing hysterically yet again. “God, Steven, what have I done?” She buried her face in the cushion as he kneaded her shoulders.

“It’s not a big deal. You had a good time, didn’t you?” His voice was gentle, soothing.

“You’re not mad?”

“Mad?” he laughed. “First time I haven’t seen you with a stick up your ass. No, I’m not mad.”

“Is this your hotel room?” she asked, stretching to see more of the suite.

“It has a beautiful view of the city from the balcony if you are up to it.”

She moved tentatively to the open terrace door and inhaled sharply. “It’s beautiful.”

Circling her waist, he leaned against her. “And so are you.” He kissed against the side of her neck and felt rather than saw her tip her head a bit to guide him deeper, but he could also feel how tired she was. “Want some tea?”

She nodded as he headed back to the kitchen area. She maneuvered carefully to the sofa and curled up with her legs tucked under her. “What floor are we on?”

"Sixth."

"I don't know if I want the answer to my next question. How did I get up here?" She covered her face with her hands. "Please tell me I walked up here."

"Sorry, I carried you." He handed her a mug of tea.

"Through the lobby?"

"No other way I know of."

"Oh, God, why did you bring me here?"

"Would you have preferred I took you to your brother's drunk? I didn't have a lot of choices."

"God, no."

"Then stop worrying about it." He sat down on the edge of the sofa and held one foot.

"What are you doing?"

"Helping you relax. These are interesting shoes you chose to wear tonight. You know what they're called?" He slowly untied the ribbon and unwound it from her ankle so he could slip it off. "Fuck me heels."

She stared at him for a long second. "You're making that up."

"Turn on your back, and I'm not making that up. Ask any of your girlfriends." He kneaded her foot in his big hands, his thumbs pressing into her arch.

"Why?"

He shook his head. "First, they get a man's attention—sexy footwear. I nearly fell out of my seat when I saw them."

She moaned. "That feels wonderful."

"But a man's eyes follow the ribbons up your calf," his hand stroked and inched upward, "to your knee. And since a woman's legs are long and fluid, the eye continues north to the thigh and to its natural junction." She pushed his hand away, and he switched to the other foot.

"You got all this from a pair of shoes?" she asked sleepily.

"Not just any pair of shoes. I'd keep these if I were you." He kneaded her other foot with the same precision, flexing her toes, pressing her arch, and squeezing her heel.

"You've done this before."

"Never," he said almost convincingly.

"You do know I'm memorizing all of this for the article?"

"Ok, close your eyes and that pretty sweet mouth."

She started to drift. "That feels so good. You keep doing that you could make me come." It took a minute before it registered then the heat crept up her neck and face. "I can't believe I said that out loud."

"I would love to see that."

"I should go home."

"You should shut up." He moved an errant curl from her cheek and tucked it behind her ear. When he was sure she was asleep, he covered her with a quilt and stretched out on the recliner. In a couple of days, they would go their separate ways. He was playing with fire. He understood Jenny's concerns, and he knew women. This one didn't do one-night stands, because she led with her heart, gave from her heart, and would only let a man in her bed when she felt a connection, a connection she wouldn't release anytime soon. Walking away from her would be painful for her, of course, though he had to admit, he liked her, and he might feel a bit more for her than he usually did. This was uncharted waters, and he honestly wasn't sure he was interested enough to pursue it. Who was he kidding? After the kiss tonight, he'd be stupid to try and deny his wanton lust for her. She had knocked him on his ass with that kiss. Damn, when had he developed a conscience? His phone rang insistently, but he ignored it. He didn't want to talk to Jenny or anyone else. Closing his eyes, he listened to her soft rhythmic breathing and wondered if she were dreaming before he slipped into a fitful sleep.

Chapter Ten

The pounding on the door woke him with a start. If the idiot on the other side of that door woke her, he was going to kick someone's ass.

"Jenny."

A look of horror crossed her face as she took in Samantha asleep on the sofa. "You didn't!" she snapped accusingly.

"Lower your voice," he growled, "before you wake her." He could only imagine her humiliation if she saw Jenny. "It's not what you think."

"It's barely seven," Jenny hissed. "It is what it always is, but this time you have really …"

"Stop," Steven said angrily. "She is fully clothed. We didn't sleep together. We were working on the article, and she crashed here." He guided her toward the kitchen and started the coffeemaker.

"Which is exactly why I stopped by. What possessed you to agree to this interview? It's a small-time magazine with a circulation of less than 10,000. You are so far beyond that sort of thing. Was it worth it just to get into her pants?"

"You don't know a damn thing, Jen. She's not like that. We had dinner, worked on the article, and that was it."

"Let me guess, you'll be seeing more of her while you are here in San Diego?"

Steven let out his breath impatiently and pulled out several mugs. "We haven't finished the article. I guess I'll see her a while longer, but when I leave it is done. It's business."

Her glare so fierce, he had to turn away. "You know how these quiet, homespun girls are. She'll hang on; they'll be no getting rid of her. At some point she'll accuse you of fathering her child. How can you be so stupid?"

"And how can you be so suspicious of everyone I meet?"

"That's my job, and you've been the golden boy because of it. I do whatever I think is necessary to promote your career and protect your interests. That is why I spoke to Victoria."

His head shot up. "And told her what?"

"To call you—you need some TLC. She understood."

"You need to stay out of my personal life." Samantha stirred on the sofa. "And you need to leave right now." He pulled her not so gently toward the door.

But Jenny wasn't leaving without the last word. "Get rid of her before you do something stupid, and I want to see this article before it goes to print. Understand?"

He shut the door in her face.

"Steven?"

He brought her coffee and sat on the edge of the sofa. "Good morning, Miss not so fine. How's the head?"

She sipped the strong slightly sweetened brew. "I'll live, but I have to go. My brother won't be worried, but he'll definitely be curious."

"Not until we plan today."

"We? Or have you already planned it."

"I have somethings to take care of this morning, but I thought some shopping, maybe get a quick bite, then we'd head to the beach later. Maybe a moonlight swim."

"Planning on drowning me? I told you I don't swim."

"You met my first challenge, dinner. Now, the second challenge."

"Slow down, Steven. You said one challenge."

"To start, of course. The second life experience is to get you comfortable in the water. I've compromised; it isn't scuba diving, yet."

"You don't understand. It's not just getting into the water and swimming. I had a bad experience, and I can't."

He looked at her thoughtfully. "You mentioned traumatized. How?"

She pulled herself to her feet and grabbed her shoes. He was surprised at how quickly she wound the ribbons and was ready to go. He didn't want to trump her, but she left him no choice. "We haven't finished the article," he said, reclining back on the sofa.

She stopped abruptly. "What exactly are you saying, Corso? Answering my questions is dependent on my getting in the water?"

"Not at all. Answering your questions is dependent on you telling me why you won't get in the water."

She clenched her fists and glared at him. "I was ten on a commercial tourist boat with my parents and brother, and I fell in." Her shoulders shook, and the tears flashed in her eyes. "I could swim a little, but the water kept pulling me under." He spread his palms over hers. "I think they had trouble finding me at first till my brother spotted this doll I was holding. It floated to the surface. Someone, a total stranger, dove in and somehow found me." She heaved a heavy sigh. "I haven't been in the water since."

His strong arms circled her, and her head relaxed against his shoulder. His familiar scent comforted her, and his soft voice caressed and soothed her taut nerves. "I'm glad you told me."

"So, you understand?" she asked.

"Of course, I understand. You were a child, and you've lived with the terror of that one day for most of your life. As a result, you are missing out on some wonderful life experiences. We are going to change that." He brushed his hand against her cheek, and she slapped it away.

"No, I can't."

"All right," he said slowly, "but we can still watch the sun set on the beach, can't we? You can't be that much of a coward."

She wanted to strike him. "Are you still going to answer my questions?"

"Of course."

"What time?"

"Sometime after lunch. I'll text."

"Fine," she snapped. "I'll see you later." She slammed the door on the way out, and he smiled. Anger was far better and less paralyzing than fear.

They met after lunch in one of the more touristy areas of downtown San Diego. The consecutive streets were littered with fast food restaurants, outdoor cafes, and a variety of gift shops that catered to budget extremes. They window shopped, for the most part, and dodged errant children with more energy than their weary parents. Steven guided her with his hand on the small of her back to the door of a very expensive chain jewelry store; the kind of store that didn't need to advertise and appealed to people who didn't have to ask the price. She stopped in her tracks.

"This isn't the kind of store you browse in, Steven. What are you doing?" she asked.

"I thought we'd look around and find you something as a souvenir of your trip here." He had a certain talent for choosing the perfect piece of jewelry for the individual woman. He had something in mind he thought would please her.

"No, I don't want anything," she said, pulling away. "Let's walk…"

"Samantha, come here, and don't be stubborn. Let me give you something pretty." He brushed back a curl and caught it around his finger.

"I don't need anything to remind me of this trip. I'm having a wonderful time, I'm getting to know you, and you're giving me the interview. I don't need anything else." She caught his hand and tried to pull him away from the store.

"Don't you want just a little something to remember your visit?"

"You want me to remember you." She turned and met his eyes. "And there's not much chance I'm going to forget you."

"Just come in and look."

"Steven, no! How many women have you given something from one of these stores?" Tears welled up in her eyes. "We're not together like that. Let this go."

There was her heart again, but, at least, she was trying to protect it. "Maybe I wasn't thinking."

Suddenly, she grinned and tugged him two stores down the block. "Still want to buy me something? Buy me something in there."

They were standing in front of a classic tourist gift shop. Inexpensive junk that made it home and ended up in a box in the basement. T-shirts with San Diego sprawled across the front, plastic toys, and, what his grandmother called, knickknacks. She wanted this?

"Please," she begged.

He grabbed her elbow and stared at her with disbelief. "I've never been in one of these stores, but you're not going to find anything of value in there."

"Value isn't measured in dollars and cents. If it's from you, it'll have value. Come on." She didn't wait for him but headed into the store.

He groaned at the life size stuffed bear with the happy face t-shirt parked just inside the door and was momentarily separated from her as a rather large family moved between them. When he found her, she was thoroughly absorbed in a large basket that held small glass bottles no more than an inch or two big. Each bottle had something inside. "I wanted the penny in the bottle, but then I saw these with the little shells inside." Her face glowed, and he had never seen a woman so radiantly beautiful. He claimed her by wrapping his around her shoulder.

"I don't want to be extravagant, but what the heck. Why don't you take both?" Her smile was enough to make him consider buying the whole damn basket. As they waited in line behind several customers, he pulled her closer. "I am still buying you a piece of jewelry." She started to protest, but they had reached the counter, and he was looking at a display of two-dollar plastic and metal rings. "Give me your hand." She watched as he tried the ring with the bright red stone on every finger, but it was much too big. He didn't like the one with the faded blue stone, because it couldn't compete with her eyes. She pointed to one, and he made a big show of examining it carefully. The deep amber stone in the center was surrounded by a ring of silver beads and, at least, it fit. "This one?" He shook his head; the total bill was less than seven dollars, and she couldn't have been happier.

She proudly slipped the ring on her finger. "My turn, how many women have you bought something in a store like that?"

"You're the only one," he said, pressing a quick kiss to her lips. "And I can guarantee it won't happen again. My turn." She fell into step beside him and waited expectantly. His tone changed dramatically. "Are you going to pick up your writing again when you go back?"

"I want to; you've given me a lot to think about. My turn. Do you speak fluent Italian?"

"I learned enough to survive parents who only spoke Italian when I was young, *Cara*, but usually I have to think about it to use it, and sometimes it just slips out of my mouth."

"Big Italian family?"

"Not your turn, but I'll answer then I get two questions. Big extended family—yes, but the close family is mom, dad, brother, Ernesto, and brother, Salvatore, and a sister, Gina. The three of them are married with kids. My turn. Isn't your brother a long way from home?"

"He went Navy for a few years and stayed here when he got out."

"Are you close?"

"Yes, he's getting married next year, and I'm in the bridal party so I have to get back on that damn plane again."

He started to say something, but she interrupted. "You got your two questions. My turn after we get some hotdogs."

"Not hotdogs. Do you know what's in those things?"

"No, and that question counts. You owe me one. And hang on to your wallet, because I want two." They approached a street vendor, bought several hotdogs, and settled in a park across the street. "So, home base is Baltimore."

"Grew up there. Family still lives there. Samantha, don't print a lot about my family. They have to put up with a lot of crap with my career. I don't want them being bothered more."

"I understand, Steven. Who said he didn't want hotdogs, by the way? Is that your third?"

He looked at his phone for the fourth time. "I've got to take this. It'll just take a minute. Hi, how are you?"

Samantha caught the tone immediately and felt uncomfortable. She hoped it was family, but she was afraid it was probably some sultry woman from Steven's past. It was none of her business, but she was feeling very protective of the couple of days they had left in San Diego to finish the article, of course.

"No, that is not a good idea," she heard him say. "She worries much too much about nothing. I'll be in Chicago in a few days, and I'll see you then." He walked casually away from her as he got more involved in the conversation. "It would hardly make sense, now. I'm done with the conference, and I'm getting some work done. You understand, don't you?"

Samantha picked up the trash and walked in the opposite direction away from Steven. In a couple of days, he would head to Chicago and her to Charleston. She really liked him even if he could be a jerk sometimes. Since she had left him this morning, all she could think about was the kiss outside the restaurant. He was right; she definitely knew she had been kissed. She realized he was making a permanent mark on her heart, but she was pretty sure it was one-sided. She was, after all, business. "Everything all right?" she asked when he caught up to her.

"Fine, how about a walk on the beach?"

"Used up another question, smart guy. My turn, do you have a favorite among the novels you've written?"

"The first one," he said without hesitation. "South Side Murder was a labor of love, though it probably wasn't my best written book. You have to start somewhere. No more questions." He took her hand and walked quietly beside her for several blocks as they got closer to the beach.

"Where did you go?" she finally asked quietly.

"Nowhere. I've been right here with you, and it's a little unnerving."

"Are you sure it wasn't the phone call that changed your mood?"

"It did have something to do with it, but not like you think. I was right here thinking about you."

"Why does that make you sad?"

"Not sad, concerned maybe. Come on. If you like shells, we can pick some up along the beach."

The discussion ended as he tugged her along, and they spent part of the afternoon and well into the evening walking and collecting shells. Some collected in her tote, and a couple were safely tucked in Steven's jean pockets. After a quiet dinner in a sidewalk café, they returned to Steven's rental and drove further down the beach. The sun was setting as they found a secluded cove to lay out their beach towels. "You even thought of towels?"

"Stole them from the hotel, but don't tell anybody," he said, silencing her with a gentle kiss. The breeze off the ocean was still warm from the day's heat, and the sand squished under the towel as Steven stretched out. The sky had turned into a canvas of deep reds and brilliant oranges. As she laid back, the sun danced on her skin and highlighted her hair in a golden halo. When she turned slightly and smiled, he forgot everything, except capturing her in this moment. His kiss surprised her—hot, hungry, greedy. Her soft gasp as he kissed along her throat to the button at the top of her shirt drove him. He easily undid the buttons and kissed along the lace over her breasts. The pretty blue bra, sky-blue, fought to hold her in while he desperately tried to get her free. One breast filled his hand as he pulled it over the top of the lace. He kissed to the sweet circle surrounding her tight nipple then drew it into his mouth. She tightened her grip around his neck, and let her head fall back in surrender. Coming back to her mouth, he delved deeper till she breathlessly pushed him back.

"Steven, wait." She cupped his face, searching for the control she was quickly losing. "I thought you wanted to go for a swim."

His head dropped on her breast, and he kissed it one last time. He smiled weakly. What was he thinking? He was acting sixteen—clutching and grabbing her on a quiet, but still public beach. His only consolation was she, apparently, was more afraid of him then the water. He gently rearranged her bra and rebuttoned her shirt. "You're right," he said finally, still trying to calm his breathing. "I did promise you a swim."

Realizing her mistake, she pushed herself up. "Or we could just sit here and enjoy the view."

He laughed softly. "You can't have it both ways, Miss not so fine." He pulled her down the beach to the shore line.

"No bathing suits," she said triumphantly, sensing she had found her out.

"No worries," he grinned, pulling his shirt over his head. "Underwear covers just like a suit." He dropped his jeans, and Samantha swallowed the hard lump in her throat. Sexy black silk boxers and an overabundance of muscle and dark tanned skin made the fluttery feeling in her core hurt with desire. Arms for holding, legs for tangling, and a chest to hold on to while…

"Are you all right?" Steven asked, an obvious awareness in his eyes. He backed into the water till it lapped at his thighs in gentle waves. "Take your clothes off, Samantha."

The words made her shudder, and her hands shook as she undid the shirt and dropped it from her shoulders. He waited patiently, but he was glad for the loose cut of the shorts as she shimmied the jeans down her slender thighs. Damn, blue matching panties with the same touch of lace.

"This won't absorb water like a bathing suit," she said tentatively.

"Stop stalling," he growled, walking back in toward her. "Hold out your hands to me." He stopped just as he reached her hands, leaving a gap between them. "Now, focus, Samantha, on my eyes. Do not look away, not up, left, or right. You just keep looking at my eyes and hold my hands." She nodded. "Trust me, honey, I won't let anything happen to you." He took a small step backward, pulling her forward. He felt her tense. "Focus on my eyes; you can trust me."

"With everything but …" She stopped talking and stopped walking.

"My turn," he said, stepping back again. The water lapped at his calves. "What's your genre? What type of novel do you want to write?" She seemed startled but kept her eyes locked on his and moved with him.

"Huh, contemporary romance—I'm a sucker for a love story."

He should have known. The water rose to his knees. "Do you believe in love at first sight? Fireworks and lightning bolts?"

She shook her head, staying focused on his eyes. "Love is sneaky, Steven. It's about getting so comfortable with another person that you suddenly miss him and want him in your life permanently. You have to find your other half, the person that completes you, and that takes time. That's my one problem with romance novels—meet, fall in love, and even marry in two chapters. Very romantic, I guess, but not real."

Steven watched her carefully and almost forgot his purpose till her gaze drifted and concern clouded her eyes. "Me, Sam, focus on me. Your turn."

She frantically tried to think of a question till she blurted out, "Favorite place? You do a lot of traveling?"

"Loved Europe—Italy, England, and I went to Japan once." He continued to step back, and the water rose to mid-thigh. "But I have a cabin outside Baltimore back home. I go there when I don't want to see anyone, and I mean anyone. Sometimes I can't even stand Jenny around me. I go there when I want to be totally secluded. Sometimes I fish or stomp around in the woods, but, mostly, I go there to write. Helps when I get stuck and can't turn the page. Maybe I should take you there."

She was still staring in his rich dark eyes. "Sounds great." She hadn't realized the water had risen around her waist.

"Listen, honey," he said softly. "Let go of my hands and slide them around my neck." Before she could argue he added, "Trust me. I'm not letting go. I just want to pull you closer." He pulled her into him. "Kick your feet. You said you knew how to swim a little." He loosened his grip when she gained some confidence and maneuvered around behind her. "I still have you. Don't tense on me." He pulled her wet back against his chest and kissed the top of her head. She suddenly pushed off him so she could face him, a slow smile crossing her lips. Still holding her hands, he encouraged her to lie back and let the water support her, but he firmly grabbed her thighs when he saw a flash of panic. Her hair floated on the water, her limp form tried to relax, and he wondered if Miss not so fine realized how truly beautiful she was. He took her hands and pulled her up. She hadn't faced her real fear, yet. He pulled her in tight again and met her eyes. "Wrap your legs around my hips and hold on tight, Samantha. Trust me, take a deep breath." She looked confused till he lifted them in the water and plunged back down. For a few painfully long seconds, he felt real panic. She stared wide eyed and clung to him in desperation—nails digging into his flesh. He brought them up quickly. Sputtering and unable to find sound for her screams, she banged angrily against his chest till she collapsed against him. "I'm sorry," he whispered softly. "You're not afraid of being in the water, *Cara*. You're afraid of being lost under it."

"I…You…How could you?"

"I want more for you. I seriously want to take you scuba diving, but you have to relearn how strong you are against this force of nature. You are not a child, but you are still ten in the water."

She circled his neck, moving closer. "I'm not sure I like you very much right now."

"See how far we are from the shore? Want me to get lost?" he teased.

"No, stay."

"Good," he said brightly. "Hold your breath." He didn't give her a chance to think as he plunged them both under the water. After several more attempts, she seemed more comfortable, not relaxed, but, at least, more patient waiting for him to push them back to the surface. Steven decided she would never relax this way; she was looking at the process as work. It was time to play. He forced her to swim with him—to remember the skills she did have as a child. To splash and bask in the light of the full moon shining brightly in the sky. And with their clothes wet and slicked against their skin, it was like holding her naked body. He kissed her, communicating his desire for her; unable to stop he skimmed her hips reverently and stroked her thighs till he ached. "Let's go back. It's getting late," he said gruffly.

"In a minute," she said, kissing him quickly. "That was for luck." She pushed off him and treaded water. "I must be crazy, but I can't be afraid if you are serious about diving. I'm going to do this myself."

He wasn't sure she was ready; afraid she was expecting too much of herself. She had accomplished a lot today, but if she could do this, he had to find a way to support her. "Are you sure?"

"Yes, I think so, maybe." She looked at him weakly but seemed determined.

"I will stay right here," he told her. "You should be able to see part of my chest and shorts. Feel for me; I won't leave you. Do you believe that?"

"Yes." She took a deep breath and dove before she lost her nerve. The first moments panicked her as she oriented herself to the direction of the surface of the water. Then she saw his hard abs, wet skin, and those damn boxers, but she didn't need to see. She felt for the waistband of his shorts and hooked her fingers. He was everything a man should be—gentle, rough, supportive, encouraging, decisive, and for a few minutes back on the beach, she had seen lust mixed with, at least, some affection. She pressed her palm against his stomach and pinpointed that moment. Something stirred within her. Maybe she was… She burst through the surface; the burn in her lungs telling her she might have taken too long. Steven had her gripped in his large hands then slammed her to his chest.

"Damn, are you all right? You scared the hell out of me. I was about to come after you, but I felt your hands, and you didn't seem like you were in trouble."

"I wasn't." She wiggled an arm free to brush back her hair. "You will have to give me some time to hone my swimming skills before we go diving, though," she said with a satisfied smile. "Is that all right?"

"Of course." He pulled her toward the shore, and as they walked in, the cooler night air made her shiver. He wrapped her in one of the heavy hotel towels and covered himself with the other. Then he cuddled her against his body. She was warm and still, and he found her hand with the plastic ring securely on her finger. He could lie on this beach forever and just hold her, or he could listen to the voice in his head that demanded he satisfy another need building between them. "Come on, Sam. We're leaving before you fall asleep."

Contented, Samantha tightened the towel around her clothes that were still damp as she nestled down into the leather seats of the rental. "Where are we going?"

"Back to my hotel room," he said, watching the road, "and I know that isn't a question."

She smiled and reached for his hand. "Then I guess it doesn't require an answer."

He waited as long as the walk through the lobby, but behind the elevator door, he couldn't stop reaching for her, surrounding her with the scent of him and kissing the breath out of her. Barely in his room, he won over the resistant hook of her bra and fumbled with the belt on her jeans. All male finesse was gone as he pressed her firmly against the door. Close, closer wasn't enough, and as absorbed as he was with exploring all the recesses of her body, he didn't miss for a minute where her hands traveled—down his back, over his ass, across the individual muscles of his chest, and between their bodies over his heat. Never had he felt the power, the insane rush of wanting one woman this badly. He awkwardly maneuvered her into the bedroom and nailed her down on the bed then lost himself in her eyes as he gathered her hair over his hand. His legs tangled with hers, her chest heaved as he stroked and sucked her nipples till they were painfully tight, and then he completely and, uncharacteristically, slammed into her body. With herculean strength, he fought to control the violent fever raging inside him. He gave her desperate seconds to adjust to his invasion, to tighten and draw him deeper, and allow her to dictate the rhythm. Once set, he claimed her mouth, her heart till the flood gates opened, and she cried out for him. And together the waves crashed, much harder, much faster, and far more punishing than the actual waves of the ocean. He fell on her and kissed lightly her shoulder as she still shuddered beneath him. *"Sei mio. Tu appartieni a me."* Then he rolled back, cradling her tightly over his heart and fell asleep.

The California sun was anything but a gentle good morning. It glowed hot through the metal blinds and washed the room in blinding light. Steven opened his eyes to Samantha's hair in his face, and her leg crisscrossed over his. He could watch her sleep but not for long. The temptation was too great to wake her, and he had done that twice during the night to amazing results. He crept quickly out of bed and pulled on his jeans. Deep in the pockets were the largest of the shells they had collected on the beach. He wrote Steven on one and laid it with her pile on the dresser, and labeled the other Samantha and returned it to his pocket. That was going with him. The little bottle of shells stood near the rest, but the bottle with the penny was nowhere in sight. He saw her stretch, and her hand with the plastic ring slipped out from under the sheet. The wave of emotion that swept over him confused him, and he slipped silently into the sitting room. He wanted to surprise her with a big breakfast so he placed an order with room service. Wanting to make the most of the day, he planned a trip to the biggest bookstore in the country and would call for reservations at a club for dinner and dancing. He wanted to hold her as they swayed to the music, maybe a little wine, and an early night back here. Of course, Samantha would continue her barrage of questions, but he was enjoying that far more than he thought he would. Truth, he was enjoying being with her and getting to know her and last night… His body tightened, and he thought of returning to bed when a sharp tap came from the door. Room service was unusually quick. Instead of food Jenny, in an extremely good mood, walked in.

"Good news. Two-day release of the new book, and you're already number five on the best sellers list. I predict another winner by the end of the month."

"That's great. We'll talk about it later," he said, trying to steer her back to the door.

"What? I thought I could have, at least, a cup of coffee."

Room service interrupted and wheeled in the lavish array of pastries and breakfast foods. While Steven signed, Jenny took a quick peek in the bedroom. She looked ill as she moved directly in front of Steven, prepared to lecture him once more. But she knew Steven well. If she pushed too hard, he'd run straight into whatever it was she wanted him to avoid. No, if she wanted him to listen, she would have to approach this differently.

"So, what happens now?" she asked calmly.

"Don't lecture me, Jenny," Steven warned. "I like Samantha, and I'm going to keep seeing her."

Jenny nodded in agreement. "I see. Are you in love with her? Are you proposing marriage?"

The question was unexpected and caught Steven off guard. "Aren't you jumping ahead quickly? We haven't known each other very long."

"But what do you know about her, Steven?" She kept her voice neutral—not judging, not even suggesting. She'd make him see her point of view and think it was his own. "Just from what you told me, she's different from other women you've known. I believe you've said she doesn't sleep around, didn't you?"

"So? What's your point, Jenny?"

"So, Steven, are you prepared for what will happen when she awakes? The adoring eyes, the profession of love, the hints at an engagement ring and wedding band. She'll think she's in love with you, and, worse, that you've made a commitment to her, because you slept with her. If she's not the typical sophisticated woman you usually see, there will be endless phone calls and cute text messages." Then Jenny took the shot she knew would make the biggest impression. "You're going to hurt the girl, Steven, whether you meant to or not."

Steven cringed. He didn't want to hurt Samantha, but in a couple of days they would be going in opposite directions. Where would that leave them? "She's a big girl," he said weakly. "We'll see."

Jenny cut him off. "I have a better idea. Let me handle things efficiently like I always do. You get your things and leave for the airport before she wakes up. Change your ticket and get a flight out of here for Chicago. Spend some time with Victoria, and I'll take care of everything here."

"Absolutely not," Steven exploded. "After I slept with her, I'm not here when she wakes. I'm not just gone, but on a plane heading to Chicago. No, that won't hurt her, will it, Jen? That's stupid. I'll talk to her."

Now or never. Jenny tore into Steven's conscience. "You're an open book, honey. She'll take one look at you, and know you never meant this to be anything permanent. She'll be devastated and humiliated. If I talk to her, I can make a reasonable excuse. I'll tell her an important business meeting in Chicago came up, and I insisted you go. In a few days she'll give you the article to read and approve, but by then you'll be miles apart. Eventually, she'll get it. Steven, it is kinder to let her down now then after a whirlwind few days in paradise." Jenny pushed him toward the bedroom. "I have never let you down. You know I am right. Get your things, and hurry before she wakes."

Steven packed quickly, but he couldn't help pausing for a moment to watch her sleep. He knew from the beginning that she wasn't his type, and he would hurt her and, yet he had stupidly brought them to this very moment. He twisted a curl around his finger. She was so damn beautiful, and he didn't want to hurt her.

Jenny paced the sitting room, waiting for Steven. No one was as innocent as that girl was pretending. She knew what a catch Steven was and sleeping with him may have given her an advantage, but Jenny had protected Steven for years, and she'd make sure this woman was permanently gone. As soon as Steven got to Chicago and Victoria, he'd forget Cinderella. She rushed him along as he scribbled a note on a pad.

"Give her this," he told Jenny. "It will, at least, collaborate your story."

"Of course, honey, now go." Steven was safely out the door when Jenny tore up the note and threw it away. Half way to the airport, Steven had a bad feeling he had made a huge mistake.

Chapter Eleven

Samantha heard voices and forced her eyes open. It wasn't a dream. She was in Steven's bed, and she had feelings for him, but she wasn't naïve. He had wanted her last night, and he was a considerate lover, making sure she was as satisfied as he was, but he hadn't made any promises. The plastic ring smiled. They had certainly complicated their business relationship, but if she went home and never saw him again, she would have no regrets. He would always have a piece of her heart, and she would have the memories of a week in San Diego. And the best part? She rolled over and stretched. She still had two days with Mr. Gorgeous, and she intended to enjoy them. Where was he anyway? She grabbed the thick hotel robe and caught his scent. Mm, maybe after breakfast, she could drag him back to bed. "Steven? Where are you?" She found Jenny instead in a brightly colored sun dress seated on the sofa. Nails immaculately done, her auburn hair pulled back in a ponytail, and her cell poised against her ear. Samantha ignored her as she finished her call and poured a cup of coffee.

"The coffee is wonderful," Jenny said, her eyes focused on Samantha. "I believe it is a special brew."

"Where's Steven?"

"Gone, Cinderella." She watched Samantha carefully.

"Gone where? Did he go out for something?"

"Poor little Cinderella," Jenny teased. "Remember the part of the story where the clock strikes twelve, and the coach turns back into a pumpkin. Your coach and your prince are gone."

"What are you talking about?" Samantha said angrily. "Where's Steven?"

"About now he is on a plane to Chicago." The cup slipped out of her hand and shattered on the floor. "Don't worry about it, Cinderella. One of the mice will clean it up."

"Why is he going to Chicago today? He wasn't going till Sunday. He didn't say anything last night." But even before

Jenny responded, Samantha was beginning to understand what Steven had done, and clearly what last night had been to him.

Jenny laughed. "I'd imagine he had other designs last night. Telling you he was leaving might have changed things. Anyway, Victoria has been calling him, and he decided to go to her earlier than he originally planned."

Samantha bit her lip. Granted, she didn't know Steven very well, but she didn't trust Jenny. "You're lying," she said calmly. "He would have awaken me if he was leaving."

"Well, I don't know what to say. He's gone, and I'm going to check him out so you need to leave, too."

Samantha dressed and gathered her things from the bedroom. She considered hopping out the sixth-floor window rather than facing Steven's smug agent again. Her hand trembled as she swiped the shells into her tote. How stupid she had been. He had used her and left without a word. Prince Charming? More like Prince Asshole. She brushed at the moisture on her checks. She would not cry over him. He wasn't worth it. She tried to ignore Jenny as she moved to the door, but Jenny blocked her exit.

"I'm hoping you will be mature about this," she said. "I would hope you wouldn't use the article to get even with Steven."

Samantha took a step back. Jenny was concerned about the interview. While she wouldn't write lies or try to hurt Steven through the article, Jenny didn't know that, and right now that felt good. "The article is about a man with good points and bad. I hope it will be balanced and honest."

"We'll sue you and your tiny little magazine."

Samantha shook her head. "Why don't you let Steven decide if it's fair? I did agree to let him see it before it is published. Good-bye, Jenny." She held her head high, though, her heart was breaking. She hadn't thought of the article till Jenny had brought it up. She still had two days in San Diego. Maybe she could lock herself up in her brother's spare room and write so that it would be done for Pete when she got back. Then she could send it to Steven and be done with him forever.

♥♥

Chapter Twelve

When Steven arrived at the airport, he checked the board for flights to Chicago. There were several scattered throughout the day. He was in no rush to change his ticket so he grabbed an available seat in a lounge area. He was already certain he had made a huge mistake. Samantha would never believe he left without waking her for a business meeting, and he wasn't sure he trusted Jenny to make the situation better. Still as lame as it sounded, he had left her a note confirming the meeting and that he would call. He still felt like an asshole, and he was already missing her. She had probably left the hotel room by now. Maybe he should call her or text her. And say what? Sorry for running out on you this morning, because I don't know how you fit in my life. Samantha was different. Maybe she would call him. Why not? That would be logical that she would expect some type of explanation directly from him. He'd grab some breakfast and wait for her call. An hour later he had picked at his breakfast, he was still at the airport, and she hadn't call. Of course, she hadn't called. She was angry, hurt, probably embarrassed, and disappointed in him for running out on her and leaving Jenny to clean up his mess. He had to fix this.

But Jenny's call interrupted his thoughts. "Not to worry, Steven. It's all taken care of, although, I don't think she bought the meeting in Chicago story. I just stuck to it and told her you were looking forward to reading the article."

Steven slumped deeper in his seat. "Did she seem more angry or hurt?"

"Oh, I don't know. Maybe a bit pathetic. She's not your usual strong independent woman."

Steven didn't have the energy to argue; he hung up and didn't answer when Jenny called him back. He took his phone and pulled up Samantha's number to text. What could he say to make things remotely better? **Sorry, I didn't realize I had to leave today.**

Her response came back quickly. **Jenny explained.**

Damn, that didn't make him feel better. Before he could decide what to type back, he got another text. **Article to you on Monday for your approval. Please answer promptly. Pete's in a hurry to put it to bed. Thanks.**

Her text was all business; she was closing the door, and that spot in his chest grew larger and hurt more insistently. His fingers hovered over the letters. **Last night was incredible.** He hit send before he changed his mind. He should be talking to her in person. This was stupid; it wasn't the way he treated any woman, but something about Samantha had him off balance—off his game. It didn't matter, because she didn't answer. He waited an hour, and she still didn't respond, but in that hour, he had time to think. While he didn't always agree with Jenny, she had a point. Samantha would want more. He knew it when he first met her on the plane. He knew it when he sat across from her at dinner, and he knew it when he held her in the water with her fingers tangled in his hair. Today, he would promise her the world. In San Diego he would be lost in her, and then when they went back to their real lives, she'd get hurt unless he wanted more. Did he? Maybe the question wasn't if he would hurt her but when? Long relationships weren't his style. At some point he'd walk away.

The new text startled him. **Has your flight left yet, or are you still waiting?** He wanted to throw his phone. He walked to the ticket counter and switched his flight. He needed to get away from his agent, and he needed to sort things out. He'd do that in Chicago, and it would be good seeing Vic. He rubbed absentmindedly at the spot that was getting larger and more painful in his chest. Maybe he should see a doctor.

♥♥

Chapter Thirteen

Steven rose to leave the plane that had just landed in Chicago. He missed Samantha. Putting a ton of miles between them had certainly clarified that in a hurry. In the cab to the hotel he texted her twice. He had said the same thing both times. **We need to talk.** But his phone remained silent. How else could he approach her? **Do you have more questions for the article? I could answer a few more if you want.** He was certain she wasn't going to respond when twenty minutes later he got a clear answer.

No thanks.

Clearly, she wanted nothing to do with him. He glanced at the incoming call and answered Victoria. "Are you in Chicago, honey? I've been so excited about your visit."

He felt sick. "I'm here, but I'm lousy company, Vic."

"I'm sure we can think of something to cheer you up," she purred. "I just arrived at your hotel and checked you in. You're in room 777. I'll be waiting for you."

Steven closed his eyes. Victoria was a beautiful woman and a very good friend. Even though they slept together, they had never claimed any exclusive dating rights to each other. Both were free to see other people, and the last he heard she was seeing a wealthy stock broker. Yet, when they both were at loose ends and needy, they found their way back to each other. Some good bourbon and a shot of Victoria would go a long way to making him feel better. Samantha was gone; falling back on old habits was a natural response.

Victoria was stylishly dressed in designer jeans and a cashmere sweater. Her short curly blond hair was spiked in all directions but looked chic and damn pretty. She held out a glass of bourbon and stepped into him as he drew closer. As he leaned in to kiss her, her hands pressed against his chest, and she murmured softly, "God, you smell wonderful."

Steven grabbed his drink and tossed it back quickly. Samantha, the plane, turbulence, inhaling, touching, the frightened look in her eyes—his brain was pulling from his rolodex of memories everything to do with her. He poured another drink and eased into a chair.

"I've been worried about you, sweetheart," Victoria said, pulling off his shoes. "You sounded very strange on the phone."

"I'm fine," he said roughly. "Would you mind?" he handed her his glass.

"Goal to get drunk?" she asked, handing him another drink.

"You my mother, too, Vic?" he asked sarcastically as the alcohol started to kick in.

"No, of course not," she said staring at him curiously. "I just thought if you needed a stress reliever, there are other things we can do."

"Not right now, but I wouldn't rule it out." He had always liked her ample ass and running his hand over it now brought his body to attention. "Damn, physical reaction; nothing more than a reflex," he mumbled with disgust.

"What is?" Victoria asked. "Look something is obviously wrong, Steven. Talk to me."

He pushed passed her and brought the bottle back to his chair. "I told you I was lousy company. Go home, Vic. Maybe I'll be better tomorrow."

"Is this about Cinderella?" Victoria asked.

"Who?"

"Cinderella. That's what Jenny calls her. I'm guessing you're Prince Charming?"

He poured another drink. "Some prince. I slept with her and left before she woke up this morning."

"Ouch, that isn't like you. You're usually very gallant even if you never want to see the woman again."

"I do want to see her. I fucked up." His eyelids were getting heavy, and the glass fell from his hand. "I do want to see her." His uneven snoring and his pained expression even as he slept had Victoria worried. She had always known someday one of them would meet someone, and they would remain just friends. She had thought she might be the one with her handsome beau, Derrick, but he had yet to pop the question, and she was still a free woman. Steven was such a virile man; it would be easy for any woman to enjoy him. But Jenny had given her forewarning. He had some kind of attachment to this girl that she didn't like, and usually her instincts were right. She had never seen Steven like this, though. For now he could sleep, and she carefully hid the rest of the bourbon in the back of the cupboard. She would order a simple dinner from room service, and she was going to make him talk to her. If he had real feelings for Cinderella, it would be a first for her friend, and she would not let him boot his opportunity by listening to Jenny.

It was very late when Steven finally stirred. "You're still here, Vic?"

"Jenny sent me your new book. I just started it, but it's wonderful."

"It doesn't matter. Something smells good."

"I ordered dinner, but maybe you'd like to shower first."

He nodded and wondered, as he got in the shower, what Samantha was doing. It wasn't supposed to end like this. He was going to take her to dinner, ply her with alcohol, twirl her around the dance floor, and take her back to his room where she'd make those soft moans that drove him out of his mind. He claimed her; she was his, and he fucked up, but he wasn't going to make a second mistake by letting her go. Funny how everything suddenly seemed to make sense. He didn't know where they were going, but he wanted to find out. And he was better than a coward, running from his feelings and worrying about what he couldn't control. He was treating Samantha like a child that needed protecting instead of treating her like the beautiful woman she was. They'd figure this out together whether they stayed together or not. The question was whether Samantha would give him a second chance.

He dried off and pulled on sweats and a t-shirt. He was such an idiot sometimes. How could he even think about using

Victoria for sex? Compounding one mistake with another would be stupid. He wouldn't touch her—not when all he could think about was Miss not so fine, his Samantha, but he was going to tell Vic everything. She understood him, and she would help him sort things out.

Over dinner Steven told Victoria about Samantha. How they met on the plane, her insane fear of flying, the article she was writing, what they did in San Diego, the workshops, the night on the beach. He told her everything and finished with how he had messed up.

"Well," Victoria smiled, "she has obviously made an impression on your heart, my friend. What are you going to do about it?"

"I'm not sure. She won't even speak to me."

Victoria grinned. "She's Cinderella, and she's waiting for her Prince Charming to get his head out of his ass and find her. Remember the glass slipper?"

He remembered the sexy heels. He wasn't likely to forget them any time soon.

"Steven, about us." He looked up to see her standing over him. "I'd like to put us on hold. You have this woman you want, and I have my stock broker."

Steven nodded. "It's after three. If you want to crash till morning, I'll sleep out here."

"I talked to Derrick while you were in the shower. He's waiting up." She kissed his cheek as she left his apartment. "Call me if you need me."

Steven was still thinking when he dumped his luggage on the bed. The t-shirt from the night on the beach was still damp and wrapped inside was Samantha's blue lace panties. He rubbed them between his fingers. Maybe it was an omen, but it told him she belonged to him, and he was going to get her back one way or another. He didn't care what time it was, and he didn't care, for now, if she answered, but she was going to get a text every hour until she talked to him. Then he needed somehow to see her face to face. Maybe he could go to Charleston, though there wasn't a break in his schedule for a while. What should he text? Go big, or go home. **I miss you and wish you were here.**

California was earlier; she'd be asleep, but she was going to find several texts when she checked her phone. An hour later he texted, **Looked on-line, closest cornflower blue, your eyes, but still not a perfect match.**

The third hour he kept it simple. **Still in San Diego? I wanted to take you dancing.** Then the following hour, **Talk to me.**

Still in the wee hours of the morning, her text came back. She obviously wasn't sleeping, either. **Stop, please.**

He had her attention. His fingers flew across the letters. **Please don't cry. Talk to me.**

Nothing. He waited, eyes glued to the small screen. **Clairvoyant, like in the auditorium? Leave me alone.**

He exhaled impatiently. **My turn, we still have the article to finish. Why won't you talk to me?**

She answered seconds later. **Article is done, and there is nothing left to say.**

He didn't have to worry about hurting her, because he had done a damn good job already. He continued his assault with text messages all that day and the next. He even tried calling her, but she wouldn't pick up. It was Sunday, and she was facing that long plane ride back to Charleston. When he realized she must be at the airport, he tried again. **Keep the shade up and your eyes open, try to relax, and don't molest the guy next to you.** His heart cringed, the spot hurt harder, and he tried to block an image of some asshole holding her hand and comforting her.

Her answer took him by surprise. **It's none of your business. I'll molest whomever I want.**

He loved her spirit. **I'll post bail when you get arrested.**

Save your money, she shot back. **I'd rather rot in jail than take anything from you.**

Maybe that was it. He got her in the water by getting her angry. **I'm going to call you when you get home, and you're going to answer, because it's a challenge.**

No, she replied.

Coward. He waited.

Coward? You're an ass, and I'm boarding.

I'm with you, Sam. He should be hugging her and walking her to the gate.

No, you're in Chicago, and I'm going home to my real life—to my cruel stepmother and two ugly stepsisters, but, at least, I got to attend the ball.

He let out his breath slowly. Jenny must have leveled the Cinderella story at her. He realized Jenny had lied to him. She hadn't told Samantha he went to some damn meeting. What did that have to do with Cinderella? He'd fire her if she deliberately tried to get rid of her. He was seething as he placed a call to Jenny

"Steven, dear, how are you and Victoria?"

"We're fine, and Vic is seriously involved with her stock broker."

"I see. Well, you know many women in that area? Lindsey Mallet always had a thing for you."

"Stop setting me up, Jen. I want to know what you told Samantha."

"Haven't you gotten over that little gold digger yet? I thought once you got out of San Diego, she'd be nothing but a distant memory."

"You thought wrong," Steven snapped. "What did you tell her? You, obviously, didn't tell her about any meeting."

"She tell you that?" Jenny asked.

"No, she won't talk to me."

"Damn it, Steven. That should tell you something. She's not right for you, even she knows it. Apparently, you're the only one that didn't get the memo."

"I hired you to manage my career, Jen, but you better find a way to get along with Samantha, because I intend to keep her in my life," he warned. "There's no point to my staying here after this afternoon. I have the one book signing that I moved up, and then I am leaving for New York."

"I will see you there soon," Jenny said quietly.

Steven went right to the airport after the book signing in Chicago. He'd be in New York sooner than he planned, but it would give him time to think through a plan to fix things with

Samantha. At best, she was communicating with him in text messages or not answering him at all. When she did answer, she was angry. That had to be the key to his plan. As he checked into another hotel in one of the most energetic cities in the world, he realized how tired he really was. He had been across the country twice in the last month, hitting key marketing cities promoting his new book. He would be glad to get back to Baltimore then lose himself at the cabin. But first he had to find a way to get Samantha back. He opened his lap top and found her email with the article attachment. He read it carefully several times. She was an excellent writer. Her style was crisp, flowed smoothly, and her word usage impeccable. He appreciated her attention to detail, and the gentle way she treated his family. She included touches of humor, personalizing the piece and treated him far better than he deserved. The piece was perfect, and he typed yes to her curt 'do you approve?' But he realized, just in time, that if he approved the piece, she was officially done with him. No reason to talk; no reason to see each other. He had nothing else to add, nothing to criticize, but he couldn't approve it, and he hadn't yet begun to get her angry. He typed instead. **Sorry, no. It's not finished.** He called Pete and left a message on his voice mail just as her response came through.

I think it is, but have I missed something?

Missed several things, he returned, **but can't talk now. Call later.**

Pete called a short time later. "Steven, I hope you are happy with the piece. I know Sam has been anxiously awaiting your approval."

"That's why I am calling you, Pete. Samantha did a wonderful job on the article. She's an excellent writer, but I feel it is incomplete, missing something so I can't approve it, yet."

"Incomplete how? Is it something Sam can fix?" His anxiety clearly humming through the phone.

"I'm sure we can work this out, Pete, and it will benefit both of us. Let me explain. I'm in New York where I'm doing several book signings and promotional deals. On Saturday, I'm on the late-night talk show with Berry Bing. My agent is involved in negotiations to turn one of my books into a movie. She's discussing the possibility of someone writing the screenplay this week. I don't see anyone quoted in the article who attended my workshops or book signings. I think my public would like that, and the bottom line is I want the press, and you want to sell magazines." Steven took several deep breaths, trying to slow his heart down to a reasonable pace. His ideas had come as an avalanche, exploding as he tried to make it worthwhile for Pete to put Samantha back on a plane—back to him.

"Wow, Steven, that is all amazing."

"Pete, understand, I didn't grant this interview lightly. I could have given it to some of the larger magazines, but I wanted the personal touch that a small publishing house would give me."

"I understand, and I want to accommodate, but my problem is meeting my deadline."

"Of course," Steven said, hoping he didn't sound overly anxious. "Here is what I propose. I need Samantha in New York now. She can shadow me and make the personal contacts with my public. I especially want her to cover the television appearance. This is new for me, too and could open some additional doors. I want her to talk to my agent about the things that are planned for the future. If Samantha stays till Sunday, she'll have everything she'll need to finish the article. It shouldn't take long since I love what she's done so far; she's just adding to it. If the whole process takes a week, can you still get it to bed within your deadline?"

"You bet I can, and it will be impressive, Steven. These new projects of yours are not public, and you are giving my magazine quite the exclusive. Can your agent provide me some pictures?"

"Yes, of course, and I think it will work well for both of us," Steven said quickly, "but I know how Samantha feels about flying. Will she come to New York?"

"Just leave it to me. She'll fly. She's committed to doing the article, and her career is on the line. I can give her much better assignments if she follows through with this."

Steven smiled smugly. She was going to kill him. "So, you will email me her flight information and talk to her about this opportunity?"

"Making her reservation right now and will talk to her shortly."

"Thanks, Pete. I'll buy you a drink next time I'm in Charleston."

Within a few minutes he had her flight information and the first of her texts.

What have you done?

He poured a drink and unwrapped his sandwich. He didn't want to answer her too quickly. **I want you to come to New York to finish the article.**

She answered so quickly, he didn't have time to put down his phone. **No, never. I'm not getting back on a plane to see you. Never, never, never.**

Don't be so dramatic. Have you ever been to New York? It will be a new experience.

I don't care about new experiences or what you need. I am not flying to New York.

Apparently, you are. He'd wait her out. He could see her spinning this to find another way to finish the article without seeing him.

She came back with her own plan. **Just tell me what you want. I'll make the changes from here. I'm sure I can fix it.**

He'd give her one last text on the subject, convincing her, he hoped, that it was futile to argue. **Discussed it with Pete. Want you to shadow me and meet with Jenny. I have your flight information and will pick you up.**

He waited again, counting the minutes. Come on, Samantha. Accept it.

Don't pick me up. I'll contact you when I settle in. You're out of your mind.

He closed his eyes tightly. That beautiful woman was coming. **I know, ever since I left you.**

Her text came back quickly, too quickly. **This is business. Nothing has changed.**

He swallowed the lump in his throat. Wrong attitude. He typed, **My turn, where is the bottle with the penny? I didn't see it with the other.**

When she didn't answer, he knew he had missed something. Silly, but it had bothered him that it hadn't been nestled together with the other. He flipped on the stereo and listened to the soft words of a man pining for a lost love—soulful, painful. He missed her.

You obviously don't clean out your carry-on. Don't make anything out of it.

He had dumped out his case in Chicago. What was she talking about? He pulled the bag onto the bed and dumped it again. Not finding anything, he checked the outside pocket he never used. He felt something cool and smooth with a crumbled scrap of paper. Samantha's little bottle safely tucked with him with a note.

You keep one to remind you of San Diego, and, of course, me. I've loved every minute with you here.

He stared hard at the tiny piece of paper, more determined than ever to get them back to where they had been in San Diego. More determined than ever to make her his again. He needed to show her, not tell her how sorry he was. He would convince her he wanted her in his life, couldn't live without her in his life, and he had just a few days to do it. He pulled her shell out of his pocket, the one he was still carrying around. I'm going to convince you, *Cara,* to give us another chance. You belong to me, Sam. You belong to me.

♥♥

Chapter Fourteen

He was out of his damn mind. Between the time change and her inability to sleep, Samantha was exhausted, and now Steven was dragging her to New York. What the hell was wrong with the man? Another plane ride, more watching him finesse his public especially the women who came to the signings, and more reminders that he had used her and left. She took the newspaper out of her tote that she had purchased when she arrived at the airport. She had stared at the picture repeatedly with the same response. It hurt like hell. The photographer had captured a picture of Steven in his pajamas kissing a woman good-bye in his doorway. The caption noted it was three in the morning, and Steven was with his Chicago beauty, Victoria Chamberlain. What hurt the most was that it was the day after he had left her in San Diego. Proof that she had meant nothing to him. She had spent some time on her computer. Steven either had great stamina, or the press had a great imagination. He had been linked to a lot of women, but the pictures with Victoria seemed genuine. There were pictures that went back several years when they were both younger, and they always seemed happy and connected. She sighed as her heart ached. She couldn't imagine what he was doing with this trip. She could have fixed the article from Charleston, saved the money and the anxiety of a plane ride, and saved her heart from pretending she didn't care about him. That would be the hardest part. This was business, and she couldn't forget it.

Pete had taken care of her air fare, but she had offered to pay for her room. That way Steven wouldn't know where she was staying. She found a small hotel in a quiet section of town and planned on checking in before texting him she had arrived. But the minute she landed, he bombarded her with texts till she couldn't keep up and called him. "I'm here. I need a schedule of where to be," she said firmly.

"Hello to you too, Samantha," he said softly in that deep rich voice that jangled her nerves immediately. "It's almost dinner time. Why don't we get something to eat and discuss my schedule? Where are you staying? I can pick you up."

Samantha took a deep breath. "No, Steven, I'm exhausted. Too many plane rides. I'm going to get a bite here and go to sleep early."

"I could come to you, and we could meet in the hotel restaurant for a little while."

"No, just text me where I need to be tomorrow."

"Samantha," Steven said slowly, "I know you're angry with me, but we have to work together. It's just dinner."

"I'm not angry. That would require me to care, and I don't. Good-night, Steven."

Damn, the whole point of getting her here was to spend time with her. It was killing him that she was here, and this guarded that he couldn't get close to her. There was an amazing city out there that they should be enjoying instead he paced his room trying to figure out how to break down her defenses. He texted his schedule for tomorrow, but she didn't respond. Maybe she really was asleep, but he had a feeling she was doing exactly what he was doing. At least, he hoped she was.

♥♥

Chapter Fifteen

Samantha bolted from the hotel lobby and frantically hailed a cab. She had tossed and turned most of the night and overslept this morning. She desperately wanted coffee, but she steered clear of the long line at the coffee stand at the door of the hotel. Maybe the bookstore later would have a coffee counter. According to Steven's schedule, he was meeting with a photographer for some promo pictures for the new book. As the cabbie made his way carefully through the crowded streets, Samantha watched the time anxiously. She had been to New York when she was a child, but she didn't recognize this particular neighborhood. In an effort to be close to on time, she walked the last block and was impressed with several art galleries and specialty shops. Maybe when she was done with Steven, she could return to do some shopping. Her steps slowed in front of a painting hanging in the window of one of the galleries; a beautiful seascape at night with stars, a gentle breeze, the cover of darkness, and the waves breaking on the shore. The tears flooded her eyes as she fought to hold them back. She had avoided Steven last night, but now she had to face him. She looked at her phone. Damn, she was late. She hurried up the block and entered the small photography studio. A well-dressed young man ushered her to a back room where another man was setting up for the shoot. There were pictures of Steven's books, several copies of the new book, and plenty of photography equipment—lens, cameras, and lighting.

"Where the hell is Samantha?" she heard from one of the dressing rooms.

She swallowed the last of her tears and pasted on a big smile. "I'm right here, my lord. Can I be of service?" She meant it sarcastically, but his hand reached swiftly outside the curtain and jerked her in. In the tiny dressing room, Samantha couldn't breathe. Steven filled it with his broad shoulders covered in an expensive looking silk shirt.

"You're late," he glared.

"I'm here. Why are you so upset?" He was close enough for her to feel his breath move lightly on her hair.

"Damn, I hate these things, Sam. Can you tie this for me?"

Samantha took the two ends of the tie. She had a feeling he could do this far better, but if he wanted to play this stupid game, she could play, too. She looped the tie like she had watched her father do a million times. When she finished, she backed into the wall to see her knot. "Satisfied?"

He nodded. "Black jacket or blue?" He held up both for her to see.

She was surprised he even wanted her opinion and more surprised, he seemed genuinely nervous. She was right when she thought despite his confidence, he could be vulnerable. "Black." She waited as he finished, because she couldn't get around him anyway. He stepped back to see his own image then picked up his coffee. Samantha's eyes widened.

"Missed your coffee this morning?"

"No, I'm perfect. Now, if you can just let me by."

"Tell you what," Steven said, backing her against the wall, "why don't you take my coffee? I'll share it with you."

He was too close. It would be so easy to lean into him, absorb his amazing scent, and feel again the power of his hard body against hers. He tipped her chin to meet his eyes. "I wanted to see you last night, but I'm glad you are here now." This was never going to work, and the universe knew it. She couldn't work with him like this. He brushed his lips lightly over her cheek, and heat flushed through every inch of her body. "You're still wearing the plastic ring?"

Samantha shrugged, trying to breathe. The oxygen had been sucked out of the tiny room. "It's stuck. I can't get it off."

"Soap and water?" he whispered, twisting her hair around his finger.

"Couldn't get it off. Believe it or not," Samantha said. "I'm considering amputation." He needed to step back, give her some space, but he seemed very comfortable exactly where he stood. "Steven, you should be out there." It didn't sound like her voice, but he wrapped her hand around his cup and backed out of the cubical. Samantha sipped his coffee to steady herself, but even alone in the tiny room, she felt the intimacy drinking from his cup. She stepped out as the photographer took several shots—serious or smiling, with the jacket or without, holding the book or not. It didn't matter. The man was still a god, and the universe was getting its revenge. It was one thing to fantasize about sleeping with Steven. It was an entirely different thing to have done it. No wonder he could have any woman he wanted, whenever he wanted. She looked away as the tears filled her eyes again.

He abruptly walked away from the camera and came to her, searching her eyes and questioning, "All right?"

"Fine, but I was thinking. These pictures will be beautiful but artificial. Is that the look you're going for?" She hadn't intended saying anything, but she needed a safe topic.

He looked at her thoughtfully. "What would you suggest?"

"Maybe some candid shots? We're in a beautiful city. Maybe try a more relaxed look at Times Square."

His photographer was nodding, and Steven agreed. "Jerry, can you bring some equipment to Times Square in an hour? Samantha and I will go back to my hotel so I can change, and we'll meet you there." He had her hand and was pulling her through the hall to the street.

"I'll wait for you here," she said, putting up little resistance against his strength.

"Don't be ridiculous," he scolded, hailing a cab. "I'm not leaving you here." He opened the door and guided her in.

"Steven."

"Don't say a word. This was your idea," he winked.

Worse idea she had ever had. She didn't want to go to his hotel room. She inched closer to the door. He had this appointment and a signing later. What could happen in an hour?

When they entered his room, Steven headed straight for the bedroom. "Come on in, Sam. I want your opinion." Could the universe be this cruel? She tried to slow down her thundering heart as she watched him throwing out possibilities. "Jeans, right? Different shirt?"

Her voice trembled. "Nice jeans—those. Same dress shirt. Upscale casual. Bring the black jacket for at least a couple of pictures. Maybe carrying it instead of wearing it for some." She took a step back, and he smiled his approval. Then he dropped his pants. Samantha gasped, turned bright red, and spun away to his quiet chuckle. She would have walked out of the room, but her legs forgot how to move.

Once dressed he moved behind her and circled her waist. "Sorry, I didn't think you'd mind. We were blissfully naked in San Diego."

She broke free of him and waited on the terrace. "You always seem to get a room with a balcony and a fabulous view."

He surrounded her at the rail and covered one hand with his. He kissed tenderly behind her ear and started a trail down her neck. "Sam, tell me what you need? What can I do to make things right?"

She shrugged helplessly as the first tear slipped down her cheek. "It wasn't anything, Steven. Let it go. I was just business, the article."

He turned her around, locking her in against the rail. "You don't believe that, do you?"

"I don't know what to believe," she said, pulling away angrily. "You not only left San Diego, but me to draw my own conclusions." He was too close, attacking all of her senses at once.

"We need to talk. Have dinner with me." Samantha's no came so fast, Steven took a step back. His eyes darkened, and his jaw set. Stiffly, he grabbed his jacket. "I guess we should go then. Jerry is waiting." He didn't wait for her but instead headed to the elevator. It was chilly in the cab. He made no move to close the space between them, touch her hand, or make conversation. If it were possible, she felt farther away from him then she did waking up alone in San Diego. He stared out the window and impatiently tapped his foot against the seat.

Samantha watched from a distance as Jerry tried to set up the pictures, but after twenty minutes he seemed happier adjusting his equipment. Steven, realizing nothing was getting done, stormed off and paced a few feet away. Samantha approached Jerry tentatively. "It doesn't look like it's going very well."

"This morning before you showed up, he was angry and impossible. He scared the hell out of my receptionist. I don't think he thought you were going to show. Then he was fine during the shoot—all smiles and Mr. Cooperation."

"Maybe coming out here wasn't a good idea," Samantha apologized.

"No, it was a great idea, but he's back to being an ass," Jerry flinched. "Look, he pays me well to do a good job. I know he's demanding, and I don't mind, but he's not going to sell many books when he looks like he's pissed at the world."

Samantha's ring caught the sun, and the amber stone gave off a brilliant glow. She rubbed her thumb over the stone like she did when thinking about Steven drove her crazy. "I'll talk to him, Jerry. Give us a few minutes."

"Want a whip and a chair," Jerry teased unsmiling.

Samantha walked up behind him and rubbed her hands over his shoulders. Neither said a word as she moved in front of him. She tried to meet his eyes, but he continued to look passed her to the courtyard ahead. "Roll your sleeves to the elbow," she said softly. "Please." He rolled the sleeves slowly without looking at her. She unbuttoned the second button on his shirt and successfully got his attention—hard and angry. "You might sell more books if you smiled." Beneath the hard exterior, Samantha saw the hurt and the struggle to check his emotions. Damn, she was stupid to think they could work together without airing out what had happened. "You asked to talk over dinner."

"And you flatly refused."

"No to talking and dinner together. Talking is going to involve some yelling, Corso, so I don't want to talk over dinner."

Steven turned to her curiously. "You'd talk to me in a more private place?"

She nodded. "Not a hotel room. Somewhere comfortable, quiet, and neutral."

He smiled at that—neutral. "Like the public library?"

"Maybe, but we would probably disturb the peace."

Steven snapped his fingers. "The Lake at Central Park. It's perfect. The view is perfect, there is a restaurant with great food and drink, and even boat rides. It'll be fun, and we can really talk, Sam." His expression turned somber, and Samantha's heart hurt.

"Sounds neutral enough," she smiled. "Why don't you go finish with Jerry now?"

He seemed lighter, and Samantha watched his charm come back. Jerry worked quickly and seemed revived by Steven's comeback. He was so damn handsome, but she had no expectation that he could explain away the mess in San Diego. At least, they could put it all out on the table and then finish the article like professionals. She'd take her broken heart back to Charleston, and... Her eye caught the silly plastic ring that slipped easily back and forth over her finger. She wanted to throw it away, but she couldn't take it off leaving his hotel room, or on the plane, or any day since coming home. It was stupid that her wounded heart refused to let go of a few days in sunny California with the man of her dreams. She'd forget Steven, because she'd have to, but as he turned toward the camera for the final shot, Samantha saw something else. Hope, how could he look so hopeful?

♥♥

Chapter Sixteen

The promo shoot took longer than expected so there wasn't time for lunch, but Steven knew the tiny bookstore well that would host his book signing. It was tightly packed with narrow aisles and stacks and stacks of books. It also had a small area for three tables, two steps up overlooking the entrance with a coffee bar and small homemade sandwiches and cookies. Samantha marveled at Steven in his element. He immediately met with the owner, a small elderly man with a full head of thick white hair and an engaging smile. They shook hands warmly, though, the older gentleman circled his shoulders and gave him a small hug. They spoke rapid Italian while Steven helped move several tables and boxes of books. Samantha moved to a table and jotted down a few notes including a comment from Jerry. Steven was already pouring coffee in two ceramic mugs and dividing a sandwich for them as she approached the counter.

"Real cups?"

"Owner has been doing business for 40 years the same way," Steven said, a note of affection in his voice. "He wouldn't think of serving his customers coffee in paper cups."

"I'm going to sit here and take some notes, Steven. I'd like to talk to some of your fans." She took a bite of the sandwich that tasted of unique herbs and Italian deli meats.

While Samantha watched, an elderly woman set down her cup on the other side of her table. "May I sit here?" she asked, looking warily at the other two tables occupied by men.

"Please do," Samantha offered. She noticed the woman clutching Steven's book to her chest as she settled in her seat and sipped her tea. Her soft gray hair was pulled back and pinned at the nape of her neck, but she had the most striking dark eyes and olive complexion. She would have been a beauty in her day.

"He is handsome, isn't he?" she brightened. "Dark and handsome, but I'm prejudiced. I love Italian men. They are so full of life, so strong, so passionate." Her cheeks turned bright pink, and her eyes twinkled with mischief.

"He is handsome," Samantha agreed.

"Are you and Steven together?" she asked, peeking over her cup.

"I work for him. I'm doing an article for my magazine about him." The woman was looking at her curiously, and it made Samantha a little uncomfortable. "We aren't together or anything."

"But he's interested in you. He hasn't taken his eyes off you since you sat down."

"Sophia," the owner of the shop called out. He waved frantically at her, but she just smiled. She waved back but made no move to leave.

"My Gianni," she grinned at Samantha. "He is such a worrier. I tell him the people come for Steven, and everything will be fine. He is a wonderful man."

"Married a long time?" Samantha asked.

"My, yes, but he makes me feel like a girl sometimes. So, you might be interested in Steven, too?"

Samantha laughed and shook her head. She needed to change the subject. "Are you getting his book signed today?"

"Oh, yes, I have all of his books, and everyone signed."

"All?" Samantha repeated. "Does he always come here?"

"He signs them for me here, or at Christmas dinner, or on my birthday."

Samantha stopped in mid-sentence with her next question when she heard Steven. He had gathered a large crowd; some scattered in the aisles, on the steps of the coffee bar, and in the doorway, and out into the street. He had his book open to the first chapter, and his deep masculine voice read the first few pages to the quietest New York crowd Samantha had ever heard. She was touched by Sophia who sat with her eyes closed listening with her heart. And her own heart fluttered with pain for this man. When he finished, people moved toward the table to have their books signed.

Sophia waited patiently. "He reads so beautifully," she said softly, tears in her eyes. "It wasn't so long ago that I read to him like that when he was just a little boy."

Who was this woman?

"Sophia?" Samantha began, but the woman rose quickly and placed her cup in the sink.

She retrieved her book and patted Samantha's hand. "Steven's a very intense man, but a very good man and worth a woman's patience."

"Steven is… I mean, he sees a lot of women."

"But he looks at you differently than the others. You must open your eyes to see." She marched off and joined her husband who was still talking to Steven. He hugged Sophia and signed her book. His gaze was tender and loving, and then he turned and looked at her. 'Open your eyes and see.' Could he see how deeply he affected her? Could she read the heat and desire in his eyes and maybe something more? It would be too easy to read too much—to see what she wanted to see reflected in his eyes.

He pulled her up and, holding tightly to her hand, guided her out of the shop. "Walk with me, Sam."

Samantha wasn't sure where he went. He was deep in thought, restless, but he didn't let go of her hand, holding it like an anchor keeping him grounded and safe. She walked along beside him dodging the pedestrians on the street and waiting for him to come back. When he finally let go of her hand to wrap his arm around her shoulders, she ventured a question.

"My turn, Sophia and Gianni are?"

"My grandparents. I grew up in that bookstore, hiding in the aisles lost in books for hours. *Mia nonna* taught me to love books and encouraged me to write. They are both almost eighty, and I worry about them." He looked away, fighting the swell of emotion—of love.

Samantha nodded. She didn't know who made the move, but she felt him gather her in and settle his head against hers. New Yorkers passed by seemingly unfazed by the couple.

Samantha moved gently back. “I’ll just go back to my hotel to freshen up. Pick me up at six at the Belmont.”

Steven raised an eyebrow. He thought he was going to fight her again for the name of her hotel. “Room number?”

“I’ll meet you out front.”

“I’m nothing if I’m not a gentleman, Sam. Please, room number?”

Samantha sighed. “312. Third floor.”

Steven put her in a cab and watched it drive away. Tonight was a turning point; he was running out of time. He had to convince Samantha to start over and to give him a chance to fix the disaster in San Diego. He smiled at the busy street, the people hurrying to work or home, at the magic of the city when the sun went down. He needed the magic to win her heart, and New York had never failed him.

♥♥

Chapter Seventeen

Samantha's stomach loudly grumbled on cue when Steven suggested dinner first at Central Park on the Lake. The restaurant was busy, but they were seated quickly, and the hostess brought two glasses of wine. Getting the attention of the waiter took a little longer, but the view was breathtaking, and neither was in a hurry to rush dinner.

"Sam, about San Diego."

"Not over dinner," Samantha interrupted. "What is your schedule for tomorrow?"

"Jerry will have the proofs for me in the morning. I hope you will look at them and help me decide what photos to use."

"I have some favorites." Samantha sipped her wine. She had no intention of over drinking tonight. She wanted to be clear headed when they finally faced the wedge between them.

"Then I have the official launch of my book at Sanders Books. It's one of the largest in New York. Three floors—small restaurant. I'll be signing most of the afternoon."

"I can't imagine writing something that people actually want to read. Would make me dizzy with happiness."

Steven reached across the table for her hand. "Did you write anymore when you got back to Charleston?"

"I wrote your article in San Diego and distracted myself on the plane by starting my own story. It's just a few pages, but I'm not really happy with it. Then I wasn't home long enough to think about it again."

"Sometimes you just need a tranquil spot away from everyone. My cabin, for instance. I go there when I need to get away and can't seem to write anything. Maybe you should go there. I could take you up there sometime and leave you till you are ready to come home."

"Your cabin?" Samantha asked warily.

"I'd promise to leave you alone. Wouldn't be much point if you don't have the space to create. You could enjoy the outdoors and write till your heart's content." He could imagine them both at his cabin, walking through the woods or swimming in the lake in the daytime and loving her during the night. He coughed uncomfortably and sipped his wine.

Samantha couldn't help but ask. "How many women have you brought to your cabin, Steven?" She stared into the rich burgundy wine till she realized he wasn't answering. When she looked up, she saw her answer before he spoke. "I've never taken anyone there, but my brothers have used it on occasion."

Samantha was grateful the waiter chose that moment to take their order. She wondered why Steven would even suggest the cabin. She was certain their relationship would end in a couple of days and suggesting anything else was leading her on, making her hope, and hurting her further. She blinked back tears as she saw the concern in the eyes across the table. "I'm not ready to jump into a book," she said lightly, "I still have a job back home, and Pete keeps me busy. I think you were right about the article; there is so much more to you—career wise, that is. I'm glad I'm revising it."

"There is more to me as a man." Steven's husky voice washed over her. "I want you to know me, Samantha."

"I thought I did know you." The tears came dangerously close to spilling so she reached a tentative hand for a slice of bread. "But, in all fairness, it was only a few days. How could anyone really know anyone in a couple of days?"

Steven exhaled and repositioned in his chair. "Trust yourself, Sam. You weren't wrong to trust your instincts in San Diego. I screwed up."

"Stop." Samantha took a big bite from her bread, hoping it wasn't possible to chew and cry at the same time. "Have some of this wonderful bread, Steven." She wouldn't meet his eyes and was mercifully spared when their dinner arrived. They ate in polite silence.

"Dessert?" Steven asked.

"No, thank you, couldn't," Samantha answered. "Coffee?"

"Mind if we take it to go?" He couldn't keep silent any longer. They needed to talk, and he needed to make her understand. He handed his credit card to the waiter. How could he make Sam understand what he hadn't understood till this moment sitting across the table from her? On the plane he was so sure she wasn't his type, but somewhere between the auditorium and the plastic ring and her hands exploring his chest under the water, she had become his exact type. Every other woman even Vic, he had easily walked away from, but this woman, fidgeting in her seat and rearranging her purse again, had accomplished the one thing no other woman had. She made him smile on the inside and broke him to his knees. If he had to follow her back to Charleston to make this right, he would, because he wanted to spend more time with her, make love to her, and hang on to her.

Samantha pulled her sweater tighter around her. The sun dress had been adequate during the day, but the chill in the evening air made her shiver. She sipped the hot dark brew and looked out at the rowboats gliding effortlessly on the lake. "Looks like fun," she said hurriedly, in an effort to stall any meaningful conversation. She wasn't sure she wanted to talk about San Diego anymore. It was over, and she couldn't imagine anything good coming out of it. She cleared her throat and turned her attention back to the man who had too much power over her. "No matter where this conversation leads," she said slowly, "we have to work together for a while longer, Steven."

He nodded. "I want to make it easier, honey, and better."

Summoning her courage, she dove in. "My turn, Jenny said you left San Diego to go to Victoria." She hated the strained sound of her own voice. "I didn't believe her, at first."

Steven stopped and held her arm. "You can't listen to Jenny."

"I know, but that much was true, wasn't it?"

He was too guarded, too angry as he searched for his answer. "Victoria was in Chicago, and I did see her, but you make it sound like I left you to be with her, and that wasn't the case."

"Wasn't it?" Damn it, the way out of this wasn't to lie. "Isn't that exactly what it was? I was just a fling till you woke up and wanted Victoria. So, without even a good-bye, you left me."

"No, that is not what happened, Sam. That's not why I left." He didn't know how bad this was; how she had truly misread his actions.

Samantha yanked her arm away and dug into her tote. Slapping the newspaper she still carried against his chest, she glared at him. "I honestly didn't think you'd lie, but the picture doesn't lie."

"What picture?" He unfolded the paper to see the picture of Victoria outside his hotel room. "Samantha, this isn't what it looks like."

"It looks like Victoria leaving your hotel room at three in the morning. Read the caption. You in your pajamas kissing her good-bye. Seems pretty clear, Steven, that you took her to your bed less than twenty-four hours after you left me. Says a lot about what we were, don't you think?" She walked quickly away from him toward the shore.

"Sam, wait, you have this all wrong." Steven chased after her. "Nothing happened between Victoria and I. The papers do this all the time."

"I know that," she snapped. "I saw you linked to a lot of women on the internet, but the difference was your relationship with Victoria was long standing—years. You looked happy with her. Made me wonder why you didn't just marry the damn woman."

"Because I don't love her." He sat down on the rocks beside her. "Vic and I have a great friendship, and we are there for each other—even physically, but not this time." He pointed to the picture. "Not this time. What did happen was I got drunk and slept it off. Then Vic and I had dinner where all I did was talk about you—everything including how I left you."

Samantha stared at the water. "She didn't want to ease your pain with a romp in the sack?"

He smiled gently and tipped her chin toward him. "She has a friend she wants a lasting relationship with. She could have stayed over, but she went home to him. Vic and I seem to be looking for something real, not just easy and comfortable. She gave me some advice about you, though."

"What?"

"She told me to go find Cinderella."

Samantha groaned. "She calls me that, too?"

"Not like Jenny," Steven added quickly. "She suggested you might be able to forgive me. Was she right, Sam?"

Samantha turned away. "If you didn't leave for Victoria, why did you go?"

He ran his hands over her shoulders and gently kissed the curve of her neck. "My turn, tell me first what you expected the next morning when you woke up?"

"Expected?" she said sarcastically. "I guess I expected you to be there."

His warm breath moved behind her ear. "Besides that, what did you expect would happen?"

She turned to look at him. "I expected breakfast, more fun in the sun, and more hot sex. Is that what you mean?"

"I mean, what did you want that morning? Be honest with me."

Once again Samantha bit back the tears. "I wanted two days in San Diego with you." She caught his surprise, and, suddenly, she had a little bit of clarity. "You thought I'd want more, didn't you? Thought I'd want what? A diamond ring? A declaration of love? You thought I was a Corso groupie perhaps? I'd declare my undying love for you, and you'd have to deal with a pathetic inexperience female? You'd be forced to hurt me? That's why you left, you egotistically asshole?" She was yelling now and walking—running away down the beach. She had to get away from him. She stumbled for a moment, regained her balance, and kept moving.

He caught up with her swiftly and held her tightly against him. She struggled angrily, trying to push him away till the tears won, and she broke in his arms. "I'm so sorry, Samantha. I was so afraid of hurting you then or in a couple of days when we parted."

She brushed at her tears. "So, you thought it'd be less painful to humiliate me and just leave?"

"I never wanted to humiliate you. Believe it or not, I was confused the next morning, feeling things for you I normally don't feel the morning after. I needed to sort things out, and Jenny suggested Chicago."

"Jenny," Samantha yelled. "I should have guessed she'd be in the middle of this somewhere. You listened to her instead of following your own heart?" Her chest heaved, and her voice trembled. "You never made me any promises that night, Steven, and I didn't expect any. I'm an adult woman. I had feelings for you, and I acted on them, and that was all there was to it. I wanted those two days with you and then I was going home with my memories without making any claim on you. All you had to do was talk to me like an adult."

"And I had feelings for you, and I wanted the two days in San Diego too. I wanted—want you in my life, Sam, if you can forgive me and start over."

"I don't know. How can I trust you won't disappear again without a word?"

"You can't, but you can let me earn your trust back, Sam. I'm not going anywhere. You don't have to believe it now, but I will prove it to you. And I don't know how, but I don't want us to end when we go home. I can come to Charleston, and you can meet me wherever. It doesn't have to end."

"I don't want to be your Charleston hookup. I don't want you to breeze in and out while I read about you and other women in between." Samantha eased back down on the rocks. "I can't be that casual about you. Maybe we could just be friends."

Steven pulled her to her feet. He cupped her cheek, drawing her hips in line with his. He teased her lips till she met his—warm and needy. When he broke the kiss, he was sure she could feel the pounding of his heart. "No, more than friends. I want you, Sam, need to feel you against me, in my arms, joined to me in heat." His fingers slid down her back caressing her hip and meeting the slightest bit of flesh at her waist. "I want you, Samantha, tonight."

"Not tonight, Steven, I can't." She couldn't breathe. He was stealing the air, bombarding her with scent, touch, and taste. The sun was setting, and dusk falling rapidly.

"I want more, honey. This is new for me—wanting someone to stick around. Be patient with me, with us, and we'll sort it out."

"I don't know, Steven."

"I know. Give us some time." He guided her lips back to his. A kiss soft and laced with promise if she could let her heart believe.

"I don't know. Please take me back to my hotel."

His heart sank. She was processing. She had let her heart lead in San Diego, and he had hurt her. She needed time to hear him, to feel him, and to trust her heart to him again. He wanted her right here, right now, but it was clearly her call, and he had to respect that. He kissed her once more at her door and texted her later good-night.

Chapter Eighteen

Steven had a restless night. No surprise he thought a lot of Samantha. He tried unsuccessfully to wipe the images of that one night together out of his mind. She was a beautiful woman and, with her in the same city, wanting her didn't seem too unusual till he thought of other women he had left behind. Beautiful women that he had enjoyed, and he could say with certainty that they had enjoyed him, but when he left, they didn't linger in his mind. If they ran into each other months later, they might spend another night together, but it wasn't like he felt the need to pursue these women. But with Samantha she haunted his thoughts, appeared out of nowhere without provocation, made him smile at unexplained moments, and tightened his chest when he thought of losing her. The hot mess from the plane was turning his life upside down.

He was taking her to the Empire State Building when he met all the duties of his schedule today. She would kill him when she learned they were going to view the magnificent sites from the top deck of the tallest building in the city. He could imagine her outrage and her fear, but it would be worth the ride, and he knew in the end she'd be captivated by the view. If they were lucky, they might even catch the lightshow from the tower from one of the local bars. He purchased vouchers for the tickets on-line during the night, and he'd surprise her later in the day. He poured a little bourbon in a glass—velvet and strong.

His conflicted thoughts turned to Jenny. He had never questioned her motives; even when he didn't agree with her, he always thought she had his best interests at heart, but she had underestimated his feelings for Samantha. He was still angry that she had tried to sabotage their relationship. He had made it clear to Sam that Jenny needed to be consulted about the article. Now he needed to make it clear to Jenny that she better be nice and cooperative with Sam. He would never deny all she had done for his career, but she had no business running his personal life.

He closed his eyes and let the alcohol seep into his tired muscles and almost fell asleep when he heard the familiar ping of his phone.

Thought you might be up. Are you? Sam's text lit up the screen.

Are you all right? He typed back. **Why aren't you asleep?**

Fine, no one sleeps in this city, and I'm beginning to understand why. It has a life, an energy that defies sleep.

Have you been to New York before?

As a child, but I don't remember much.

We're going sightseeing tomorrow. We're going to see the entire city.

In one day? You're crazy.

About you. Sleep, I need you well rested tomorrow, love.

Good-night, Steven.

Steven stared at the amber liquid. She should be here with him, warming his bed and his body, smiling at his bossiness, and sleeping tucked in close to him. Yes, she should be here, and they both would sleep better, at least, for part of the night till he wanted her again—needed her in a way that made him weak. He wouldn't quit till she surrendered, because that was the only acceptable outcome—surrender. Just as he had surrendered his heart, he needed to recapture hers.

♥♥

Chapter Nineteen

Steven was late, and Samantha paced the small hotel room impatiently. She suspected he was never late for anything and, yet, he was nearly half an hour overdue from the time he had demanded she be ready. His schedule wasn't nearly as tight as yesterday so maybe he had lingered over a second cup of coffee. She leaped at the door when she finally heard an insistent tap. Throwing it open, she stopped in mid-sentence at the sight of Mr. Gorgeous carrying several stems of the most beautiful shade of blue orchids. "Sorry," he grinned. "I had the cab driver stop at three florists looking for this unique flower, ocean breeze orchids. I'm still looking for a match to your eyes."

Damn, the man was almost perfect, and the orchids were beyond perfect. Samantha found a small container and set the flowers on the counter. "What made you think of flowers this morning?"

"I don't know, but it wasn't this morning. More like the middle of the night and to your next question, no."

"No what?" she asked, looking confused.

"I've bought a bouquet or two for a woman, but, unimaginatively, typical roses, never orchids. I thought you'd prefer something unique." He let his hands drift over the soft curve of her hips as she kissed him lightly. "Mm, we have so much to do today, and all I want to do is stay here with you, Sam."

"You promised me sightseeing later which is about the tamest thing you've suggested since I've met you. Nothing crazy or risky so I am holding you to it. Jerry first. I'm dying to see the pictures."

Steven shrugged. "Just remember later, you wanted to go sightseeing, love."

Jerry was running late when Samantha and Steven arrived. The young man behind the desk cringed and cowered relaying the news to Steven. "We'll wait," Samantha intervene. "We'll take a walk. I want to show you something anyway."

She walked him back to the gallery where the seascape still sat in the window. He liked the colors and the way the night played off the water, but he pulled her away when he spotted Jerry waving frantically from his cab as he arrived.

"I'm so sorry, but I worked late on these last night and overslept this morning." He laid the pictures across the table for Steven to inspect. "Remember these aren't finished, but they are good quality proofs."

They were amazing. Samantha picked out her favorites immediately, but she waited as Steven's critical eye glanced over them several times. "I don't know," he finally said. "I should probably leave this to Jenny."

He left too much to Jenny. "Steven, they are all wonderful, but think about your purpose and your audience. This one, serious businesslike but sexy as hell, to sell in New York. This one, more casual, smiling, and still sexy as hell, in California. And this one I want, because it's just sexy as hell."

Steven laughed. "I'll take them with me, Jerry, and let the ladies decide."

Jerry wrapped up the pictures. "She has a good eye, boss. She was right about the location shots. You should think about hiring her."

He definitely had plans for Miss not so fine, both professionally and personally, and that thought widened the smile on his face.

They stopped for coffee and a breakfast sweet then headed to the bookstore. It was huge in contrast to the tiny shop from the day before. This one had three floors with a real restaurant that served light meals all day long. Jenny greeted Steven immediately, and Samantha decided it was too soon to deal with her. She headed upstairs to check out the layout for the signing.

"So, have you seen this morning's paper?" she asked, a smile spreading across her face. "I'd imagine Cinderella won't like the notoriety."

"Don't call her that," Steven snapped, "and what are you talking about?"

"There's a brief piece on the new book in this morning's paper, honey, just a couple of paragraphs, but the pictures are worth a thousand words. Can't say I didn't warn you."

Steven looked at the paper and cursed loudly. One picture seemed innocent enough of dinner at the Italian restaurant, but the other was when he had carried Sam through the hotel lobby. Someone might conclude she was asleep, but the caption noted the time of night, the dinner and the drinking, and insinuated she was his new toy for the moment. The picture could be picked up and used anywhere including Charleston. She would be embarrassed in front of family and friends. Steven turned his anger on Jenny. "I'll talk to her about this. I'm sure she will handle it. She's also going to talk to you about the article, and I'm telling you to be polite to her. She's going to be around."

"A while? Temporarily? Waste of energy," Jenny concluded.

"Not a while, not if I can help it," Steven replied. "Any more crap from you, too, and our next conversation will end with you're fired."

"No offense, honey, but I've seen you chase a woman before. It's short lived, at best."

"Not this time," Steven repeated.

Jenny had only seen Steven angry with her once before early in their relationship. She could be patient till he realized how wrong Cinderella was for him. "All right, Steven, I'll play nice, but you'd better tell her. I picked this up on the back shelf. She may see it, and we don't need a lot of immature theatrics."

Steven sought Samantha at a back table on the second floor where she was jotting down questions in her notebook.

"Something wrong?" she asked as he approached her.

His brow knitted together as he opened the paper before her. "I told you they do this with everyone I'm with. It goes with the territory, Samantha, but the good news is that they will see you're not going away." He watched her expression but couldn't read her thoughts. "Say something, Sam."

"Anyone can pick these pictures up, can't they?" she asked.

"Anyone, anywhere," he answered still anxiously awaiting a reaction.

"My folks and my brother will see this, but my biggest concern is Pete. I just wanted him to see me as a complete professional. He's going to think you threw me the article, because I slept with you." Her voice faltered for a moment then she sat back in her chair.

"You know that's not true, Sam. What you did was more than professional. It was an excellent piece, and when you add to it, it can only get better." He watched her eyes carefully as the blue appeared to change—darken to yet another shade he couldn't define.

She let out her breath slowly. "I guess I can't undo it, and it was my fault. Don't worry about it. Maybe no one will even see it."

"Samantha, I'm really sorry."

"Don't be, and you still have a lot to do." She relaxed into an easy smile. "There are worse things than being romantically linked to you like flying, drowning, or molesting a stranger on a plane. At least, they didn't get a picture of that."

Steven laughed and squeezed her hand. "By the way, I talked to Jenny. She won't give you a hard time when you talk to her."

Nice to know, but she still wasn't ready to talk to her.

Steven became busy with his public; he greeted them at the door and made small talk. At designated times during the day, he met the group who had gathered, reading passages from his book, answering questions, and finally signing his coveted signature. Samantha stayed out of the way. She didn't want to be recognized after the picture in the morning paper, she didn't want to talk to Jenny, and she didn't want to be distracted by the intense looks Steven threw her. She spoke to several people, trying to get a great quote for the article and needing a cup of coffee, she descended back down to the main floor.

The coffee warmed her as her gaze fell on a young girl in the children's section of the bookstore. She appeared alone among the books but glanced occasionally to the second-floor book signing. Samantha guessed her mother was seeing Steven while the little girl amused herself. She moved closer and watched her carefully lay three books on the tiny table in her section. Then she spun around, dancing in a graceful circle, arms over her head, and leg extended in a leap. Samantha slid into one of the overstuffed chairs on the outer edge of the section, and the little girl smiled a sweet childlike innocent smile. She squatted down to check her books again while Samantha observed her. Her long blond hair was divided into two beautiful long pigtails, and a silver tiara rested on her head. Undecorated, her dress was still dressy with the white bodice and the full blue skirt. On her tiny feet were ballet slippers; she spun in her circle again and leaped and twirled. Her smile was endless and lit up the room.

"That is such a pretty dress," Samantha commented.

She smiled shyly at first then burst into uncontrolled chatter. "I'm Katy, and I'm seven. I take ballet lessons then my mom and I come here to pick out books."

"Do you like to read?" Samantha asked.

"Oh, yes, I read, and mom reads to me, too. My most favorite book in the whole world is Cinderella. Have you ever read that book?"

"A long time ago," Samantha admitted. "Do you want to be a dancer?"

Katy looked at Samantha thoughtfully like a seven-year-old with a huge problem. "I love to dance." She twirled again to make her point. "But I want to be a princess like Cinderella." She carefully took the book off the table and brought it to Samantha. "See," she said, pointing to the last few pages of the book. "Her prince comes to find her. He tries the glass slipper on everyone, even her two ugly sisters. Then even though Cinderella is dressed in rags, he tries the slipper on her, and it fits." She spun away again—pure joy. "And the princess gets her prince. I want my prince to make me a princess."

"You will be a beautiful princess, sweetheart," Samantha said as the story took on a new meaning. "And what happens after the prince finds her, and he makes her a princess?"

"They live happily ever after, of course."

"Katy, you aren't bothering the nice lady, are you?" A young woman carrying Steven's book draped a protective arm around her princess.

"She's a delight—a beautiful child," Samantha told her. "I've enjoyed talking to her about princesses and dancing."

Her mother laughed. "Her two favorite things. She loves her ballet classes and then we come here. I couldn't miss Steven Corso. He's so hot, isn't he?"

Samantha grinned. "Enjoy his books?"

"I save just to buy his hardcover books. I love the feel of a real book and the pleasure reading his mysteries. And, of course, Katy gets to read Cinderella for the millionth time." She smiled tenderly at the little girl who was carefully returning her books to the shelf.

"May I buy this book for Katy?" Samantha asked. "I don't have any children, and I would love to see Cinderella in the hands of someone who would really love her."

Katy looked astonished and hopeful. "Please, Mom. My very own copy of Cinderella."

"Are you sure? That is very generous."

"I would love to. I just need to peel the bar code for the cashier, and the book is yours, princess." She stuck the price to her hand.

"Thank you. Could you sign my book?"

Samantha knelt down in front of her. "I didn't write the book, honey. Usually the author signs it."

"But you are giving it to me like a special present," Katy insisted.

"Like a signature on a card." **For Katy,** she wrote. **May you find your prince like Cinderella. Keep dancing. Love Samantha.**

As Katy and her mother left, Steven circled her waist from behind. "Make a new friend?" he teased.

She grinned. "I bought her a book; she was a sweetheart. Jenny still upstairs?"

Steven nodded. "She's in a mood." He rolled his eyes as Samantha took his hand and stuck the tag on it.

"Pay for this for me. I need to talk to Jenny." Samantha nearly skipped as she climbed the stairs.

"Hey," Steven called after her. "So, I bought the kid a book?"

"Seems fair," Samantha replied over her shoulder. "Her mother bought yours. She thinks you're hot if it matters."

Steven couldn't take his eyes off her as she made it to the top of the stairs and ventured around back to where Jenny was packing up his books. God, he loved that woman. He...loved...her. Paralyzed he couldn't move away, could only watch till she disappeared from sight. Of course, he loved her. Why else would the thought of losing her cut through his heart like a dagger? He had never thought about a woman in those terms before. He handed the sticker to the cashier and prayed Jenny was nice, because if anyone was leaving, it wouldn't be Sam. He loved her.

As Samantha approached Jenny, she straightened up and met her with a nasty smirk. "Well, if it isn't Cinderella."

Samantha's plan was to back Jenny down. She needed her input, because Steven had asked, and because she probably knew him better than anyone short of his family. It would be necessary to her article, but Jenny had seen too many woman come and go. If she wanted her to, at least, be civil and work with her, she'd have to command her respect. Deep breath, Samantha held out her hand. She was starting over. "I generally go by Samantha, Jenny. Nice to actually meet you."

Jenny glanced up at her warily and shook her hand. She returned to packing the heavy box of books.

"Steven asked me to talk to you." She put her hand down on the box, demanding Jenny's attention. She straightened begrudgingly and stared unimpressed. "I'd like to talk to you about the career plans you are working on for Steven. I know you are looking at a movie deal for one of his books."

"Yes, I am and a few other things."

"I haven't mentioned it to Steven, yet, but I'd like you to answer some questions too about your relationship with him. You've been with him a long time, know him well, and I know my readers would love to hear what he is like from your perspective, employer and friend."

Jenny smoothed the not-existent wrinkles from her skirt. "I could do that."

"Good, I know Steven has a meeting with his publisher tomorrow. Can we meet for breakfast? I assume, you are staying at the same hotel as Steven. I could meet you in the dining room at eight. Would that be all right?"

Jenny nodded. "Doable."

"Wonderful. I think my readers should have a glimpse of the woman behind the man." She turned to walk away feeling confident, but Jenny's words stopped her.

"Whatever Steven wants, Cinderella."

Samantha turned slowly, a pleasant smile on her lips, "Whatever Steven wants? Has it been a long time since you've read Cinderella? As I recall, in the end the prince finds her—wants only her. She gets her prince, and they live happily ever after." Jenny's jaw dropped. "I'll talk to you tomorrow."

Chapter Twenty

Samantha was excited when they finally left the bookstore. She spun around grinning at Steven. "Where do we start? Rockefeller Plaza, Times Square, Staten Island, Statue of Liberty, Central Park, a museum or art gallery. What's the plan, Corso? You usually have one."

"Today is your lucky day, lady. All of the above."

"But where are we starting?" she whined, climbing in the cab he offered.

"At the top," he smirked, "so you can see it all."

Samantha got suspicious in the cab. "What does that mean, Steven? You're hiding something from me."

He shook his head nonchalantly. "You'll see shortly."

"No surprises. The last surprise I nearly drowned."

"Don't get melodramatic on me. This is definitely not under water."

The cabbie pulled to the curb. "Empire State Building, Sir."

Samantha cleared the cab while Steven paid the fare. She looked straight up to the tallest building she had ever seen. He took a firm hold on her hand and started walking to the entrance.

"Steven, slow down. Where are you going?"

He pointed without looking at her. "Up there."

Samantha yanked him to a stop. "Up there? In the clouds?"

"Lower than an airplane, but definitely up there." He kept pulling while she was digging in trying to stop him.

"Wait, you think you are taking me up there?" Samantha asked. "No way."

"Sam, the view is amazing. You can see the whole city. I've done it, and it's easier than being in a plane." He held her eyes. "Come on, trust me."

Samantha caught sight of the very long line, wrapping around the building and trailing for a couple of blocks. "We'll be in that line forever."

"No, I bought vouchers on-line last night. We'll trade them for tickets at the office."

"You need to sleep at night."

He yanked her arm and pulled her into the lobby. As he exchanged the vouchers, she could already see the marble walls and the gorgeous mural. "Beautiful, isn't it? I paid a little more for an express pass to avoid another line. This way." They quickly passed through a second entrance to the security line. Much shorter, he had them in the lobby within a few minutes. She stood in awe and forgot her fear as she examined the mirror images of the marble and the artistry of the space. As he guided her to the elevator with his hand planted firmly in her back, she screeched to a stop again.

"How high are we going?" she demanded.

"The top, of course. It is the smaller of the two observation decks, and it is enclosed."

"How high, Steven?" she repeated.

"A mere 102 floors," he coughed.

"How many?"

"102, but it's not as bad as it sounds."

"No, it's worse. I'm not going." She turned to flee, but he caught her around the waist.

"We'll make the next elevator. This is a life experience you need, honey. Relax."

"I don't need this. I just wanted to walk around, and you've got us on a stationary airplane."

"If you don't want to then don't." Abruptly, he let her go; he angrily headed to the elevator.

She debated for a second then followed, grumbling all the way. "All right," she said breathing deeply. "But you are going to do this my way."

He held back a smile as long as he could. "Always your way, sweetheart." He pulled her closer, but she pushed him back.

"Don't even pretend this is my decision, Corso, but I'm going to do it. If I panic, you need to kiss me so I don't embarrass myself or molest someone else."

"Always willing to help, honey."

The elevator continued the marble décor of the lobby and seemed like every other elevator except every six seconds it climbed ten floors. Of course, some genius decided the passengers needed to view a clock that ticked off the floors as they ascended. She turned into him; her cheek pressed to his chest. "You're doing fine," he said, watching the floors climb to sixty and seventy. He brushed his lips against her ear, lower till he met her mouth. The elevator came to an abrupt stop, and some of the passengers were staring as Steven swept her up in his arms. "Newlyweds," he mumbled. "Hey, Sam, any chance you want to see why we are up here."

Samantha raised her head but still held tightly around his neck. And then she gasped as she took her first look at New York from above. "Oh, my God," she whispered as he set her down.

"Look," Steven pointed out. "That way in the distance. Can you see it?"

"Is that the Statue of Liberty?" Samantha asked, pulling his arms around her waist.

"And Ellis Island. We got a good day; a clear day for viewing." She seemed rooted to the spot, but she gradually relaxed, and he led her around the 360-degree view. "Rockefeller Plaza and Times Square over there, and we have to find the Brooklyn Bridge. Try the binoculars, Sam."

"You can see the whole city, can't you?"

"When you don't have a lot of time, this is one way to do it, love."

She handled the ride down better, though, he got them off at the 86th floor. "How do I know this place?" Samantha asked.

"Several movies were shot here. Bet you're a sucker for *Sleepless in Seattle*."

"God, yes, that's where I saw this. I love that movie."

Steven smiled at her joy. He knew she would love it if he got her up here. "The building has a reputation now for romance. They do weddings here on Valentine's Day."

"It's open," Samantha said tentatively. "I think I liked it closed in better."

"You're just a coward, my love," Steven answered, squeezing her hand.

She backed him up to the wall and stretched to meet his lips. When he released her, she whispered, "I think you said newlyweds?"

The hunger in his eyes translated to the next kiss. Breathless, Steven pulled back. "I could easily forget where we are, beautiful. Keep your hands and lips to yourself." He spun her back to his chest, and she moved several steps back into him. "Somebody wants to play," he mumbled, tasting her neck.

"Is there a gift shop?" she asked.

"Next stop," he said, moving her back to the elevator. "Although, I don't know how I could buy you anything better than that rock on your hand."

She laughed as she stared at her hand. "It's silly, isn't it?"

"I don't know," Steven said somberly. "It could double as an engagement ring. I might have to marry you."

Neither laughed. Newlyweds and engagement rings—what was he thinking? He pulled her off on the 80th floor to see the exhibits and to shop in the gift shop.

He shook his head slowly. "What crazy souvenir can I buy you here?"

Samantha knew immediately. "The water globe with the skyline of New York."

Steven took it from her hands. "I don't know. It's pretty touristy."

"I'm a tourist, aren't I?"

"Oh, this will break the bank. $25?"

"Could be worse. I'm starving. Wait till you see what dinner costs you."

It was getting dark as they exited the building. Steven walked her across the street and several blocks down to a bar and grill. They could still see the tower and expected a spectacular light show in a little while. In the meantime, he ordered two beers, two burgers, and an ocean of fries. As she sipped her beer, her mood shifted.

"What's wrong, pretty lady?"

She reached across the table for his hand. "I leave tomorrow. I think my flight is almost midnight."

He kissed the top of her hand. "I'm not letting you go, Sam. It isn't good-bye."

She swallowed another sip of beer as she fought down the tears again. "I know, sure, we'll keep in touch. I was just thinking of the plane ride home. That's all I meant." She grabbed a fry and dipped it in ketchup.

Steven knew she was lying, but it wouldn't help to call her out. "Hey, look at the tower." The light show reflected jungle animals, exotic birds, and fabulous colors from LEDs. The entire building was washed in colorful lions, wild birds, and butterflies.

The music continued to blare, and for a while Samantha hummed along till she couldn't sit any longer. She let loose on the dance floor swinging her hips and shaking her hair. Steven would have followed, but he couldn't move. He was completely captivated by her beautiful body, her shapely hips, and her wild dancing to the hard beat of the music, and he wasn't the only one. She captured the attention of the male population in the bar and, in a few minutes, three or four guys had joined her on the dance floor. They circled around her, jockeying for position in front of her and gyrating too close to suit Steven. He launched from his seat and used his broad shoulders to muscle his way between two guys. His hands fisted when one asshole protested. "Hey, Dude." Was he for real? Samantha circled his waist, linking her fingers in his belt loops as he grabbed firmly to her hips, but she continued to rock, moving dangerously closer to him. "Samantha," he growled against her ear. "You swing these hips for me—only me. Understand?"

"Only you," she whispered against his chest.

The music slowed, and she cuddled closer. His scent penetrated her senses, and his hard body pushed her passed the ability for sane thought. "Steven."

Tensely, he swayed with her, protecting her from the hungry looks from other men. "What, Sam?"

She ran a gentle hand down his cheek. "Are you mad at me?"

"No, of course not," he pulled her tighter, "but if you're done, let's go."

They walked for a while; the night was beautiful, even if a little cool. The city was alive and breathing as they made their way through the late-night partiers and shoppers.

"I have a meeting in the morning with my publisher," Steven reminded her.

"I guess you want to get some sleep. I'm having breakfast with Jenny."

"No, that's not what I want." His eyes so dark and intense stared at the fullness of her lips without reservations. It was clear what he wanted. He brushed his fingers along her jaw to her chin then followed along to the top of her tank between her breasts. When he pulled slightly on the fabric, he saw the blue lacy bra. "Same one you wore in San Diego?"

She could barely hear him over the pounding of her heart. "Yes, the only blue one I have."

He couldn't stop the smile. "I have the matching panties. I found them in Chicago tangled up in my t-shirt."

"Really? I wondered where they went. I searched the bed and the floor before I left your room." She stopped as the thought of waking to him gone rushed back.

"Don't, Sam, don't." Steven said, pressing his forehead to hers. "That's not what I want you to remember about that trip. That night was so damn good. You know it was."

She nodded. "It was." Her mood flipped again. "Are you going to return them to me?"

"No," he said too quickly. "They're mine. Come on. Too many people, traffic. We should go somewhere quiet."

"Not yet," Samantha said, stepping away. "My turn, you said something that night in San Diego. Something in Italian that sounded beautiful, but I didn't understand the words. I've been wanting to ask you what were those words, Steven?"

He thought for a long minute as he pulled her back to him. “I said, *Sei mio*, you’re mine. *Tu appartieni a me,* you belong to me. You do, Samantha, you do belong to me.” A single kiss joined by a tear that escaped her eye and traveled to her cheek to her smile.

“Get a cab, Steven,” she whispered. “I think it would be easier to meet Jenny tomorrow if I stay at your hotel.” She wanted tonight, and she wanted him. She’s wouldn’t spoil it by telling him she was falling in love. ♥♥

Chapter Twenty-One

Steven listened to her shallow breathing, the gentle rhythm of Samantha sleeping quietly beside him. He had awoken early, anticipating his meeting, but he couldn't pull away from her, yet. He lightly trailed his hand over the curve of her back and down her hip. God had created beautiful creatures with women—long sleek artistic lines combined with bold curves. If he could draw as well as he wrote, he would only draw women, and only this woman who held his heart in a way no other woman ever had. He had almost told her last night as he branded her again that he was in love with her, but it was such a completely foreign feeling to his heart that the words had bounced within him never reaching his lips. And tonight after meetings and the talk show, he would take her to the airport where she would board a plane for Charleston with his heart. He kissed her shoulder, knowing he shouldn't; he should let her sleep. His weight pressed her gently as he moved her hair and kissed another curve along her neck. He brushed the side of her breast and awoke the tender warm flesh and kissed lower to the firm perfectly rounded ass. God had made her absolutely perfect just for him.

"Steven," came her sleepy hoarse voice.

He rolled her back, brushing back her hair and gritting his teeth against the pressure building in his body as she stretched beneath him. Her smile was dazzling, and he'd miss that little bit of sunshine tomorrow.

Her arms tightened around his shoulders. "Sad?" she questioned.

He didn't answer with words. Kissing her was like living through an earthquake. The rumble started in his chest as the kiss teased, nipped, and pulled him in. Quickly, the tremors became more intense, knocking him off balance as he explored her mouth tangling with her tongue. Finally, the earth shook violently as the force of the kiss moved his hands over her breasts to the heat between her legs. Such kisses raised the intensity till the earth split, and he fell hopelessly into the fire that was Samantha. She wiggled beneath him, intensifying the contact till he couldn't breathe with want and could only feel the need and desire for one woman. She stoked his fire with every touch of her fingertips, every kiss on his body, and every shift of her hips till being one with her was the only thing his brain could process, his heart would accept, and his soul relentlessly sought. He cupped her face as his body slid together with hers. Tight and hard without effort, they held to each other as they released, panting and sweating till he collapsed on her. He kissed her once more before rolling to his side. With clear conviction, he resolved to find a way to get her to Baltimore and to move her into his home.

"Sorry," he said, tucking a stray curl behind her ear. "I didn't want to wake you, but I didn't want to leave for my meeting while you were sleeping."

"It wouldn't be the same thing, Steven. I knew about the meeting." She traced the hard muscles in his chest. "Something bothering you?"

"No," he lied. "Maybe just a little nervous about the talk show."

She grinned and slid closer to him. "You'll be great. All you have to do is smile and answer questions, and we've been practicing that a lot. You'll be wonderful."

He kissed her forehead. "I'm going to shower and get dressed. If you're asleep, I'll see you later."

"I'm up. I don't want to be late to breakfast. Don't want to give Jenny another reason to hate me. Sure you're all right?" she asked again when she caught him staring.

He didn't want to spend their last day together for a while tied up in work, but he'd keep her close. He kissed the top of her hand. "I'm fine. I'll meet you back here. Maybe we can do something before we have to be at the studio tonight." Maybe he could drag her back to bed.

Samantha left before Steven, hurrying through the lobby to the dining room for breakfast with Jenny. Somehow, she had to convince Jenny to be civil and give her a chance. She settled at a nice table and ordered coffee. Jenny was late, most likely on purpose to irritate Sam, but she expected it and used the time to jot down her questions. After they ordered,

Samantha tried to make small talk, but Jenny was obvious that she wanted to conclude their business as quickly as possible. She asked the usual questions pertaining to Steven's career and about the new projects she was working on. In addition to the possible movie deal, Jenny was working on a book tour starting late in the year hitting fourteen cities in three months and ending with a trip to London. Steven's books did well in England, but she liked to keep him in front of the public eye for good measure.

Jenny was a bit thrown when Sam changed the direction of the questions to the more personal side of her relationship with Steven. She knew the business well, but Sam was interested in how well she really knew her client, and she acknowledged Jenny as the driving force behind Steven's success.

"You care about him, don't you?" Samantha said, holding her gaze.

"I care for all of my clients." She had a hard shell—hard to crack and hard to understand. "I watch that he is not misled or used by people impressed with his success."

Samantha shifted in her seat and sipped her juice. "By people you mean women?"

A hostile smile crossed her lips. "May I be honest with you Cinderella?" She didn't wait for an answer. "Steven has had relationships with women over the years, but they didn't last long. Most of the time he was smart enough to have his little fling and move on, and he is careful to choose women who aren't clingy and dependent. Things can get messy then."

So much for winning Jenny over. "So, I'm not Steven's usual kind of woman?"

"Not at all," she growled, "and I won't let you get in the way of his career. I loathe scandal so have your little fling, then slink back to Charleston and leave him alone."

Samantha closed her notebook. "Lucky for me wherever this relationship goes is up to Steven. I go home tonight, and he knows where to find me. One last question, Jenny, do you want him to be happy? Meet someone and marry? Maybe have a family? Or is he supposed to be an author and nothing more for the rest of his life?"

"Someday he'll look around and see what he's missed. He'll see what has been right in front of him and available to him all along, and he'll have all those things you mentioned." She stood to go; her cheeks flushed.

What the hell was Jenny's problem? Samantha didn't understand why she was so flagrantly hostile toward her. Was she just protecting her investment? Or was there something behind her overprotectiveness where Steven was concerned?

She changed clothes and packed before Steven returned. Then they stopped at Rockefeller Plaza before heading to the studio. He needed to be there earlier to meet with the host and discuss how the interview would be handled. Berry prepped him on the type of questions he would ask, and Steven relaxed. Usually the interviews were very casual, more like conversing with a friend in front of the viewers at home, and, apparently, he was to meet with several people to check his wardrobe, hair, and makeup. Make up? What had Jenny gotten him into? Samantha stayed close but was careful to stay out of the way. He made sure she was welcomed backstage and that she was within his sight. He looked even more gorgeous than usual, and Samantha wet her dry lips as she waited for him to find a few minutes to spend with her. Berry Bing's show was live and was known for pushing the limits of his guest's comfort zone. Steven held tighter to Samantha's hand as they watched several other guests join Berry first on his comfortable set with reclining chairs, a unique coffee bar, and fresh flowers.

"You'll be wonderful," Samantha whispered as he was introduced to the audience. Steven spoke easily before people. He appeared confident discussing his book and plans for the future. Samantha's heart swelled with pride. It all seemed too easy till Berry crossed the line and took a gigantic leap into Steven's personal life.

"So, Steven, the papers have you linked to yet another woman recently," Berry began.

Samantha gasped and felt the not so gentle grasp of Jenny on her arm. Their eyes met in an almost simultaneous look of panic till Jenny took a deep breath. "He can handle this."

Steven waited as a smirking Berry laid his trap. "She's a pretty girl, but a virtual unknown. How do you know this Samantha?"

Steven cleared his throat and sipped his coffee. The lighting was making him unusually warm; he wished he hadn't worn a jacket. "As a matter of fact, Samantha is doing an article on me for the magazine she works for, *A Writer's Life.* It's a relatively new magazine still in its infancy stages, but they are first rate."

"So, you are involved with someone who works for you?"

"Not involved. We have a professional relationship even if the papers are trying to make more out of it."

Berry stared at the newspaper he suddenly produced from his table. He flipped it around for the camera to see. Samantha covered her face and groaned. She was going to strangle the universe. "Interesting picture," Berry continued, goading the audience. "Wouldn't you say so, folks?" The audience hooted and howled as Steven set his cup down; his jaw locked and his eyes icy, he met Berry's gaze.

"No story here, Berry," he tried to say lightly. "She's no one special."

The color drained from Samantha's face. She didn't know what was worse—hearing Steven say she was nobody or seeing Jenny's I told you so expression. She didn't want to see or hear anymore. She found an empty dressing room and tried to calm down. Steven must have had his reasons for dismissing her so completely. Berry had caught him by surprise, and as Jenny put it, he handled it. He couldn't possibly think that, could he? Samantha fought down the panic. She heard applause and rose to find Steven, but she caught the image of herself in a mirror. In a few hours she'd leave Steven and go back home. He had said he wasn't letting her go, but what did that mean? He hadn't made any promises—never said he loved her. What would happen when he was in Baltimore, and she was in Charleston?

"Samantha." She was suddenly wrapped in him. "I couldn't find you. I was afraid you left."

"No, I just needed some air. Didn't mean to worry you. I'm sorry."

"You're sorry? You have nothing to be sorry about," he replied angrily. "I specifically told the ass that my personal life was off limits."

"You should be angry with me. The picture was my fault," Samantha argued, her hands fisting the fabric of his shirt.

"Sam, definitely not your fault and none of Berry's business." He tried to see her eyes, but she stared with fascination at the tiny green buttons on his shirt. "What, Sam? What else is wrong?"

Her misty eyes finally met his briefly. "Nothing, I have to leave for the airport."

"You have time. Tell me. Oh, God, you didn't believe that nonsense I was telling Berry, did you?"

"No, of course not."

"Baby, look at me. You are everything," he said softly, holding her eyes. "But the press can be relentless when they smell a story. I didn't want them hounding you in Charleston. Samantha, we were quite visible in California and here in New York. I don't care who knows about us, but I want to protect you for a little longer till one of two things happen."

Samantha moved in closer, pressing her hips to his. "What?"

"Either we break up, or we don't. I'm betting we don't, because I'm not letting you go. As for the press, until we make some decisions so there aren't hundreds of miles between us, they won't get a confirmation from me. Understand?"

She nodded. "If you are still saying us, I won't see you in the papers with other women?"

He kissed the top of her shoulder. "They print what they want. I can't help that, but I promise you, I won't be with anyone since you. And if some asshole takes an interest in you, I'll break his face."

Samantha unexpectedly pressed her lips hard against his. She cradled the back of his neck and pulled through his hair. The words were there, but she couldn't say them. Holding her, Steven already felt the loss. She was leaving. The words were there, but he couldn't say them.

With one more hug and kiss, Samantha darted for the tunnel under threat of last call boarding. "Sam, wait," Steven shouted as he held up his phone. "Smile."

She swallowed her tears as she smiled her brightest, and he took his picture. For the first time she realized, she was boarding a plane, but her fear was replaced with an overwhelming sadness. A sadness that would stay with her all the way home.

Chapter Twenty-Two

Samantha worked on the article all day Sunday. She hoped to send it to Steven, get his approval, and present it to Pete with the pictures on Monday. She dreaded the avalanche of work she knew would be stacked in boxes waiting for her. Young talented and not so talented writers who were depending on her to clean up their manuscripts and praise their efforts. Samantha was grateful, at least, that she didn't have the final say in whether a book was published. Pete had a team that took her recommendations and reread the manuscripts then made the contacts with the much sought after yes or the much feared no. She carefully fixed punctuation, grammar, and spelling mistakes, but she never changed content. She offered advice, but it was up to the author to decide on any changes.

Much as she expected, the work was overwhelming as she wedged her way into her chair. Some of these would have to go home with her if she was going to make some kind of dent in the pile. She flipped on her computer and had a response from Steven already.

Love it, Samantha. You have my approval and an attachment with the file of pictures. Use whatever you want.

She opened the attachment and found all of the pictures Jerry had taken. She picked out two and added them to a new file for Pete. Steven's note hadn't said much, but she had talked to him briefly since she had been back, and he had just returned to Baltimore last night. He had a busy schedule returning home, and if she heard from him, it would be late in the evening. She found Pete in his office intensely staring at his computer.

"I sent an email, Pete. Steven approved the article and gave you a couple of pictures. You're all set to go."

"Well done, Sam," he said with a satisfied grin. "I guess I'm going to have to give you the raise Corso suggested."

Samantha nodded. "You did like the article, didn't you?"

"Very much. Very perceptive and poignant, but you were in a unique position to get to know the man." His eyes danced as he smiled at his own humor.

Samantha didn't get it. "What unique position are you referring to?" she asked.

"You enjoyed your trips to California and New York, didn't you?" he asked innocently enough. "Personally, it is none of my business how you got the man to open up to you."

Anger flashed, and her body tensed. "What are you saying, Pete? I hope you aren't insinuating that I…"

"If you did, the net result was well worth it." His eyes met hers. "I didn't think it was your style, but this is a demanding business. A girl has to do what she has to do."

Samantha slammed Pete's office door shut. "This girl didn't sleep with Steven to get his story. If you remember correctly, you sent me to San Diego for the workshops."

"And after meeting you, he was willing to do the interview. Why would that be?"

"Damn, Pete, maybe he just thought I was competent or thorough. I don't know."

"Sam, calm down. I'm not judging." He shoved the daily newspaper across his desk to rest in front of her. "Nice picture."

The color drained from her face, but she tried to salvage her dignity. "Picture is misleading, Pete. I wasn't sleeping with the man at the time."

Pete sat back in his squeaky chair, and let his gaze travel over the young woman who had worked for him for several years. "You know his reputation, Sam," he said in a conciliatory tone. "He will eventually hurt you."

"I don't want you to think I used sex to get to Steven. We talked a lot, I shadowed him through his daily life, and I got a glimpse of what he is really like. If you are pleased with the article, I'm glad, but there is nothing but mutual respect between us." The moment the words left her mouth, Samantha realized she had said exactly what Steven had tried to tell Berry Bing. "I have work to do, and you might think about sending

Steven a thank you and an advanced copy of the magazine when it is available."

"He plugged the magazine on Berry Bing's show a couple of nights ago. I wanted to thank him for that, too." Pete turned back to his computer. "Planning any more trips?"

"You'll be the first to know, but that pile should keep me busy for a while." She slammed the door again as she left. She knew it. Pete was the one person she worried would think she had done the unthinkable to get her story. Now that Pete had seen the picture, she worried about who else would see it. Her mom and dad? Her brother? Friends? Would they all think her success was classic—ambitious girl sleeps her way to success?

She flipped through the first three manuscripts on the pile, and one caught her attention. Avery Sloan—so it was fiction writing now. She had met the self-centered but very good looking young man through her brother. They had been very good friends in the Navy, and on one of Ray's visits to Charleston, he had brought Avery. The two were thinking of going into business together after the military, but Ray hated all of Avery's ideas. As she recalled, he was thinking of starting an escort service, a security squad made up of his military buddies for young women, or a boot camp/fitness center in the woods with late night romantic campfires and extracurricular activities. It all boiled down to the same thing. Sex sold, and Avery wanted a piece of the action. Ray's friendship with Avery ended when he made San Diego his home and got a job as a mechanic working on expensive boats. Samantha had gone to dinner a couple of times with Avery when he was in town, but she spent most of the evening listening to him brag about his military exploits and his budding future. Not surprising, the relationship didn't go anywhere; he had never even kissed her, and now it looked like he had detoured into writing. She set it aside as she weeded through what she needed to finish before taking on more.

Just before lunch her phone rang, and Samantha was surprised the screen lit up to an old friend she hadn't heard from in months. Gabby was several years older with a gorgeous face and a 'let's live for the moment' attitude. They had drifted apart when Gabby did more traveling for the modeling agency she owned, and Samantha had missed her. She brightened a room and lifted Samantha's spirit on those days when the manuscripts were closing in on her.

"Samantha, honey, how are you? It's been too long."

"I'm not the one with her own business to run. What have you been doing?" Gabby did make her feel like she was standing still sometimes, but it acted as motivation, and she usually went back to her writing after a visit. "Seeing anyone special?"

"Funny, honey, I was going to ask you the same thing. How's the career? A new man in your life maybe?"

Samantha inwardly groaned. Gabby's one negative trait was she was transparent and intrusive. She'd bet she had seen the picture, but she was proud of her article. She could tell Gabby that. "I've been in New York, Gab, doing an article for the magazine."

"On Steven Corso? I caught him on Berry Bing the other night."

Damn it, didn't anyone sleep at night anymore? "Yes, the interview will be out next week."

"Come on, honey, tell me the good stuff. What's going on with you and that gorgeous man?" Gabby moaned. "Is he as good as all those women say he is?"

Samantha's breath hitched. "Steven and I are friends, Gab, not much to tell really." Her eye caught the light off the amber stone. Maybe she should tell Gabby she had a two-dollar engagement ring. She momentarily laughed to herself till she heard Gabby's prattle.

"After I saw the picture in the paper, I went online, honey, and discovered there are lots of pictures of the two of you having a good time. Some touristy places in San Diego and the Empire State Building in New York. Just friends? Really?"

Annoyed, Samantha knew Gabby was persistent. "We should get together for lunch sometime, and I'll spill everything. How about I call you later in the week?"

"Sounds like fun, Sam. Don't forget to call now."

Samantha stared at her phone then she deleted Gabby's number. She was looking for dirt, and Samantha wasn't letting anyone pressure her where Steven was concerned. It was none of her business. It wasn't sordid; it was beautiful, and the overwhelming sadness came back. She pulled up Steven's number and sent a quick text. **Know you're busy. Just wanted you to know I miss you.**

Steven replied quickly. **Tied up, but missing you, too. Call tonight.**

She ran her fingers lightly over the text. How was this ever going to work?

Plunging back into her work, she cleared away the last of her to-do list and attacked the pile of manuscripts. When Samantha was at her desk, she organized the submitted manuscripts as they came in. Guiltily, she sighed, as she noticed the manuscripts had been tossed haphazardly. Avery's had been sitting for several weeks. What had he written anyway? Samantha laughed when she read a 'Navy Seals paranormal romance.' Sounded like an awful lot of something. She began reading, and it didn't take long to realize Avery was in way over his head, and, worse, she couldn't edit it. She couldn't follow the story that kept jumping between a main character in the Navy Seals, strange abnormal happenings, and a love story. He needed to narrow down his focus and follow a story rather than stringing together a series of events. Maybe it would be better if it wasn't paranormal or if it wasn't a Navy Seal. Samantha always tried to emphasize the positive first, but the best thing she could say was Avery did a good job with spelling. She tried to read more. Maybe it would get better, but the longer she read, the more confused she became till she jumped to the last chapter. There she found new characters, possibly for a series, but she wanted to scream, it's a romance novel. You don't kill off the girl. Where is the happily ever after? She looked at her phone. She had wasted all afternoon on Avery's novel. She grabbed her recommendation form and curtly wrote her review for the team. ***Disorganized, lacks an understanding of the genre, tried to do too much and accomplishes nothing but confuses the reader, not for us***. She signed the form, tucked it inside the manuscript, and passed it to the next table. She felt bad for Avery, but he could try one of his other ideas. Writing wasn't for him.

Late that night after a hot shower and take out, she flipped on the television. She had brought home another manuscript, but she was too tired to read, and she hoped Steven would call soon. Her eyes filled with tears, and the remote fell in her lap when she saw the little boy at the top of the Empire State Building. *Sleepless in Seattle* was on so the universe could once again get the last laugh. God, she missed Steven. It was nearing the end of the movie, and Samantha leaned in as Jonah and Sam returned to retrieve his backpack and to run into Annie. Samantha dissolved in uncontrollable sobbing, not just because she had a shitty day, but after one day, she missed Steven so much. How was this ever going to work? She leaped on her phone when it rang.

"Sam?" Steven could barely understand her as she sniffed and cried into the phone. "Sam, baby, what the hell is wrong?"

"Wait," she squeaked out, trying to calm down.

"Sam? Are you all right?"

"Yes, yes, I'm sorry, Steven. I'm fine."

"No, you aren't fine. What the hell happened?"

"Empire State Building, Sam and Annie and Jonah," she said sheepishly. "Sorry, I lost it before you called."

"You were watching that movie," he chuckled. "At least, I know you miss me."

"You have no idea how much," she said softly.

"I do, because I feel the same way. Come to Baltimore, Sam. I can't get away right now, but you can come here. I want you to see my house; I want you in my bed. Get a flight out tomorrow." The slight stir of emotion in his voice, whether lust or something else, sent a shiver through her.

"Tempting, Steven, but Pete will kill me. He thinks, by the way, we are sleeping together because of the damn picture. It hit Charleston."

"We are sleeping together if I can get us in the same city."

"No, he thinks that's why you gave me the interview, and that is just what I didn't want him to think, but he is pleased with the article and the pictures."

"I got an email from him that I forwarded to Jenny with the article. You really won't come to Baltimore—not even if I promise you fine wine, soft music, gourmet food cooked by your own personal chef, and hot, very hot, sex?"

"Mm, you make a strong case for irresponsibility and quick flights to Baltimore, but I can't. I just have too much catch up to do."

"Did your folks see the picture?"

"I don't think so. I would have heard from them, but it's just a matter of time. Steven, is it my turn?"

"I'll defer to you, honey. What's your question?"

"I know you've been to Charleston. Ever been on the carriage tours of the city?"

"Not yet." She could hear the smile in his voice.

"Well, if you ever make it here, my treat; a night time carriage ride, or we could charter a boat. I can walk you through history and take in the plantations or Fort Sumter."

"Would I get the tour of your apartment, Sam?"

Her pulse quickened. "I couldn't let you go to a hotel. You'd have to stay with me, wouldn't you?"

"Damn, you're killing me, babe. I'd be on the next flight if I could."

"I know. We'll make a hole in our schedules somewhere, right?"

"Soon, promise you won't give up on me."

"Cross my heart. Good night, Steven."

"Good night, Samantha."

♥♥

Chapter Twenty-Three

Samantha made a decision on the way to work. She would have to go to Steven in Baltimore. His schedule was much too structured for him to leave now, and her plans would only impact Pete. Since he wasn't her favorite person at the moment, she didn't feel too badly about leaving him with a stockpile of manuscripts. Besides, she had pleaded with him for months to hire another editor, but as long as she did the work, he didn't budge. Now, he would have to budge if she took time off. She would see how much she could get done non-stop in a week then she was going to Baltimore. Before she got to work, she got a text from Ray.

New boyfriend or just a California fling? Pictures don't look like the antics of my baby sister.

Samantha rolled her eyes. Not a surprise, but her brother usually stayed out of her personal life. Yes, he was supportive, but he didn't judge. She returned. **Your baby sister is a grown woman. We are together for now. Don't worry.** She loved Ray, and she hoped that would end it.

If he hurts you, I'll kill him. Take care of yourself, Sis.

I will. Mom and Dad know? Samantha held her breath.

I heard about it from them.

And that meant she'd be hearing from them soon. She looked at the silly ring on her hand. She needed to get back to Steven.

Samantha settled in at her desk and ignored the whispers from her co-workers. That had started late in the day yesterday, though no one had mentioned the pictures or Steven to her. She started another manuscript that had an intriguing plot and soon got lost in the book. She wanted to ignore the insistent ringing of her desk phone.

"Samantha Westerly. Can I help you?"

"I hope so, honey. This is Avery Sloan. Do you remember me?"

Samantha set down her coffee. Avery could only be calling about the manuscript. "Of course, Avery. How are you?"

"I'm good. Still working for my father right here in Charleston."

Damn, she hadn't heard he was living in Charleston. He was too close; she didn't want to see him.

"I was wondering if we could get together," he continued. "I got an email this morning, a rejection of my book, *Twisted Fate*. The email said you reviewed it. Since we know each other, I thought you might be able to give me some insight, some suggestions. I'm open to constructive criticism."

Samantha inwardly groaned. How could she tell him the truth? This book was his baby, and if she were honest, she'd tell him to throw it out and start over. "I've been out of town, Avery, and I'm so far behind at work. I don't know when I'll be free."

"I have a suggestion," Avery countered. "My father's company is having this awards banquet tonight. It's just dinner and a few speeches. I'm supposed to get an award for something. Highest volume sales this month, I think. Anyway, it should just be a couple of hours. We could have dinner and talk after."

"This is business, right?" Samantha clarified. "It's not a date or anything, because I am seeing someone."

"Well, I do need a date for the event, but I do understand. We'll call it a business meeting." His voice dropped lower, softer, almost a whisper. "I don't want to be in sales forever. I think writing is my niche."

Samantha closed her eyes. She could be wrong. She could suggest he pitch it to a literary agent or another publishing company.

"How's Ray?" Avery asked. "Is he still in San Diego?"

"Yes," Samantha finally said. "I'm sure you know he's getting married next spring."

"Looking forward to it. I'm sure I'll see you there, too. About tonight?"

"All right," she heard herself say. "What time?"

"Pick you up at six. Black tie affair."

"I'll be ready, but I have to work in the morning. It won't be a late night."

"I will have you home before your carriage turns into a pumpkin, Cinderella." He laughed enthusiastically and hung up.

Samantha was stunned. Cinderella again and Steven. Plan A she wrote in her notebook. Finish as many manuscripts as possible, go to the stupid affair with Avery, avoid mom and dad for a while, and get to Baltimore very, very soon.

She was nearly dressed that night when Steven called. "I'm glad you called now, Steven. I'm going out."

"Going out? As in a date?" he said tensely.

"No, not at all," Samantha answered. "It's a business meeting. I reviewed Avery's manuscript, and it wasn't very good. His rejection listed me as the reviewer, and he called me. He wants my advice on how to improve his book."

"Samantha, who is this idiot? You can't go out with a stranger," Steven said angrily.

"That's the thing. He's not a stranger; he's a friend of my brother. They were in the service together. I kind of feel like I have to help him."

"Are you sure he isn't expecting more than editing advice?"

"He's not. I made it clear this was business before I agreed, but I don't know what to tell him, Steven. The book is bad."

"Can it be fixed? How bad is it?"

Samantha sighed. "Throw it away bad."

"Ouch. You have to be honest with him, Sam, brutally honest. Although, he might take it better from a total stranger than a friend. He's not going to like you much."

"I don't care how he feels about me, but he's still Ray's friend. He's invited to his wedding in the spring."

"Am I?"

The question caught Samantha by surprise. “You want to go with me to Ray’s wedding?”

“I’m saying I plan on keeping you. Don’t you think it would be nice to go to a family function together?”

“I’d love that. So, you think we’ll still be together then?” Her heart tightened.

“I know so. We’ll fly from Baltimore to San Diego. I’ll book the flight now if you give me the date, and I’ll make sure I’m free.”

“We’re flying from Baltimore?”

“I want you here with me, Sam. We have to talk more about getting you out here. I know you have a life in Charleston, but we have a life together, a life we need to start living.”

Samantha sniffed back her tears. “I’ve been thinking about that too.” She noticed the time when she heard a tap on the door. “I’m sorry, Steven, Avery is here, but we need to talk more.”

“I know. Later?”

“Maybe, oh, the wedding is May 17th if you’re serious, but I have to be there a few days before for the pre-wedding activities.”

“May 12th early enough, babe?”

The knock grew louder. “Perfect. I’ll call you later.”

Samantha took one last look at the blue cocktail dress that draped her body loosely and shimmered to her knee. She wore Steven’s favorite heels and several bangle bracelets. Good enough for a stuffy awards banquet, she thought, opening the door.

Avery filled her doorway in a smart black tuxedo, pale green shirt, and tie. Clean shaven, he smelled of a woodsy cologne and breath mints. She wondered why he had never married. He was handsome, built like a Mack truck, toned and hard from hours of military physical training, and he had money. Daddy paid him well.

“You look amazing, Samantha, but we need to hurry.” Avery took her hand and led her to his car parked out front. The expensive sports car stood out in her modest neighborhood. Yes, Daddy paid him well.

The Carlton Hotel's banquet center was decked out in lanterns and candles in silver and blue with Sloan Enterprises' logo displayed at the end of the room behind a standup podium. Samantha's head spun as she was introduced to countless guests including Avery's father. He was loud and borderline obnoxious as he welcomed his colleagues and clients and passed out cigars. Their table was labeled Avery Sloan and guest and was near the front. And most annoying was the photographer who repeatedly bothered them for pictures—holding up their champagne glasses or standing in tight with Avery's arm around her shoulders.

"Why does your father need pictures?" she finally asked Avery.

"There's a section on our website called events. He puts all kinds of pictures there. Maybe if you're free, you'd like to come with me to one of the holiday parties."

No, that sounded too much like a date. "I'll probably be out of town, Avery."

Through the awards, Samantha did notice Avery was well liked and very successful. Not only did he receive the award for most sales but also for most promising. Maybe he should stick to Sloan Enterprises instead of writing. Maybe in a tactful way she could suggest it. Dinner was exceptional, and finally, as the party started to break up, Avery brought up his book.

"Honestly, Samantha, you liked the book in general, didn't you? Maybe it just needs some tweaking?" he asked hopefully.

"Avery." Samantha reached over and covered his hand sympathetically. "I'm just one editor. Maybe you need to pitch your book to several others. See how the opinions compare."

"Maybe, but I could improve it first with your suggestions."

Samantha heard Steven's voice whispering in her ear. Brutally honest, do it. She took a deep breath. "I think you need to narrow your scope, Av. There's too much going on, and it can be confusing in spots."

"I thought it was clear if you're any kind of reader. Besides, it was meant to be suspenseful." He looked hurt, and Samantha realized he didn't want help with his book. What he wanted was a pep talk, because the rejection caught him by surprise.

"Were we the first publishing company you submitted to?" Samantha asked.

He nodded. "I can't tell you how much time I've spent on this book. I really thought it was special."

Samantha bit her lip. "Does he have to be a Navy Seal?" she asked. "Maybe if he wasn't always running off on a mission in the middle of the paranormal activity, he could devote more attention to his lover and the circumstances."

Avery considered that. "No, that's where his strength is. He has to be a Seal."

"And why did you kill Ellen off in the end?" She tried to keep the edge out of her voice. "It's a romance novel; your readers want a happy ending."

"I was trying to be realistic. Life isn't a fairy tale like Cinderella." Avery sat up straighter and pushed aside his glass. "You said you have to work tomorrow. I'll take you home."

She felt awful; she had hurt his feelings and dashed his hopes. "As a first time writer, you might self-publish. When publishers see you can sell, it will make your material more marketable."

"That's actually not a bad idea. Thanks, Sam." He walked her to her door and kissed her on the cheek. "I'll see you at Ray's wedding then."

Never again. Samantha shed her clothes and stepped into the shower. She had started another novel since coming back from New York, and for the first time she was excited that it might be a good beginning, but then she thought of Avery. She thought every writer probably got shot down before they published. He needed to toughen up, really listen when someone offered advice, and pray to the universe, because everyone knew a little luck couldn't hurt. She wondered if Steven had ever received a rejection, and how he had handled it. What had given him the drive to keep writing? She remembered from the workshop 'the voice within that had to be heard'. Did she have that voice?

She curled up in bed and wrote. Out of nowhere the words came, filling one notebook till she needed to grab another. She loved her main character; he was handsome and strong and decisive and loving. He was Steven. She wanted to call him, but it had gotten late so she put away her notebook and snuggled down in the covers. She would call him in the morning and tell him she might be an author after all.

♥♥

Chapter Twenty-Four

For the next two days Steven and Samantha played phone tag. Samantha left messages, but Steven just hung up. She tried texting, too, but the one text he did return said only that he wanted to talk to her. Finally, as she entered her apartment after work with a few groceries, her phone rang.

"Steven, at last. I've been trying to reach you," she said breathlessly.

For a moment, the line was silent. When he spoke, the sound was tight, angry. "When are you coming to Baltimore, Sam? That's all I want to know."

"I'm working on it," she stammered.

"I'm tired of your excuses. I want you here in the next twenty-four hours. I don't give a damn about your job or anything else," he yelled. "Get on a plane and get here."

"Steven, what's wrong? Why are you so upset?" Samantha asked.

She heard the rage as his breathing escalated rapidly. "I said you're stalling. Get here."

"I'm not stalling. I'm trying to finish things at work."

He cut her off. "Why are you really reluctant to leave Charleston, Sam?"

Samantha paced the living room. Why was he so angry? "I want to come to Baltimore," she said softly, "to you, Steven."

"Where were you last night?" he demanded. "Did you go out again?"

She fought down her own anger. What the hell was wrong with him? "No, I was in the shower when you called, and when I called you back, you didn't answer."

"I'm not appreciating the games, Sam. If you have something to tell me, get it over with. I saw the pictures."

"What pictures? What are you talking about?"

"Got your laptop handy, sweetheart," he hissed. "Pull up Sloan Enterprises."

"I got it," she whispered. She had a feeling she knew what pictures he meant.

"Click on events at the top. Then Awards Banquet. Tell me what you see."

Samantha followed his directions to the pictures taken with Avery. They were all there. Every last one of them. How could he think?

But he was yelling again. "So, what do you see, hon? See what I see? I love the first one with his arm around you. Not as good, though, as the one with the toasting champagne glasses. Damn it, Sam. Did you forget to mention the party was in a hotel? I don't remember you mentioning it. And that damn dress, and God, the heels. Did you sleep with him, because he's a real idiot if he didn't get you into his bed?"

"Steven!"

"Not yet," he growled. "Last picture says a lot, my love. Are you really holding his hand?"

"Steven," Samantha pleaded, "you have this all wrong. I didn't know where the party was. The pictures were just promo pictures for the web site. They don't mean anything. He doesn't mean anything to me. You have to believe me and trust me."

"Right, Sam."

"I called you last night," she added apologetically.

"I went out." He let that hang in the air between them.

"Out? You had plans?" she asked. What had he done?

"Out to a bar to get drunk, and yes, honey, I could have gotten laid if I wanted." There was a long silent pause. "Are you coming to Baltimore, or are we done?"

Panic took over, and she fought for control, for rational thought. She could straighten this out. "Steven, we are not done. Nothing happened between Avery and me. You of all people should understand how pictures can look misleading." She heard the tinkle of ice in a glass.

"You looked beautiful, sexy," he said softly. "I don't want to talk to you anymore."

When the line went dead, Samantha went cold. What had just happened? Were they really done? She loved the idiot; she couldn't lose him over Avery. She called him back several times that night, but he didn't answer. In fact, over the next two days, she called over and over, and he didn't answer. She knew what he wanted. If she had to drop everything and fly to Baltimore today, she would. She'd show him that he was everything to her, but she wouldn't tell him she was coming. She didn't know if he still wanted to see her, and she wasn't taking any chances. That Saturday she booked her flight and waited impatiently at the airport. Pete wasn't too happy with her plans, but she told him she needed a vacation. Where was none of his business. Her mother called three times, but she didn't answer. All she could focus on was getting to Steven and straightening out this mess.

An hour in flight she got a text. **I'm about to board a flight for Charleston. I'm tired of waiting. I'm dragging you back to Baltimore.**

Oh, God, no. They were going to crisscross in the air. No, no, no. She tried to text him back, but she couldn't get the text out. One of them didn't have reception. She guessed he had turned off his phone. This was insane. She burst into tears—loud, mournful, heart stopping sobs heard from first class to coach. The impatient gentleman seated next to her groaned, leaned away, and finally covered his ears while more sympathetic concerned passengers were standing in their seats and in the aisle trying to help. Her sobbing wracked her body and filled the plane. A pretty stewardess draped an arm around her shoulders and brought her to the front of the plane. Between sobs, Samantha managed to tell her that the man in her life was mad at her, she was flying to Baltimore to fix it, but he didn't know she was coming, and, at that very moment, he was boarding a plane for Charleston. Most of all, she hated the universe.

The stewardess patiently squeezed her shoulders. "Let's see if the captain can help." She guided her into the cockpit and retold her story to the captain.

He watched Samantha sniffling and in need of a tissue and picked up his radio. "Baltimore tower, we have a problem—nothing urgent, but we could use a little assistance."

Steven closed his eyes as two young female fans approached him for an autograph. He didn't want to be rude, but they had already called first boarding, and he didn't want to miss his flight. He had been such an ass. Maybe that's just what love does to you. He had stared at the pictures and didn't see anything to indicate she was anything but bored. He needed to get to her, beg her forgiveness, and move to Charleston if that was what she wanted. He approached the gate and the young attendant looked at his ticket and called over two airline security. Big men whom Steven wouldn't necessarily argue with, but he had to get on this plane.

"Is something wrong? I need to get on this flight."

"You won't be flying with us today," she said quickly. "You need to go with these two men."

They flanked him on either side. "It is Mr. Corso? Please come with us."

"Wait, am I being arrested? What's wrong? I need to get on that plane."

"Just come quietly with us, sir. Mr. Flax will explain everything to you."

He was taken to a part of the airport he had never seen. He imagined not many people saw this area unless airport security had a problem with them. He hadn't done a damn thing. What could they possible want from him? Maybe they had him mixed up with a terrorist. Maybe he should call Jenny or his lawyer. He was ushered into an outer office and, eventually, called in to see Mr. Flax, a short bald man who probably didn't see a lot of excitement during his day, but he seemed genuinely amused to see Steven.

"Sit down, Mr. Corso. You're probably wondering why you were brought here."

"Yes, and I've missed my flight to Charleston."

He laughed. "Well, that's a funny story. I believe you know," he picked up a scrap of paper and adjusted his glasses, "Samantha Westerly."

"Yes, is she all right?" he asked with alarm.

"She is now. Apparently, she discovered you were on your way to Charleston, and she had a melt down on flight 469. The pilot asked us to detain you till she arrives."

"Samantha is on her way here?"

Mr. Flax grinned. "She is indeed. Her flight should arrive on time in about 47 minutes, gate 25."

Samantha was coming here soon. What had she done to get the cooperation of the pilot? "Am I free to go?"

"Of course, just a question, though. Don't you ever talk to each other? You could have missed each other and still been divided by two cities. You should talk more often." His lips twitched in a half smile as Steven thanked him and headed to gate 25.

Families were gathering as the time drew closer for flight 469 to arrive. It was still on time, and Steven waited on the outer fringe of people to see the tunnel, to see Sam when she came off the plane. She had done it—dropped everything and had come to Baltimore for him. He was such an idiot.

He knew she wouldn't be the first off the plane so as some of the passengers and their families moved away, Steven moved closer. There she was, scanning the crowd looking for him. She was a mess—hair falling out of the pins, her mascara darkening her lower lids, and red eyes and tear stained cheeks. He wanted to fall at her feet and beg forgiveness, but instead he had to laugh. She was dragging that damn purple bag. His heart craved her, but he needed to get closer, because he could see the concern, the fear in her eyes. "Sam, Samantha, over here," he waved.

She tucked in her head as she pushed through the crowd till she stood in front of him, his hot mess. She hesitated then threw herself in his arms. He held her so tightly to him, trying to stop her trembling body. "I was afraid I missed you," she whimpered.

"I'm here, Sam, and I'm so sorry."

She stayed close but looked up at him, and he couldn't stop the fierce need that ripped through him. He cradled her head as he leaned down to meet her lips. Not gentle, not sweet, but with the desperation of a man too long denied the woman he wanted. He kissed her hot, hard, with longing and need, and when she parted her lips seeking more, he turned her against the barrier partition and fitted his body flush with hers. "I am so sorry, Sam. I've been acting like an idiot."

She brushed at the tears still needing to escape and cupped his chin in her hands. “All my fault. I’m sorry. God, I’ve missed you.” She tugged him back to her, devouring his mouth in a feverish frenzy.

“Home,” he said softly, trying to breathe and pressing his forehead to hers. “I’m taking you home, and I’m never letting you go again.”

“I may have to stay,” she said with a weak smile. “They may never let me on a plane again.”

♥♥

Chapter Twenty-Five

Steven didn't press her in the car. He held her hand and drove through Baltimore to the residential neighborhood he loved. She pulled the remaining pins from her hair and shook it out, trying to get herself together.

"The stewardess was sympathetic," she said, avoiding his glance. "Then she told the pilot my problem, and he stopped you from getting on the plane."

Steven smiled slowly. "I have it on good authority you had a meltdown."

"I guess I lost it. I couldn't imagine you in Charleston and me in Baltimore. I couldn't stop crying. But to make it worse, the stewardess announced all was well, and you would be waiting for me in Baltimore. Everyone clapped and cheered. I thought I would die. I wanted to crawl in my bag."

He was laughing hard, and Samantha smiled. It was so good to hear him laugh. "Steven, can you forget about Avery? That was absolutely nothing."

"I know." He kissed her hand and pulled into a driveway. "I couldn't stand you so far away. I acted foolishly, and I am sorry, but I'm glad you decided to come." He parked and reached for her. "I don't want you to see my house when we go in. I want you to move here; I want you to see yourself in your home with me." He brushed a gentle hand across her cheek.

"I look awful."

"You are beautiful—the most amazing woman I have ever known."

Samantha took her first real look at Steven's house as she circled around the front of the car. "It's beautiful and big."

"Got it for a steal a few years ago, because it needed a lot of work. I contracted some of it out, but I did a lot of the work myself. I'm pretty handy." He circled her shoulders and pulled her closer to drop a slow tender kiss on her lips. Still holding her hand, he brought her into the foyer with a winding staircase and corridors in several directions. "Can we start with a tour of the house?"

She nodded already absorbed in the paintings in the entrance and down the hall. "These are beautiful."

"I'm not a big fan of art, but I know what I like," he said, guiding her into a large open area on the left. In one corner was a piano and arranged around a fireplace was a sitting room. Behind them was a well-stocked bar. "My sister plays. She's the only one who had any interest." Down the end of the hall, the house opened up to a huge gourmet kitchen.

"Do you have help, Steven? Who cleans this house? Makes the meals?" Samantha asked, sitting down at the counter.

Steven pulled two bottles of water from the refrigerator. "I have a cleaning lady who comes in once a week, but I rarely see her even when I'm in town. I swear she's invisible. I cook. My mother made sure we could all make a decent dish of pasta. I'll cook you something you'll like tonight."

"You don't have to go to any trouble."

"I love to cook, and you will be my very capable assistant." He ran his hand over her arm. She was real and felt amazing.

"I don't know how capable, but you can bark orders if you want," she teased.

He pulled her off the stool and led her through the double doors to the patio and the pool. "See? This is why you have to swim, my love." He wrapped his arm around her waist and backed her into his chest. "Moonlight swims, with or without clothes." He kissed along her neck till he reached her ear and tugged gently at the lobe with his teeth. She backed even closer to him, tilting her head, and giving him more access to the delicate flesh of her shoulders.

"Show me more house."

"Right, this way, back through the kitchen and across the hall is the rec room."

"Man cave," Samantha laughed. Biggest wide screen television, video games, stereo system, several recliners and a sofa, another well-stocked bar, refrigerator, and pool table.

"You have the ideal man cave. Most people could live in this room."

"I do spend a lot of time here when I'm home. Come on, upstairs." He grabbed her bag where he had left it at the foot of the stairs and led her up.

"How many bedrooms?" she asked.

"Five, but they come in handy when I have the whole family here. No one goes to a hotel. This room is mine," he said, his hand on the knob of the closed door.

"Did you do all the decorating?" Samantha asked, peeking into one of the bedrooms.

"My sister is an interior decorator. I pretty much turned her loose. She has great taste, and I trust her. There were two exceptions, though. I completely did the library which doubles as my office—the place where I spend my time writing and the master bedroom. Those are my spaces, and I decorated them." Samantha lingered outside one of the spare rooms. "What are you thinking, hon?"

She let out her breath. "Have you brought women here?" She immediately got flustered, and cheeks flushed. "Of course, you have. This is your home. Forget I said that."

She swiped at her cheek, and Steven caught her hand and her eyes. "I have brought a woman here on occasion. Vic has been here, but I've never brought anyone into this room—not my room. I used one of the spare rooms on those occasions."

"Why?"

"Never wanted anyone in my space around my personal things till now. It seemed to mean something bringing someone in here, Sam. Now, I understand why." He opened his bedroom door and let her walk in first. "Where do you want your bag? Over here by the chair all right?"

She nodded, completely absorbed by the room that was so him. Four poster bed in a dark walnut stain and two matching dressers, linens in white with a variety of pillows, a valet stand, another recliner, a fireplace, his personal things on the dresser, and a walk-in closet with his suits all neatly hung and shoes lined up. She shook her head. "Are you sure, Steven? We could go across the hall."

"I'm sure. I want you in here in my space."

Her mouth twitched into a crooked smile. "You won't mind if I lay my stuff, my toothbrush in your space? Scatter my clothes on the floor?"

"Counting on it," he said with a glint in his eye. "I want you to be comfortable in here. Move things around if you like." He watched her move around the bed and stop in front of the nightstand where he had printed and framed her picture from the airport.

"I did the same thing. Put your picture in exactly the same spot in my room."

"I've laid in that bed, talked to you in that bed, and I want you in that bed more than I can tell you."

Samantha turned away as the tears flooded her eyes. "Oh, my God, Steven." Completely forgetting herself, she knelt on the bed moving closer to the wall behind the bed. "The seascape from New York. The one I showed you. You bought it?"

"I had the cab driver stop before I left for the airport."

She ran her hand along the frame. It was even more beautiful hung on the wall amid all of his things. "I can't believe…"

"I hoped it would erase the part of the San Diego trip I wanted you to forget. I knew you loved it, and I intended to send it to you when I got home, but I thought it was a memory for both of us, and it should be with both of us. So, I took down the picture that was there and hung the seascape, because you belong here, Sam. I want you to know that. You belong here with me."

"You're persistent and persuasive, but there so much to think about."

"This isn't a vacation, Sam. Relax and think about it as home, and we'll see. Now, I could climb all over you like I'd like, or I could make you something to eat." He smiled easily, content. "Freshen up, and I'll meet you downstairs."

The bathroom off the bedroom was shockingly beautiful with a circular shower and a large tub. The heated floor tile was soft shades of brown while the vanity continued the dark masculine look of Steven. His razor and shave cream sat on a shelf, and his toothbrush waited for hers in the holder. Her home. Could she make a home here with him? Would he ever say the words she longed to tell him but couldn't? Damn, would her mother ever stop calling? Later she'd call her. Not now when she needed to wash her face, brush her hair, and go help the chef with dinner.

Chapter Twenty-Six

"So, what's on the menu, Chef Corso?" she laughed, catching sight of his apron with **Kiss the Cook** emblazoned on the front.

"It is very important to follow directions," he said, his tone serious and commanding. "So, get over here and kiss me. Then you can pour the wine."

Hard and broad she skimmed his back. How would they ever get through dinner? He turned, reading her thoughts, and grinned a wicked smile. "We've been apart too long. I can tell. Come here." He pulled her against him by pressing her hips and digging into the soft flesh of her cheeks. He brushed her lips as she hungrily reached for his. Closing in on a demanding hot kiss that curled her toes and shook her to the core, he mated their tongues and brushed against the side of her breast, and nearly burned the onion and garlic sautéing in the pan. He pushed her back with a jerk as he grabbed the pan and expertly flipped the vegetables in the hot oil.

"What are you making?" Samantha asked, sucking in her bottom lip and grabbing the red wine on the counter.

"*Pasta e piselli*," Steven answered. "Pretty easy, but comfort food Italian style." He added chopped pieces of prosciutto, an Italian ham, and peas. Samantha handed him his glass of wine as he measured the small shell shaped pasta. "Your job, assistant. When the water boils, dump in the pasta. We don't want to overcook it. I hate mushy pasta, and my mother would kill me. Nine minutes should do it, and then we'll taste it. You can stir it occasionally."

She memorized him at home in his kitchen, confident, competent, and just a beautiful man. "Do I smell warm bread?" she suddenly asked. "You don't bake bread, too, do you? Hell, I could get off on a man who makes hot Italian bread." It suddenly got too warm. Was it the kitchen, or Steven looking at her like she was dinner? "I meant."

His laughter filled the kitchen, and he winked. "I know what you meant, my love. No, I didn't bake the bread, but I thought you might like it warmed. Now, I guess, I'll have to learn how to bake bread."

Samantha sipped her wine and darted her eyes away from the man who made who lose control of her mind and her mouth. She watched him dump the pasta and season the sauce with parsley and basil. Tossing everything in a big bowl, he liberally covered the pasta with Romano cheese.

"Sit, Sam," he said, grabbing the bread before coming to the table. "A toast first to breakfast, lunch, and dinner here with you for the rest of our lives."

She tapped his glass and waited while he scooped the fragrant meal onto her plate. "Mm, amazing. You can cook for me anytime, Corso."

"I'm an amateur. My mother is the real chef, and my father isn't half bad." Samantha saw real affection for his parents.

"Your family close?" she asked on her way to the refrigerator, helping herself to the butter.

"Too close sometimes, but I do love them. Couldn't imagine my life without their support for my dreams. They keep harping on my love life. Want me to find a nice …"

Samantha finished his thought. "Italian girl?"

"Look, honey, they came here as immigrants before I was born, but as proud as they are of their adopted home, they still hang on to the customs and traditions of Italy." Steven refilled her glass and set it closer to her.

"Will I ever meet them?" she asked.

"Been thinking about that. Thanksgiving is only a couple of weeks away. If you stay, you'll meet them all at once."

"I'm not Italian. Strike one?" She looked at him tentatively.

"They want me to be happy. They'll love you."

"They'll stay here? How will they feel about you and me in your room?" She pushed her plate back and sipped her wine.

He laughed again. "I think I'm old enough to decide who I want in my life and in my bed. They wouldn't say anything. Don't worry, Sam, and should I take that to mean you'll stay till Thanksgiving, at least?"

"I didn't give Pete a specific time, but two weeks is more than I planned. Then I'd have to make my excuses to my mother, speaking of which." Samantha stared at the call coming in on her phone from her mother. "I need to call her soon."

"Won't she worry you're not answering?" Steven asked.

"They're not like that," Samantha answered. "They're good parents, but they don't worry about me and aren't overly affectionate. I know they love me, and I love them."

Steven's heart tightened. "You may be a little overwhelmed with my family then. Their hugs are the best, and they aren't afraid to touch you, hold you, protect you. Do you want that, Sam? I would love to share my family with you."

"They are important to you." Samantha covered his hand. "I do want to meet them, but I have to deal with my own parents first. I know my mother is upset about the pictures—not because of what I am doing, but because they are public."

"I'm sorry about the pictures, but you can reassure your parents I have only honorable intentions," Steven teased, but Samantha's expression didn't change. "I'll meet them at your brother's wedding if not before." He tore off a piece of bread and dipped it in the oil. Resting his elbows on the table, he leaned in and pressed it to her lips. As she took it into her mouth, her smile returned.

"Let me talk to them first."

Rising, he squeezed her shoulder as he kissed her. "Mm, you taste better than the pasta." He gathered a stack of dishes and carried them to the sink.

"Slow down, chef." Samantha moved around him with a pile of her own. "You cooked so I'll clean up. It's only fair."

"Leave it for the housekeeper, Sam."

"The invisible one? You don't even know when she comes. These could be sitting for days. Take a break, and let me clear up the dishes. Finish your wine." She smiled the sunshine he had missed.

"Sam, how long has it been since I picked you up at the airport?" he asked quietly.

"I don't know," she said, filling the sink with warm sudsy water. "Maybe three or four hours. Why?"

"Because I've waited long enough." She looked up to see his gaze land on her breast, trail down her hips, and return to her lips. "Come here."

Her smile broadened. "Patience, let me finish these. You'll thank me in the morning."

"Don't make me come get you," he growled impatiently. Moving behind her, his hands gripped her hips and slid up to cup her breasts. "Now." Turning her around, he picked her up by circling her thighs and tossed her over his shoulder.

"Steven Corso, what the hell are you doing?" she laughed. "Put me down." She clung to the only part of him she could reach as he climbed the stairs to his bedroom. Once inside he shoved the door shut with his shoulder and carried her to his bed.

"Now, what am I going to do with you? Oh, right." He tossed her down on the bed, immediately pinning down her hands to either side of her and resting his body on her.

"You're part caveman," she giggled.

"Want to guess which part?" His arms slid around her, freeing her to reach for his t-shirt and pull it over his head. Pressed against her, he lingered over the fierce pulsing in her throat and the soft valley between her breasts. "Too damn many clothes," he mumbled, rolling back and pulling on her jeans as she released her breasts to the dark longing in his eyes. "You're here in this house, in this room, and in this bed," he said almost reverently, "and better than I could ever imagined." He caressed her breasts in deliberate circles with the tips of his fingers till he drew in the little peak that stood at attention in breathless anticipation. In spite of the need building within him, Steven wanted the first time in his bed to be slow and unhurried. He was keeping her in Baltimore somehow. There would be many nights. This was one he wanted them both to remember. Switching to her other breast, she moaned softly arching her back to press closer to him. The words were there; he wanted to say them, but he was drowning in her scent, in her touch, in the way her body moved against his in a longing they both wanted and couldn't hold back. He wedged his hips between her thighs and rocked against her core till her nails dug into his flesh, and her legs wrapped around his waist. "Say you're mine, Samantha. Say it."

"All yours, Steven," she cried as the waves broke over her. Her pleasure aroused him further till he broke with her and fell exhausted on the bed. He gathered the pillows around them and wrapped her tightly to him. She'd stay in Baltimore; he smiled as they drifted off to sleep. He'd make it impossible for her to leave.

Chapter Twenty-Seven

Samantha stretched in a cocoon of soft pillows and cotton sheets. She reached for Steven and, for a moment, panicked when she realized he wasn't there. Then she remembered she was in Baltimore, and he was probably fixing breakfast. She quickly dressed and made her way to the kitchen where a note waited on the counter. **I'm somewhere in this big house. All you have to do is find me.**

He was crazy. Samantha made a piece of toast, poured a cup of coffee, and went in search of her missing writer. She wanted to explore the other corridor to the right of the staircase anyway so here was the perfect opportunity. The first room she peeked in was nicely painted in a soft yellow with hardwood flooring. No furniture—just an extra room. The next room was a weight room and fitness center with a treadmill and various ecliptic machines. No wonder Steven was so fit. Next, a bathroom but still no Steven. Her anticipation grew, imagining him behind the last door. She knocked gently, but he didn't answer. Maybe he wasn't inside, but she still wanted to take a look. When she pushed open the heavy wooden door, a velvety voice greeted her.

"Come in, Sam."

"Am I interrupting?"

"Not possible. Just let me finish this thought." His fingers flew across the keys which gave Samantha time to take in his space. It was again so Steven; so masculine, heavy on the dark woods, flooring, desk, and an entire wall of books. The shelves were packed with classics and current novels, mostly adventure, mystery, or detective. Steven's books were displayed on the shelf at approximately eye level and centered on the wall. Surrounding his desk was his computer and printer while he worked intently on his laptop. Yet, another picture of a seascape hung on the only bare wall, though it was predominately sailboats adrift in the water. Samantha lingered over the sketches on the table beneath the picture and the file of Jerry's photos.

"Sorry, just didn't want to lose the thought," Steven said, crossing the room to her. Moving back her hair, he nuzzled her neck and kissed behind her ear. "Tentative sketches for the cover of the next book," he pointed. "Jenny's been on my back to write faster, but I was distracted with you in Charleston. I woke early this morning, and the story just seemed to come together in my head so I came down here to work."

"Is that how it is?" Samantha asked. "You suddenly get a burst of creativity, and it just has to spill out?"

He sat on the edge of the table, staring at her intently. "Have you experienced that? Are you writing?"

Samantha nodded, though she was embarrassed by Steven's interest. "I started a new novel on the way back from New York. Forgot I was on a plane, and I've been working on it here and there." The color rose from her neck into her cheeks as Steven continued to stare.

"Are you happy with this one?"

"I think so, but it's still early and not polished—just a very, very rough draft, but I like the story concept and the main characters. It's just…"

"What? Stalled out?"

"No, I just don't have the time. You said in the workshop, writing shouldn't be something you dabble in if you're a real writer. Between my job and my life that's what I'm doing."

Steven smiled. "I'm glad you were listening at the workshop. A possible solution—move here, and we'll fix up the empty room down the hall for you to write. I can throw a computer and printer, some furniture in there, and anything else you want."

"But if I quit my job in Charleston and move here, I have to find a job. Plus, you would be a huge distraction." She pressed her palms to the front of his shirt. "It would be the same situation."

"No, you don't have to find a job. Your writing would be your job just as it is mine."

"What if I'm no good?" she whispered, voicing her worse fear.

Steven pulled her to him. "That voice in you wants to be heard even if you don't publish, but the odds are in your favor. If the article is any indication, you have talent."

"Different kind of writing," she said, pulling back. "Steven, Avery thought his book was good; he was wrong. What if I am too?"

"What if you're not wrong? There's only one way to find out. Write, Sam, and we'll see."

She moved to the bookcase and ran her hand along the bindings of his books. "Did you ever get a rejection for a book?"

"Ah, yes, not a rejection, many. I have Jenny to thank for taking a chance. Truthfully, my writing has improved, but she took a risk on the first book, and here I am." He watched her debating in her head. He needed to push her over the top, make her commit to leaving Charleston and moving here. "Move in with me. Let me give you the time and space to discover where the writer is within you. If you get bored, or don't want to write anymore, you can always get a job."

"Tempting, very tempting, Steven." Then she surprised him. "You are pretty certain we are for real, not just a passing thing?"

His heart hurt for the doubt he saw in her eyes. Lightly he brushed his fingers over her cheek. "I believe in us, Samantha. When two people should be together, they are good for each other. I'm writing this morning, because you are here, putting my universe in perfect order. I was lost without you. Trust how you feel." He leaned down and captured her mouth with his while she tugged him closer to her. "A kiss doesn't lie, does it?"

"No. I'll think about it. You should write, and I'll call my mother and wander around. When it gets closer to lunch, I'll make something." She looked back to catch him roll his eyes. "I can cook enough so we won't starve."

"I have no doubt," he laughed, returning to his laptop.

Samantha wanted to put off calling her mother just a little longer. She refilled her coffee cup and settled on the sofa in the sitting room. Steven had offered her an opportunity—not just to stay with him but to work at her art without the responsibilities of life getting in the way. But what if she gave up the life she had created in Charleston and moved away from family and friends, and they didn't work out? She knew in her heart what she felt for him was real, but he had known a lot of women. What if he grew tired of her in three months or six months? It would break her heart. He had said many times he wouldn't let her go. Was that the same thing as saying he loved her? Why hadn't he said those three simple words?

The pictures on the mantel caught her attention. Family photo, Steven's mom and dad with their four adult children sitting in a cozy casual room around a Christmas tree. They were a handsome family with their dark features. A second photo looked like a deliberate family photo that included the spouses and children of Steven's brothers and sister. Didn't Steven want that? Something permanent in his life, a wife and kids. He looked younger and happy in the picture. No wonder his parents wanted him to settle down with a nice girl. That would complete the picture. Samantha wondered if Steven had ever lived with a woman in this house. Not that it really mattered but had he ever thought he had found the right woman and moved her in his home? Restlessly, she rose from the sofa and watched the leaves blow across the front lawn. He expected her to change her whole life; he could answer a few questions. She marched down the hall to his office and pushed open the door. Steven looked up, surprised to see her. "I don't want to bother you, but it's my turn." He sat back and waited, deliberately not interrupting her. "Did you ever live with a woman in this house?" Despite her directness, Steven sensed her vulnerability and her confusion. She was weighing where she fit in the chapters of his life.

He studied her carefully. "Fair question, no."

"You've never lived with a woman?"

"You said in this house. The answer is still no, but I lived with someone in college for a semester."

"Why didn't it last?" Samantha asked.

"Mostly, I didn't want her in my space or my life, I guess. What's going on, Sam?" He could see the wheels turning in her head, and he wasn't sure if it was to his advantage or not.

"I noticed the family pictures on the mantel. Does it bother you your brothers and sister are married with kids? Do you want your own family?" She stayed in the doorway still holding tightly to the knob. "We don't really know anything about each other."

Steven thought about that for a minute. "Doesn't bother me. I fully expected to find the right woman eventually to share my life. Samantha, you know …"

"I know I should call my mother," she interrupted. "I'm sorry I bothered you."

Something didn't feel right. "Sam, wait." He came around his desk and circled her waist loosely. "I'm asking you to move in here, because you are important to me. I want something more with you. You understand that, don't you?"

She leaned into him, and let his physical strength overpower her. "Yes, I want that, too."

"Mm, maybe," his heart quickened, "I should drag you back to bed."

"Maybe you should go back to work," she smiled reluctantly. "I better call my mother."

She closed the door softly and retraced her steps till she sat in the center of Steven's bed. How was she ever going to explain Steven to her mother? She would ask all the right questions. Unfortunately, Samantha doubted she'd have the right answers. And by the end of the conversation, she would know where she was spending Thanksgiving. If her mother was too angry, she'd go home. Wait, if she couldn't tell her mother where she was spending a holiday, how was she going to tell her she was moving to Baltimore? She couldn't leave Steven again, and that realization frightened her. She wanted him, needed him more than he wanted or needed her, and, in the end, she'd take the ultimate risk. She'd risk her heart. She fell back against the pillows holding back the tears. At the moment she decided, once again, to wait to return her mother's call, her phone rang. She heard what she dreaded in her mother's tone immediately. The controlled anger, the disappointment, and the guilt were trademark responses for Mrs. Westerly. She questioned not only Samantha's behavior but her common sense. Surely, she understood the word discreet. Surely, she understood how this had embarrassed her parents before their friends. She grilled Samantha on who Steven was, why she was chasing him around the country, and why she was behaving like a hormonal teenager over a man she barely knew. Samantha apologized the first time as she always did when she disappointed her mother, but soon realized her mother wasn't listening. This conversation was meant to be completely one sided; her mother talking, and she, the obedient daughter, listening. As the conversation came to a close, Mrs. Westerly reminded Samantha that she loved her dearly, and dinner on Thanksgiving was at four. Samantha fell back on the bed.

"About Thanksgiving, Mom, I don't think I can make it," she said slowly.

The bedroom door opened, and Steven walked quietly to his dresser to retrieve some papers. He watched Samantha try to reason with her mother.

"Of course, I love you and Dad, but … I was going to meet Steven's parents… No, we aren't engaged, but…" She rolled her eyes helplessly at Steven. "I know Ray is in California, but…" Samantha knew exactly what Steven was thinking as he stared at her. She had landed in the place she hated the most—the middle—between her parents and Steven. "All right. I'll be there. Love you, too."

Steven focused on controlling his anger as he sat on the end of the bed. She wouldn't look at him; she couldn't. Pulling at an imaginary thread in the spread, Samantha swallowed hard. "I need to go back anyway. Pete's going to be angry if I stay that long."

"Samantha, look at me," Steven said, trying to calm down. When her beautiful eyes met his, he softened a little. "Are you moving in here, my love?"

God, nobody was playing fair. How could she say no to him or her mother? She nodded, still holding his gaze. It was impossible for her to look away. “Yes, I want to live here with you, but I can’t just walk away. I have an apartment with a lease I have to deal with, a job I have to quit, and parents I need to talk to in person. I know it isn’t in your schedule, but I wish they could meet you before I make this move.”

“I’m not letting you go,” he said firmly. “I was crazy after you left New York especially after our misunderstanding. No, we will take care of all those things when I can go with you. After Thanksgiving I can take a long weekend, and we’ll get everything done.”

“You’re busy. You don’t have to do that. I’ll get it done quickly. I can be back in a week or two,” Samantha pleaded.

“No,” his temper slipped, “we aren’t doing this. Thanksgiving is here. The next day we’ll fly back to Charleston.”

“So, just like that I’m supposed to call my mother back and tell her I’m not coming?” she argued.

“You’re an adult woman. Figure it out.” Steven angrily left the room. He knew he was being unreasonable, admittedly selfish, but San Diego and New York had taught him leaving her was not an option—not at this stage of their relationship. Besides, he had told his family she would be there, and he desperately wanted them to know her. He was being demanding and hard headed. Drop everything and come to Baltimore. Now, drop your family and stay for Thanksgiving. Life use to be so damn easy when he did what he wanted and didn’t feel guilty.

When Samantha finally came down, she went right to the kitchen to start lunch. She expected Steven to be pouting in his study trying to work. Instead, she found him outside on the patio in a ratty sweatshirt staring at the pool. Quickly, she organized two plates and set the table. Mustering her courage, she pushed open the glass doors. “Lunch? I made lunch.” He nodded and followed her back into the kitchen. Filling two mugs of coffee, he sat down at the table and cleared his throat.

“If you really want to go to Charleston, I’ll go with you.” He hoped to God he knew her well enough to believe she’d say no. “We’ll get a flight out on Wednesday.”

"Your family is coming here," Samantha reminded him. "You've got all the food, and it would be wrong for you to bail on them this close to the holiday."

He bided his time wanting to agree, but it had to appear to be her decision. "My family will understand. My brother lives a couple of miles from here. I'll deliver the food to him, and they can have it at his house." He avoided looking at her, because his eyes would deceive him and let her know just how much he wanted a Baltimore Thanksgiving.

Samantha looked at him thoughtfully. "No," she finally answered, "I haven't even met them yet, and I'm disrupting their holiday and taking you away. No, you have to be here."

"Then you do too," he said, threading their fingers together, "because you belong to me, Sam. We're just starting out as a couple, and these are the things we share."

"Thank you."

"For what?"

"For putting me first. I know how important your family is. It was sweet of you to offer."

He let out his breath slowly as she cleared the table. He ignored the nudges of guilt that he feared would push him to do the right thing. The right thing, he rationalized, was to keep her in Baltimore. "What are you going to do about your parents?"

"I don't know. You heard my mother, and normally when she gives me an ultimatum, I cave. I guess either way one of you is going to be mad at me."

Steven pulled her down on his lap. "You'll stay here, and we'll figure out how to appease your mother." He considered hiding in his study the rest of the afternoon, but he didn't feel like writing so they took his car and drove through Baltimore. Overly quiet Samantha retreated far away—Charleston; it was calling her back, and, at some point Steven was afraid she'd leave. Her mother had saddled her with guilt, and his good girl was going to give in. Damn it, this shouldn't be so hard. There had to be an answer they were both overlooking.

"Why do you love Baltimore?" Samantha asked.

He tossed her a sideways glance and smiled brightly. “For me it’s everything; it’s home. It’s centrally located, just half an hour from DC and a couple of hours from New York while it retains its own beauty and charm. It’s wedged in history, and yet, has the vitality of a modern city. I’m taking you to one of my favorite places, Fells Point, on the Chesapeake Bay.”

Steven had spent a lot of time at the Point in his reckless youth. With over one hundred bars in the historic neighborhood, young people spent nights drinking, listening to live music, and enjoying the local seafood. In those days he cared little for the history of the Point; the cobblestone streets, the mix of immigrants, or the ship building industry that the rest of the country relied on, but as he grew older, he appreciated more of the city that would always be home. During the day Fells Point was a gathering place for tourists. Steven took Samantha to specialty stores where she purchased several candles, antique stores where she marveled at the craftsmanship, and the local market where the smell of hot breads and pastries definitely resurrected the smile he had come to love. The weather was brisk but perfect for a cup of hot apple cider and a generous meal of crab cakes and oysters on the half shell. And as night fell, they walked along the waterfront—the moon playing on the water, the scent of fish and nature, and the sound of water lapping rhythmically against the shore. Steven cradled her shoulders in a possessive hold and drew her in till his lips joined hers. Without hesitation, her body sought his heat and turned into him till she could circle his waist and lay against his shoulder.

By the time they returned home it was very late, and while Steven took a quick shower, Samantha crawled into bed and fell asleep. As much as Steven wanted sleep too, his brain wouldn’t shut down. She was happy tonight; after a while she had forgotten about her mother and had relaxed. He loved how she was tentative, but he could coax her into a new experience. She had never eaten oysters, but she had finally given it a try. Of course, with the warm bread he bought, she’d probably have eaten anything. He loved how she was open and unpretentious.

He loved her smile and that unique blue of her eyes. He loved her.

He closed his eyes and cuddled against her back, but the tension fired through him, and he couldn't relax. He couldn't sleep. "Sam, wake up," he whispered against her ear. "Sam, wake up, honey," he repeated, sliding back and rolling her with him.

Her eyes fluttered sleepily and attempted to focus on his face. "Is it morning?" she asked.

"No, baby, it's still dark, night, but I want you to wake up, please."

Samantha's smile broadened and moving closer she linked her hands behind his head, pulling him till their lips met. Steven smiled against her lips. "Nice, very nice, but I really want you to wake up."

"Why? Is something wrong?" She brushed her hair away from her face and tried to read his expression.

"Nothing is wrong." He pulled on a pair of sweats and didn't bother with a shirt or shoes. "Come on." He yanked back the covers, and she squealed in protest as the cool room met her naked flesh. "Here," Steven said, wrapping her in his robe. "This will be good, but watch you don't trip."

"Where are we going?" She continued to protest. "Is the house on fire?"

Steven didn't answer. In the big sleeves of his robe he found her hand and tugged her reluctant body toward the stairs. "You are going to break your neck." He swooped her up in his arms and carried her down to the kitchen.

She could only stare at him. "Hungry?" He shook his head. "You want to have sex in the kitchen?" Had he lost his mind?

"Destination isn't the kitchen, my love," he answered, shifting her in his arms and opening the glass doors to the patio. A blast of cold air hit them hard in the face.

"No," Samantha screamed. "What the hell?"

He put her down on the side of the pool and walked the short distance to the pool house to grab a handful of towels.

"I'll have to close up the pool after Thanksgiving, but we can get, at least, one swim in tonight."

"Did you say swim?" Samantha groaned, stomping her cold feet on the pavement and tightening the robe around her.

Steven laughed and shoved down his sweats. He backed up a couple of steps before jumping off the side of the pool into the water. "It's great, Sam. Take off your robe, and get in here."

"You're crazy. It must be 45 degrees out here."

"43, I checked my phone before I woke you."

"You need some serious help, Steven."

"Drop the robe," he said insistently.

"No, normal men roll a woman back and make love in bed, a warm cozy bed. They don't drag her into a pool in the middle of the night so she can get pneumonia," she argued.

"Are you done?" he smirked, swimming to her side of the pool. "Get in, Sam."

"Naked swimming. What if someone takes a picture? My mother will stroke out if she sees a naked picture of me on the internet."

"You are such a coward," he challenged. "I had the place landscaped for privacy. There's never been any pictures from here. I'm counting to five then I'm coming to get you."

"No, no, no. I'm freezing, and I'm going…"

"To walk to that end of the pool, drop the robe, and walk down the steps into the water." His eyes met hers defiantly. "One!"

She glared at him. "No."

His eyebrow lifted. "Two!"

Her anger weakened as she realized he had every intention of coming for her. "Steven, we are both going to be sick tomorrow."

"Three!"

"Stop counting," she yelled, stomping to the far end of the pool. If she felt cool in the bedroom, she couldn't imagine how cold she'd feel when she dropped the robe. She held his eyes. "If I do this, it is only because I am going to kill you when I get in."

He grinned, slowly treading water. "Water is heated, Sam. Four!"

"All right, all right." She closed her eyes and tensed. Just do it like tearing off a band aid. The robe fell at her feet, and her skin protested in one giant goose bump. "Cold, cold, cold," she screamed, scrambling down the steps. She felt the warmth when the water hit her knees. Pushing farther out, she bobbed till she was enveloped in warm water beneath her chin.

"Better?" Steven asked, pressing and wrapping his thighs around hers. "And I'm going to make it even better." He crushed her chest against him as he kissed her quickly cooling shoulder. He slid deeper into the water, searching her eyes as she relaxed in the heat.

"My lips are cold," she whined.

Steven brushed her lips playfully then delved as a starving man to bring them intimately together in the first rush of heat. She leaned in to kiss his muscles, clearly outlined in his chest, till her fingers rolled his nipples in gentle strokes. He gritted his teeth as the second wave of heat rolled over them and noticed Samantha was no longer covered by the water. She didn't seem to care that the water was around her waist as he gripped her ass and caressed the back of her thighs. She moaned softly against his cheek as the water helped him easily turn her back to his chest. "You are addictive, Sam," he whispered softly. "I can't get enough of you."

He paddled with one hand moving both of them to the side of the pool where he held her between him and the tile. Steven relished the moment; he had often written the aha moment, but it wasn't often he had the chance to live it. He focused completely on her face, on the wet curls clinging to her neck and shoulders, on the blue of her eyes darkening against the moon's glow, and the pink swollen lips that parted and waited in anticipation of him. Clearly, he saw the love; she may never have said it, but it was there in every thought, every touch, and every look she gave him. He wondered if she could see it in him, because he wanted her to know. He pressed her lips, sealing his heart with hers. "I love you, Sam." Her eyes widened, and she mumbled something, but it was lost in her gasp as he brought them together and ironed out every wrinkle in the universe. She held tightly to him and let the water support her as she descended the heat of the moment and whispered softly, “I love you, Steven.”

Wrapping his arms around her shoulders, he lowered her shivering body down under the water and held her head against his chest. “Stay here for a minute, love.” Using the side of the pool, he boosted himself out of the water. He quickly dried off with a towel and tied it around his waist. Then he lifted Samantha, drying her quickly, and wrapping her in his robe. “Damn, it’s cold,” he mumbled, catching her eye. “Whose idea was this anyway?” Slamming the door behind him, the house roared with a blast of heat, and Samantha headed for the stairs. Steven stopped in the kitchen long enough to grab two glasses and a bottle of wine. “Warmth,” he answered Samantha’s quizzical look, “and a small toast to finding love.”

♥♥

Chapter Twenty-Eight

Wednesday morning the blitz began. Mrs. Westerly, like any good general, went on the attack enlisting the help of the rest of the family to get Samantha to Charleston for Thanksgiving. Her father called first reminding her how much her mother had sacrificed for her. A second call from Ray, who felt guilty enough living in California, brought her to tears when he explained their mother felt abandoned by both of her children. The difference was Samantha lived in Charleston and could go home easier than he could. And even knowing how manipulative her mother was acting didn't stop the blitz from working. When her mother called finally with more questions, Samantha felt her last shred of resistance failing. Was she married? No. Was she engaged? No. Was she even in a long-established relationship with Steven? No. Then her place was with her mother and father who loved and expected her. The guilt hit the target, and Samantha sighed. She had to go home, but every time she brought it up Steven had kissed her senseless. Since the night in the pool when they had opened their hearts to love, he was even more insistent her home was in Baltimore, and her place was with him on Thanksgiving. He was going to be so angry with her.

She packed her bag before she lost her nerve and carried it downstairs to face him. Instead, she found a note that he had gone to the store for a few things, and he'd be back shortly. Samantha reread it three times; it was the coward's way out. It was wrong to just leave a note and head to the airport. He said he loved her; maybe he was just going to have to prove it.

Dear Steven,

I have to go to Charleston. Please try and understand. Spend Thursday with your family and come to me on Friday. I know this isn't what we wanted, but I don't know what else to do. I love you, Sam.

Samantha pulled her purple bag through the holiday travelers. One of the busiest days of the year for air travel, she prayed she couldn't get a seat. She swallowed her tears when the clerk swiped her credit card and handed her the boarding pass. Steven was right; she was home and should be with him. She settled in a waiting area for her flight which was scheduled to board in ten minutes. Her hands shook and palms turned sweaty. Was it the flight, or was she disgusted with herself for not standing up to her mother? Or was it the panic knowing Steven would find her note and think she was a coward again? The airline called first boarding, and she sat. Her brain refused to tell her legs to stand.

"Miss Westerly? Samantha Westerly," a deep male voice addressed her.

She looked up to a very tall man with dark eyes and a square jaw. Somewhat handsome with a five o'clock shadow, he placed his hand under her elbow and pulled her to her feet. It was then she noticed he was in uniform. At her other elbow was a second man, younger and shorter, with light hair and freckles wearing the same uniform.

"Wait, who are you? What are you doing?"

"Baltimore police," shorter guy said. "Please come quietly."

"My plane," she insisted. "They've already called my flight."

"I'm afraid you'll be missing your flight. You need to come with us." The taller officer looked at his phone then pushed her through the remaining passengers. People were staring, but Samantha had little time to absorb the scene around her.

"I'm not going anywhere with you two. Are you really cops? I haven't done anything." She pulled away stumbling over her bag.

"I didn't want to do this, but you leave me no choice. You have the right to remain silent. Anything you say can and will be used against you in a court of law." Samantha stopped listening. They were arresting her. "Do you understand your rights, Miss Westerly?"

Samantha nodded. She needed to call Steven. "I want to make a phone call."

"All in good time when we get to the station," the officer said.

"I didn't do anything. What's the charge?" Samantha demanded.

The two officers looked at one another. "Desertion," tall cop finally answered, pulling out his handcuffs. He gently pulled Samantha's arms back and cuffed her. Temporarily stunned, Samantha walked through the airport to the waiting patrol car parked out front, dragging her bag. The arresting officer pushed her head down as he helped her in the vehicle. Steven would be so angry. What the hell was wrong with the police in this city? Didn't they have anything better to do than arrest innocent people? Too late she realized the words were tumbling out of her mouth, and she wasn't finished.

"I'll have both of your badges, and I'll sue the damn city," she yelled. "You can't do this in America." Both officers exchanged a look then taller cop texted on his cell, looking downright amused. Samantha sank back in the seat as much as she could with cuffs. Turning her attention to the street, she noticed they were driving through a nice residential neighborhood. Was a police station hidden in here? They drove down a street that looked vaguely familiar and turned into... Steven's driveway? Steven came out of the house, and tall cop met him half way. They talked briefly in Italian, and both were smiling. The door opened, and Steven helped her out. She stared at both of them waiting for an explanation.

Tall cop grinned at her. "Nice to meet you, Samantha. I'll see you at dinner tomorrow."

"Dinner?" She turned back to Steven who was pulling her away from the car. "Who was that?"

Steven wrapped an arm around her as the officer tossed something to him through the window. He waved and moved her towards the front door. "I think I told you about my brother, Ernesto."

"The police officer?" Samantha said, understanding a piece of what had just happened. "You had your brother arrest me? Drag me out of the airport in cuffs?"

He chuckled softly. "I didn't know he'd go that far, but he said you were uncooperative. Honey, I was on the phone with him when I found your note. I blew up and told him I'd tear the airport apart till I found you. He was pretty sure with my temper I'd end up in jail. So, he offered to give you a ride home."

Samantha shook her head. "I will never be able to set foot in that airport again. How could you?"

His eyes narrowed. "I could ask you the same thing. How much courage does it take to write me a note and leave?"

"Take off the cuffs," she said, ignoring his question. "And for your information I don't know if I would have left. I couldn't seem to move till your brother yanked me out of my seat."

Steven stifled a smile. "I'm sorry, Sam, but maybe I have a solution."

"Take off the cuffs," she repeated. "Your brother must think I'm crazy. Great way to introduce us."

Steven dug the key out of his jeans and turned Sam around. "You made a wonderful first impression," he grinned, unlocking the cuffs. He rubbed her shoulders gently. "He called you *briosa,* spirited and *una buona partita per me*, a perfect match for me."

"Really?" That pleased Samantha, and she really did want to stay in Baltimore, but there was still her mother to deal with. "Did you say you had a solution to my mother?"

Steven kissed her and wound his arms around her. "Wasn't sure you caught that. Yes, I was thinking of it earlier, and while this won't be the solution in the future, this time will be the exception. Call your mother, Sam, and put your phone on speaker. I think it's time I meet her."

Samantha paled but made the call. What did she have to lose? Prince Charming might be able to finesse her mother, and if not, she was ready to stand up to her. Maybe the adrenaline was still pumping, and maybe her courage was coming from almost getting arrested, but either way if Steven didn't handle this, she would.

"Hi, Mom. I want to introduce you to the man in my life, Steven Corso."

"Hello, Mrs. Westerly, I look forward to meeting both you and Samantha's father soon, but for now I'd like to tell you how important your daughter is to me." Steven's voice was strong yet, soothing and commanding. Samantha melted, and wondered if her mother could resist this powerful man. "I'm concerned that she has been very unhappy over this whole Thanksgiving situation."

Mrs. Westerly took the opening. "Samantha should be with her family on Thanksgiving, don't you agree, Mr. Corso? From what I understand your relationship with my daughter is new and should be secondary to her parents."

Samantha started to speak, but Steven pressed his finger to her lips. "I assure you our relationship is not frivolous, Mrs. Westerly, but I prefer to discuss that with you and your husband in person. Are you aware Sam is with me in Baltimore?"

"No, you haven't said anything, Samantha."

"I've been here almost two weeks, Mom. Steven invited me after he finished his tour in New York." Biting a fingernail, she looked uncertainly at Steven. The line was silent.

"Maybe we can make everyone happy this holiday," Steven continued. "I understand you have the holiday meal later in the day. My family gets together early; we'll be eating by noon. I'm looking online and can book Samantha and I on a flight to Charleston at four. We should be at your home by 6:30. I know that is later than you planned, but if you could wait for us, I think everyone would be happy." Samantha felt the moisture collecting in her eyes.

"Well, it's just the four of us. If you are coming, we can celebrate a little later," her mother was saying, "and I would like to meet you, Mr. Corso."

"Steven, please. I'll text you from the airport to let you know we are on schedule," Steven added, as Samantha's tears silently slipped down her cheeks.

"Please do. I will see you both tomorrow." Mrs. Westerly ended the call, and Samantha launched herself into Steven's arms.

"I can't believe you did that," she whimpered against his chest. "I know the last thing you want to do is leave your family and travel on Thanksgiving Day."

"Honey," Steven cuddle her closer. "It's not the best solution, but I don't want you miserable with my parents tomorrow, and I sure as hell don't want you in Charleston without me. We'll make it work, and," he grinned, brushing aside her tears, "you owe me big time. Might get you in the pool again."

"Too cold, but I offer my services in the kitchen," she smiled back. "I know you have a lot to do."

"I'm packing you up, talking to your landlord, quitting your job, and pacifying your parents, all in a four-day weekend. You got a problem with that, love?"

"No, I'd say that's impossible, but I'm learning nothing is impossible when Steven Corso makes up his mind. He gets what he wants." Her eyes glistened with admiration for the man that held her future and her heart and lived life with a passion.

"Good, now, you're on sous chef duty. You do what I tell you, and we'll get along just fine. The bird is the primary focus and breads and dessert. The family is bringing the rest. So, can you take orders to make this dinner happen, Sam?"

"Order away," Samantha laughed. "Seems to be something you are very good at." But she couldn't hide the tightness in her chest or the love in her eyes for this amazing man that she knew loved her—Samantha Westerly, Miss not so fine.

♥♥

Chapter Twenty-Nine

Steven's family could only be described as passionate. In a house that had been so quiet with just the two of them, it suddenly came alive, pulsing with the energy of this family and their children. And they all loved Steven; he was son, brother, and uncle. Steven embraced his family with unconditional love and joy. Samantha watched from the sidelines carefully waiting to be introduced and welcomed to their celebration, but she didn't have to wait long. The Corsos didn't stand on ceremony, didn't stand on formalities, and she was quickly pulled into their loving embrace, figuratively and literally. Ernesto approached her sheepishly. "Hello, Samantha," he greeted her, pulling her into a hug. "How's my favorite collar?"

She struggled to keep a straight face as she narrowed her eyes, but before she could respond, a pretty woman with thick black hair and eyes, wearing a sweatshirt with a big orange pumpkin nudged him. "I still can't believe you did that to this poor girl, Erno. You and Steven are serious trouble." She hugged Steven affectionately. Oldest of the Corso grandchildren, James, Joseph, and Lillian, belonged to Ernesto and Angelina and were already dialing up the Baltimore Ravens pregame.

Salvatore, youngest of the Corso brothers, dutifully carried in pans of stuffing before pounding Steven on the back in a big bear hug. "I hear you've resorted to having women arrested to keep them, big brother," he grinned. Graciously, he turned to Samantha. "A beautiful woman. I see why you are hanging on to this one."

"Do none of you have any manners?" his wife, Maria asked, handing their youngest to him. As tall as her husband, this woman stood out in this family with her red hair and freckles. "Welcome, Samantha. It's always good to have another woman to even things out around here. These two, Sarah and Rachel, are ours, and the little guy is Max."

Steven took her elbow and borrowed her, pulling her into the kitchen. "Mom, this is Samantha."

Mrs. Corso looked up from where she was plating the potatoes and stuffing. She wiped her hands quickly on her apron as she came around the counter. Samantha clearly saw the resemblance to Steven in the sharp perceptive eyes and the soft olive skin. She brushed back a dark curl that had escaped the long ponytail that hung loosely down her back. She was warm and welcoming, hugging Samantha and asking about her family. "Steven, we are just waiting on Gina. Go see if she is here."

"Can I help?" Samantha offered. She glanced at Steven just as he was leaving. "I'm very good at taking directions."

His mother had the most beautiful smile. She handed her the bread to plate. "Steven has never brought anyone to a family dinner. You must be very important to him."

"He's a very special man," Samantha said, meeting the woman's eyes.

"He can be exasperating to a mother's heart sometimes. He's so unsettled, restless. It worries me, but he is a wonderful son." She brushed at a solitary tear.

"You have a beautiful family."

"Steven, be careful. If you drop," she stopped in mid-sentence, staring at Samantha. "You must be Sam." Gina, the youngest of the Corso siblings, threw herself in Samantha's arms. "Thank you. Thank you so much."

Samantha was thoroughly confused. "Thank you for what?" she asked, catching Steven's confused expression.

"For putting up with my bossy brother," she said with a smirk. "You're doing all of us a big favor."

"Somebody's not too big to spank, Sis," Steven threatened.

"Ok, tough guy, I get it. She's special, and we all have to behave," she grinned, grabbing a carrot stick. "But she might as well learn now, this family isn't normal."

"Gina," Mrs. Corso interrupted, "where are my grandchildren?"

"Tino and Julia are with Daddy who is probably fighting the kids for the TV. Mark said we have to eat before football starts."

Seated around the dining room table off the other side of the kitchen, Samantha was overwhelmed by this family that might one day really be hers. She was amazed, as they passed plates of food, at the love she saw between the husbands and wives, the children and their parents, and the respect they showed their grandparents. At the head of the table with the golden-brown turkey in front of him, the patriarch of the family, Steven's father led grace, passed the wine, and more than once, Samantha caught the wink or the look that passed between him and his wife at the other end of the table. At one point he raised his glass. "I am thankful this Thanksgiving to share another day with my beautiful wife who has blessed me with four children and their families." Samantha sipped her wine as Steven held tightly to her hand underneath the table. What a beautiful family and so different from her own.

"Dad makes that toast every year," Steven whispered. "He loves her more every day."

When everyone had eaten, the table was cleared for desserts. Left out, the 'help yourself and clean up after yourself' rule was announced. Football was in the man cave, and the kids took turns pulling Steven into their play. He colored with the little ones and played video games with the older ones on the smaller TV till Steven slipped away to remind Sam they were leaving. He caught the hesitant look.

"Steven, I feel worse now dragging you away."

"Come here. Haven't hugged you nearly enough today." He leveled her with a hot hard kiss that was promptly interrupted by his sister. "Your timing is awful, Gina, as usual."

She stared him down in a familiar sort of way. "She's a keeper, big brother. Don't blow it." She squeezed Samantha's shoulder and went in search of her husband.

"I have no intention of letting you get away, but we are going to miss our flight if we don't hurry. I'll get the bags. They know we are leaving."

Steven said his good-byes while Samantha was more apologetic, but they seemed to understand, and they were welcome to stay at his house. They were nearly the last to board which didn't leave her much time to actually worry about the flight. Steven took both her hands in his. "They loved you just like I knew they would."

"They were wonderful; I liked them too, but my family is so different," Samantha laughed softly, "so much quieter than yours."

"New experience for you and for me. I assume you are entertaining me at your place tonight?"

She smiled seductively. "I guess I am."

The flight was uneventful, but still Samantha rested on the edge of panic as she tried to forget the images of plane disasters dogging her memory. Steven waited till the seat belt light flashed as they neared landing before taking her hand and asking if she was worried about telling her parents about the move. Pulling something from his shirt pocket, he thought he had a possible solution.

"If you were wearing this, they would probably take it better," he said, slipping a solitary diamond engagement ring on her finger.

"Oh, my God," Samantha gasped. "You don't have to do that."

"I don't have to do anything," he answered, holding her eyes. "I love you, and this seems to me to be the next step. Seemed like the right place to ask you since this is where we met."

Samantha stared at her hand then at Steven; her voice completely silent.

"I think this is the time you say yes, my love."

She shook her head, still staring at the ring. "No, I can't."

Steven paled. "Can't? We aren't on the same page on this?"

"I love you, and yes, I want to marry you," Samantha said hurriedly, "but being with your family I realized, there is a lot we don't know about each other. We've only been together a few weeks. I don't know if you've ever had a dog or if you like cats."

Steven would have laughed if she didn't look so damn serious. "So, if I tell you my pet preference, you'll take my ring?"

She sat back, eyes still riveted to the ring. "There's so much more, Steven. Do you want children?" Blue met caramel. "Now? A year from now?"

"So, if I'm understanding you, you want to marry me, but you want a little time to get to know each other better before we make it official?"

"Is that stupid?"

The plane touched down. "No, not at all, but how much time? Not years, I hope."

Samantha laughed and kissed him. "Not long, I promise. We'll just ask more questions like we've been doing, and we'll know when the time is right."

"Do you want me to hold the ring?" Steven asked.

"Absolutely not," Samantha grinned. "It is so beautiful and perfect. I'll wear it with my cross for now." People were retrieving their bags and heading for the exit. "Did we land?"

Steven nodded. "You were preoccupied staring at your ring, and to move this process along, I like big dogs—not yappy little dogs, and I hate cats. If you want one, keep it away from me."

"Understood, and you're not mad, right?"

"No, baby, not mad, just one more thing you owe me."

Steven rented a car and drove the freeway to the Westerly condo just outside Charleston. It was stylishly decorated, sized down for two people, and comfortable and homey. Steven hit it off immediately with Samantha's father, opening the discussion about football, fine cigars, and brandy, all of which waited after their second turkey dinner. Samantha's mother would take more effort to win her over, but he knew woman. A little compliment sprinkled here and there, some casual but simple displays of affection for their daughter, and a willingness to help and pitch in would, at least, begin to bring down her defenses. Steven's latest book rested on the coffee table where both parents thought it wise to read one of Steven's books before their first meeting, and each gave it positive reviews. They were pleasant people, thoughtful and accommodating, but Steven couldn't help compare them to his family. They didn't touch. Neither parent hugged Sam, though she didn't seem to expect it. She stepped right into the role of dutiful daughter, bringing food to the table and pouring the wine. At some point the conversation turned to where their relationship was headed, and Steven candidly spoke of his love for Sam and his hopes for the future. He asked about her brother, and he noticed her mother visibly brightened. When she spoke of his life in California and the beautiful girl he was marrying, Steven realized Ray was the golden child, the favored child. Samantha smiled easily, not seeming to be effected at all by her mother's unusual openness and warmth, but he was grateful that his own parents had never treated them differently. They were all special and unique and so was Samantha. He would make sure she knew that.

When he pulled into the parking lot of her building, she looked exhausted. "Thank you," she whispered, "for everything you did today." She leaned into him as they climbed the stairs and fell asleep quickly when her head hit the pillow. Steven slept briefly, but while it was still dark made his way to the kitchen to create a plan to get Sam back to Baltimore by Monday. Three days wouldn't be enough time to get everything done, but for this trip, he'd devise shortcuts. Samantha soon joined him when she rolled back, and he was missing. She made coffee then straddled his lap. "Mm, sorry, I fell asleep." She breathed in the scent of man and sleep and kissed slowly down the side of his neck. She searched his eyes for why he seemed distracted. "What are you thinking?"

"Just trying to figure out how to get everything you want done in a short time," he said, grabbing a notebook. "I think it best if we don't do everything at once. We can rent a storage unit and a truck, then pack everything you don't know what to do with, yet. As we pack, clothes and other personal items you will want in Baltimore can be prepared for shipping and dropped off before we leave. We'll find your landlord, and tell him you're moving and will continue to pay the rent till the end of the lease or until he rents the unit. That's fair."

"And that would take care of the apartment?" Samantha's fingers played through Steven's longer hair that was in need of a cut.

"Pretty much. Next, text Pete so we can meet him somewhere for a drink."

"So, I can quit?"

"Quit? Yes, or I was thinking, you probably get email submissions as well. If you want, he could forward one or two a week if you still wanted to do that," Steven suggested, "but I don't want you to neglect your own work. It might be more of a favor to Pete till he replaces you."

"That's a great idea. Genius as well as gorgeous," Samantha said, her hands sliding down his chest to the waistband of his shorts.

"Anything I've missed?" Steven asked, closing his eyes and just feeling her fingertips.

"I'd still like to introduce you to my Charleston. Can we squeeze in a carriage ride and dinner somewhere? I'd like to take you to *Frank's* for a drink. It's just a rundown bar, but I used to work there before Pete hired me. It has a mechanical bull that I'm kind of talented on."

Steven caught her hands. "You've been on a mechanical bull?" He couldn't imagine her bobbing up and down and all around, pumping and …"

"I got good while I was there. Bet I can stay on longer than you. Wait? You've never been on one, have you? You mean I finally have a life experience you don't have?"

Steven smiled. "We'll make time for everything." He slid his hands over her bare thighs. "Still dark. We have some time."

"We could make a big breakfast," Samantha said innocently enough. She moved tighter against his core. "Or we could do something else and grab toast and coffee later."

"I vote for something else." Steven stood, carrying her up with him, prompting Sam to wrap herself around him. "Definitely."

Peeling off her robe, he dropped her on the bed and sucked hungrily against her throat and the pulse that beat in time to his heart. "Ernesto," Samantha groaned.

What the fuck? Steven's head jerked back as he caught her smiling eyes. "My brother?" he said, his fists tightening.

Samantha's hands slid down his back and gripped his ass. "I'm multitasking—asking my questions to get to know you while you keep doing what you are doing. Please, keep doing what you're doing!"

"That's insane. Now, you want to talk about my family?" he groaned.

"Sooner the ring goes on my finger." Her leg wrapped around his, exposing the intensely soft inner skin against his unforgiving hard muscles.

"Talk then," he said, gritting his teeth.

"Angel said you two were trouble." Samantha moaned as Steven gripped her thighs and kissed closer to her heat. "What was the worst thing you did?"

"Borrowed a truck," Steven said, fighting to put together a coherent thought. "Neighbor, old truck, broke down three blocks from home."

"You stole…oh God, Steven ….a truck?" she moaned again.

God, that was damn hot. "Didn't get busted by cops—by dad. Much worse, beat the shit out of us then worked our asses off around the house for months. Flip over on your stomach."

"How? How old were you?" she tried breathlessly.

"Fourteen, Erno was sixteen." He tugged on her hair and kissed over her shoulder and down her back.

"God, don't stop, Steven. Are you close to Gina?"

He shook the image of his sister out of his head. "Samantha, shut up."

"Are you close?" she insisted.

"Close? Yes." What were they talking about? His body was damn close.

"Were you her protective big brother?" Her hands clutched the sheets in tight fists.

"Beat up most of her boyfriends. They were losers."

"Till Mark? Steven, I need you now," she cried.

He raised her hips against him. "I tried to run off Mark, but he stood up to me. He wasn't giving up Gina even if I killed him." And plunged inside. "Shut up, Sam, please."

Samantha moved into his thrusts and lost the ability for speech as well till they both shattered. "Warm jello. That's what I feel like."

"Don't you ever do that to me again, Sam. I enjoy focusing on you. Ernesto and Gina shouldn't be anywhere near my thoughts."

Samantha glowed. "You were amazing, and it didn't seem to bother your power of concentration. I'm getting dressed while you think of a question to ask me."

Steven shook his head as he watched her move around the room. "My turn, where do I get you some serious psychological help?"

She tossed his jeans his way. "No time, hon, too much to do today."

Renting a storage unit didn't take long, but finding a very big truck the day after Thanksgiving took a little longer. Luckily, they also sold boxes. Steven intended to make one trip to move her from the apartment to the unit. Thankfully, she lived modestly in the small apartment. By early evening most of her things were packed in the truck or in boxes for shipping. He'd break down the bed in the morning, load it with any last-minute articles, and spend a good part of Sunday unloading in the unit. So, if they were going to enjoy Charleston, it had to be tonight. Revived after a hot shower, Samantha drove the rental car to the carriage rides in the heart of her city. The horse drawn carriages that weaved down the city streets screamed this was Charleston. It mixed the old buildings, the historic sites, and the outdoor market places with the new high rises, the malls, and the tourist business that thrived in Charleston. This was the city she loved and would miss. She stroked the head of one of the horses as they waited to board then snuggled tightly together under a blanket as the wagon showed Steven the real city, the real history.

Afterwards, Samantha took them to *Frank's Bar and Grill* but warned Steven not to eat the food. It was technically a bar. The food had only been added to attract tourists and, unfortunately, the owner had never hired a real cook. The food was, hands down, the worst she had ever eaten, greasy and tasteless. Steven didn't mind. He was more interested in seeing her ride the mechanical bull. He ordered two beers as she said hello to the bartender and several of the waitresses. He couldn't imagine her in this bar, coming every night to work. He also didn't miss the guy in the Stetson sitting by the bull who hadn't taken his eyes off her since they walked in. He was sure he knew what the asshole was thinking as his gaze checked her out from head to toe. He was about to straighten him out when Samantha returned to the table, tapped her beer against his, and took a long drink. "Tough place for a young girl," he observed.

"Young and stupid," Samantha agreed. "But I never really felt unsafe." Asshole caught her attention and tipped his hat. "Ricky," she explained, reading Steven's reaction. "He runs the bull and acts as a bouncer. There should be a couple more guys in here, too. They were very good about watching out for the girls when some jerk had too much to drink and got fresh. I guess it's pretty seedy, but I had nothing else till Pete hired me."

"Another beer?" Steven asked, his chest hurting in that familiar spot. There was something about this bar that reminded him how little he knew about her, and wasn't that what she had been trying to tell him?

Samantha nodded. "It used to take two to get me on the bull. So, Corso, I bet you, I can ride the bull till the buzzer, and first timer, I bet you can't."

He felt the familiar tug at his heart. Damn, those blue eyes could bring him to his knees. "Stakes?" he questioned.

She leaned in for only his ears. "Beat me, and I'll ride you tonight."

His hand wrapped quickly around her neck, and a low growl escaped his lips. "That's going to happen either way, sweetheart. Go, take your shot."

She pulled a rubber band from her pocket as she made her way to the bull. She leaned in to talk to Ricky who nodded while focusing on her lips. Steven watched, and his fists clenched. What the hell was his deal? He seemed too familiar with her. Friend? Maybe they had dated? Maybe they had slept together? His anger stilled when he noticed Samantha staring at him, waiting to meet his eyes. Her arms were over her head, pulling back her hair in a tight ponytail, but before securing it, she changed her mind and winked at him. She shook out her hair and flipped the band on the table. God, she had his attention, and every other guy in the bar. Deliberately, she tossed a denim clad leg over the bull and settled her knees and thighs hard against the metal animal. Steven's pants tightened, and his mouth went dry as she fisted the rope in one hand and held the other over her head. She waved at Ricky who started the fierce contraption in a slow steady pace to prepare the rider. It rocked Samantha back and forth then circled around. She adjusted her position, straightening out her back and extending backward to hold on. After a minute, she waved at Ricky who increased the speed. Steven was mesmerized by the fluidity of her body—long and lean as the muscles beneath the jeans tensed to hold on. Her body swung with the bull following the motion. Once more she waved her hand, and everyone in the bar stood. She was breathtaking as her hair flew out in a spray behind her, her smile fierce. She was one with metal and machine, and she was the most beautiful sexy woman Steven had ever seen. He reminded himself she was doing this for him as he tried to ignore the hooting and hollering of the appreciative men. The buzzer sounded. As the bull slowed, Samantha slumped forward, and Steven saw her shoulders shudder. Was she all right? Many moved, but Steven plowed through them; she was his to claim. "Sam? Honey, are you all right?"

She reached for him and allowed him to pull her off and to him. "Just need a minute," she whispered. "I'm a little dizzy."

"Not uncommon," Ricky butted in. "Booze and bull will do that." Who the hell asked him?

Samantha ignored him and smiled smugly at Steven. "Your turn."

"Another beer first," Steven said, pulling her towards the bar.

"Really?" she laughed. "Need a little courage? You who jumps out of planes? You're having trouble getting up for this?"

He jealously pulled her into his side, ignoring the looks he was getting from around the bar. "Getting up is the problem, sweetheart. You were sexy as all hell on the bull, but I think you know that."

Samantha ran her hand over his thigh. "So, sitting on the bull is the problem?"

Steven let out his breath slowly and set his hand over hers. She wasn't going to win this one without a fight. "This is the problem—you. Hot sexy you, but if you can behave, I'm going to beat you on the bull."

"That's my Steven," she purred. "Gorgeous, brilliant, and cocky as all hell."

His smile widened as his thumb grazed her lips. "Kiss for luck?"

"You don't need luck." Samantha closed the gap, pressing his lips in a soft tender kiss.

Steven took his turn on the bull as Samantha moved closer to get a better view. The bull again started slowly and gradually picked up speed, and while he lacked grace, his powerful body had muscles in all the right places to hold on. Samantha hooted and hollered as he rose off the animal just enough to absorb the sharp turns and the circling motion, but just before the buzzer sounded, Steven momentarily lost his focus. His foot grazed the floor to prevent him from toppling off. Game over. Samantha won by one second. She grabbed his hand and barely gave him time to catch his breath before pulling him into a hug. He guided her back to the table, but not before Ricky brushed up against her. He wasn't even sure she noticed as she congratulated him on his first ride, but he noticed, and he wanted answers before he pounded him into the ground.

"My turn," he said angrily. "What did you have going on with asshole when you worked here?"

"What are you talking about?" Samantha asked. "Who?" She followed Steven's glare directly to Ricky. "Are you kidding?"

"Do you know me well enough to know when I'm kidding?" he asked sarcastically. "Did you date?"

"Hell, no. Never."

"Did you sleep with him?"

"Don't you know me better than that?" she countered. "Where would you get such a stupid idea?"

"I don't like the way he looks at you—hungry," Steven sneered. "And I don't like him touching you. Apparently, he doesn't get you're with me." He slammed his beer on the table.

Samantha bit her lip and slid around the booth. "I get it, and isn't that what's important? I didn't even notice him." Her voice dropped as she stroked his upper arm. "We were having such a good time, and you did amazing your first time on the bull. If Ricky annoys you that much, send him a clear message I belong to you."

"I'm considering breaking his face." He continued to scowl across the bar at Ricky.

Samantha turned his face back to her by guiding his chin then brushed his lips with her fingertips. "Better idea. Kiss me like I'm yours. Leave no doubt who owns me."

Steven straightened up and met her eyes. The sparkle ignited by heat changed the blue to a lighter, brighter hue that matched the glow in her smile. His hand caressed her cheek, soft and tender under his fingers. She bent forward, and her hair fell over his shoulders, tickling his neck as she whispered, "I remember a kiss in San Diego outside a restaurant." He leaned in, his forehead brushing hers as she tilted her head a fraction to align their lips. Two men at the bar were arguing over something, but it seemed far away. Time stopped; they were alone in a private space. His lips touched, soft, tender, lingered briefly. He inhaled deeply as he circled her shoulders and claimed her lips once again with more pressure, more urgency, more need. She twisted, trying to slide closer, but the table was in the way. Steven turned, pulling her tighter without breaking the kiss, one hand pulling through her hair till the strands were tangled in his fingers, the other hand caressing the small of her back in soft squeezes. "Sam."

"Take me home, Steven." Her eyes, explicitly expressing her desire for him.

Did she even know how beautiful she was when she wanted him? When her eyes and her touch called to him to make love to her? "Home is in Baltimore, my love," he answered, kissing lightly against her cheek.

"Home is wherever you are, Steven." ♥♥

Chapter Thirty

Breaking down the bed and packing the last of Samantha's things, Steven finished loading up the truck. On the floor, she packed her clothes and her books in boxes labeling them for shipping to Baltimore. Pouring the last of the coffee in two mugs, Steven handed her one while taking a seat on a box. "Everything is going as planned, sweetheart."

"Almost," Samantha sipped her coffee. "My mother wants us to stop by before we leave. Something to do with the wedding."

"Probably have to be tomorrow morning before our flight. Something urgent?" he asked.

"I'm sure, probably daisies or lilies or pink linens or rose."

"Not big on weddings?" Steven smiled. "Or is it just your brother's wedding?"

"A lot of anxiety over too many details," Samantha answered. "Oh, with your family you are probably expected to have the big wedding with all the trimmings."

"Expected? Yes, but it will be whatever you want it to be. It's your day, too." Steven stacked the boxes by the door.

"The beach in San Diego would be pretty, but your family is in Baltimore," Samantha said, "and weddings are for families. Yours has been waiting for you to get married for a long time."

"And your parents are in Charleston so please yourself, Sam, because the odds are you won't be able to please everyone. Look at how Thanksgiving turned out, and we haven't even faced Christmas, yet."

"Still," Samantha said thoughtfully, "you have to include the families in the planning."

Steven laughed. "I can't even get you to put on my ring. I don't think I want to deal with our families till then. Have you given that anymore thought?"

Samantha fingered the engagement ring at her throat. "All the time, but I can't take off my big.."

"ugly, plastic ring? Seriously, Sam, in another week I'm calling that your engagement ring, and I'm taking the other back."

Her eyes darkened. "Do you want children, Steven?"

"Of course, but only if they have your eyes," he answered quickly.

"I don't think you can control that. How many kids do you see us having?"

"As many as you are willing to have, honey. One or ten, it's up to you." He rubbed gently over her arms.

"I want to write for a while. Can we wait a little bit?"

She looked tentative, timid, almost reluctant to ask; he hated seeing her like that. "I'm not going to dictate a schedule, Sam. When we are ready, I'm sure we'll know it."

The corners of her mouth barely turned up as she asked, "Will we raise toddlers who take risks on the playground like jumping off the swings or diving down the slide, or are you going to be an overprotective daddy especially with a daughter?" Her smile brightened.

"A daughter?" Steven groaned. "We'll have to have boys to protect her. Put the ring on, Sam."

"I will. Soon, I promise." She saw the question in his eyes. "By the first of the year."

Filling the storage unit took longer than expected, and Sam texted Pete they'd be a little late. It did nothing to improve Pete's sour mood when they finally showed up. "I guess I'm not surprised," Pete said, learning of Samantha's move to Baltimore. "It was pretty clear something happened between the two of you a few weeks ago."

"Pete, I'd like to still edit email submissions," Samantha offered. "I'll have some time to read through one, maybe two a week."

"Charity?" Pete asked. "There's no need to feel guilty."

Steven sat back and sipped his drink. "Good business, not charity. When Samantha and I get engaged, we could give you the exclusive."

Pete brightened. "I could send one of my guys to Baltimore to get engagement photos in your hometown."

Steven agreed. "Keep it simple, but yes, that would be fine. It'll follow up the original story nicely. Now, if I can just get this woman to take my ring." He reached for her hand and threaded their fingers together.

Pete chuckled. "And I had to practically beg you to go to San Diego."

After dinner Steven drove to visit Samantha's parents one more time. Since her apartment was empty, it made sense to get a hotel room by the airport before their flight out on Monday. The only drawback was they had to fit her parents in tonight. Mrs. Westerly had a catalog of bridesmaid's dresses to show Samantha. The bride had selected her three favorites, and Samantha was to pick the one she wanted. All in sky blue she showed Steven before she settled on the taffeta A-line, V-neck, backless dress with ruching and beading at the waist. Steven left nothing to the imagination as he nodded his approval at her choice. Absentmindedly, she thumbed through the book looking at the colors and styles.

"Getting some ideas maybe?" Steven asked, unable to read her expression.

She shrugged as her mother came back with a tape measure. "Faith needs your measurements to order the dress. Then, hopefully, it will fit when we arrive for the wedding." Sam sighed impatiently and, finally, maneuvered them out the door.

"Something wrong?" Steven asked.

"Tired and cranky," she admitted.

"Those are things I can fix," he boasted. "Besides, you owe me, and, I think it is time to collect. Make as both feel good."

"Steven, I'm tired," she repeated softly.

"I know, stretch out. You need some serious pampering." He squeezed her shoulders; his thumbs pressing into the knots. "What has you so wired, my love? Is it talk of a wedding or this move to Baltimore?"

"No, I want both of those things, but you have to admit your life moves pretty fast. I just want to settle in, do some writing, and get to know you better, but that would be boring for you."

"Cara, you are a mystery to me. Every day I keep unraveling more about you. I have to get down to writing again, too. My next book in the series is supposed to be in bookstores by August, and it will get hectic promoting it in the fall, but I need."

"What, Steven?"

"Come here." She crawled to lay against his chest. "Not I, we need some alone time. Not family, not my career, just you and me and a laptop. Remember I told you about the cabin where I go to hide when I've had enough. It's time."

"But you're busy."

"I'll find a few days. I should be hearing from Jenny when we get back."

Jenny had made herself scarce since the last book signing in New York. With other clients needing her attention and the coming holidays, she had given Steven some space to think through this infatuation he had with Cinderella. Surely, his return to Baltimore, a return to his roots, and a heartfelt holiday with his family would reground him and make him see the ridiculousness of his attachment to this woman. But just to make sure Jenny made a note to drop in on Steven on Monday. It would have to be in the early evening since she was finalizing a talk show deal for him earlier in the day in Baltimore. She sensed his weariness, but that was a plus. He'd go home, forget about Cinderella, get back to writing to meet his August release date, and be ready for the whirlwind tour in the fall. That tour would end with a week in London in the middle of December. Perfect, and she could stop worrying about him.

The plane landed late in the day, and Steven was glad to be home. He'd do anything for Sam, but they were going to have to find a better way to deal with the holidays than flying back and forth. He was genuinely worried about her after their last night in the hotel. He understood bone weariness that sleep alone did not relieve. She had changed her life and now needed to settle in and make Baltimore her home. He'd squeeze out a couple of days away from everything to clear her head and then they would get down to the business of living. As for the next round of holidays, he had briefly mentioned to her father that they were welcomed in Baltimore for Christmas, hoping he could bring both families together and skip another plane ride. With the lengthy holiday season between Christmas and New Year's, it would be expected at some point. Maybe if they had good news for both families, he could encourage her parents to join them, but that would depend on whether Samantha would be wearing his ring by then. Climbing over the suitcases still in the foyer, he answered the door to a festively dressed Jenny.

"Steven, happy holidays, honey. Oh," she exclaimed, "are you coming or going?"

"Just got home from Charleston," Steven replied, expecting a lecture,

"Visiting Cinderella?" Jenny asked, her distaste apparent.

"Samantha had Thanksgiving here, then we went back to Charleston for her parents." Steven wondered if Jenny would ever understand how he felt about Samantha. How she was different from other women he had dated.

"Isn't that cozy?" The sarcasm was impossible to miss. "Are you ready to put all that business with her behind you now and get back to work?"

"She's moved in here." Steven met Jenny's cold stare.

"For how long?"

"I've asked her to marry me. I hope that means forever."

"Steven, you don't even know this woman, and in a few weeks you'll tire as you always do and walk away. Except she'll hold on for whatever reason. Money? Career?"

"She couldn't possibly love me back, could she, Jen?" Steven moved behind the bar and offered a drink.

"Yes, something strong. What does she want, Steven? Oh, of course, love."

"She wants to be with me," he said fiercely. "She wants a family and to finish her book."

Jenny swallowed hard. "She writes? That explains it. She wants you to help her get published, and I was worried about how she would take it when you walk away. I think I should have been worried about you. She'll walk away, and you'll finally understand what it is like to get your heart broken."

Samantha poked her head in the room. She sized up the situation quickly, though she hadn't heard their conversation. The tension was lethal. "Steven, I can take the bags up or start dinner. Are you hungry? Hello, Jenny, happy holidays."

"Hello, Cinderella. I see you're still in the picture."

"I'll get the bags later. Something easy for dinner." He kissed her cheek quickly and tried to reassure her with his eyes. Steven watched as she headed for the kitchen.

"She's not wearing a ring," Jenny observed.

"She doesn't want to wear it, yet." Steven took a large swallow of his drink. "She wants us to get to know each other better."

Jenny's eyes narrowed. "I never thought you a fool," she said quietly. "She's moved in here and, supposedly, loves you, but she needs to think about marrying you. Sounds like she's plotting her escape."

"Damn it, I've heard enough." His voice boomed through the house. "Samantha is here to stay, and, frankly, it's none of your business. If we are going to continue to work together, you need to change your attitude toward her and get along with her."

"None of my business?" Jenny glared. "Talk show is tomorrow night; I'll send you the details. Your friend at the university is Thursday, and I'll be sending you a tentative schedule for the fall tour soon. I assume," her obvious anger and frustration evident, "that any planning or reservations should include Cinderella?"

"Yes, include Samantha."

Jenny slammed her empty glass on the bar and headed to the door without a good-bye. Maybe it was better that way, and maybe only time would convince her Samantha was here to stay.

"Jenny leave?" Samantha asked. "I was going to invite her to dinner. Lots of turkey leftovers."

"She's busy." Steven added another splash of whiskey.

"And you're angry which means her opinion of me hasn't changed," Samantha observed.

"Everyone has an opinion. Doesn't mean it's worth something. The cabin is sounding more and more like the place we both need. We'll drive up Friday and stay the weekend. Even a couple of days will help."

Samantha pushed aside his drink. "Your family labeled all the food. We could have a feast of our own." She moved into his arms and held on tight. She was discovering the Steven's life had a lot of twists and turns, and if she wanted to be a part of it, she had better learn to hold on—hold on tight, because if she loosened her grip Jenny, family, or the press could ruin their happiness. "At the end of the day," she whispered in his ear, "it's just you and me."

"The way it should be," he answered, kissing her cheek. "The way it should be."

Chapter Thirty-One

The Bailey Show was live late night television in Baltimore. Steven was a last-minute addition after the holiday rush, and while it was small time and very local, it gave him exposure, practice, and a friendly audience. The hosts were the husband and wife team of Maggie and Jay Bailey. Steven had met Maggie at a book signing once, and she had seemed polite and professional. He had never met Jay who was known for asking the tough questions. Neither, though seemed like the kind of people that worried about ratings or might press for dirt. They hosted local political figures, athletes, and celebrities from the Baltimore area or the state of Maryland.

Steven fidgeted back stage while Samantha held his hand and reassured him he'd do well. "You're the hometown boy, Steven. They love you."

"These shows are never scripted so you just never know where their questions will go," Steven said, picking up his jacket.

"We have nothing to hide, right?" Her eyes met his with such warmth he had to pull her in tight.

"Nothing," he repeated, nuzzling her neck. He wanted to go home, take her to bed, and skip the damn show, but Jenny was nudging him toward the curtain.

"You're on next, Steven, and don't forget to smile. People hate brooding authors."

The interview started well, focusing on the new book, and Maggie skillfully put Steven at ease. She leaned forward, creating an air of intimacy like their conversation was private as she finally brought up his personal life. "I don't have to tell you how special you are to Baltimore, Steven, so you know everyone wants to know about the woman in your life."

Steven reacted automatically wanting to shield Samantha. He sat back and adjusted the fabric of his jacket. "Is that a question, Maggie?"

She smiled invitingly, gentle without malice. "We've seen her in the papers with you in different cities and in different situations. Are you seeing someone?"

Steven forced the air out of his lungs. "I've been seeing a beautiful woman from Charleston. We're still exploring where it's going."

"Really, Steven, you've been linked with a lot of women. You think this woman might become Mrs. Corso?" Maggie took her husband's hand, and he was beaming.

It was interest, not sordid, and the words tumbled out of his mouth before he had a chance to think. "She's backstage," Steven announced. "Would you like to meet Samantha?"

Samantha gripped the curtain. He didn't just invite her to join him on television. He didn't. He wouldn't. Jenny gripped her arm.

"Pull it together, Cinderella. You're going out there," she growled.

"No," Samantha dug in her heels literally. "I'm not dressed. I can't go out there in jeans." Someone was pulling a comb through her hair and trying to put on some gloss. "I can't."

"You can, and you will if you care about him. He's claiming you before Baltimore. Do you want to make him look foolish? Smile and get out there," Jenny glared.

"All right, but I'm going to kill him later." Samantha took a deep breath, put on her smile, and crossed the stage to Steven. He rose to meet her, taking her shaky hand in his and seating her beside him. Jay took over the questions.

"We're all pleasantly surprised to meet you, Samantha. How long have you known, Steven?"

Samantha cleared her throat as Steven rubbed gently down her arm. She relaxed against him as she tried to focus on Jay. "Only a few weeks. We met on a plane to San Diego."

"Were you a fan of his books?"

"I didn't know who he was on the plane. We were just seated next to each other, but I love Steven's books."

Samantha felt like everyone was staring at her. She focused on the two hosts and looked away from the cameras and all the people on the set and in the audience. Jay had asked her a question, but she had no idea what it was. He looked at her strangely, and she answered honestly. "I'm sorry." She stole a glance at Steven. "I didn't expect to come out here. I'm a little nervous."

"Understandable," Maggie took over. "Why do you enjoy Steven's mysteries?"

"Oh, his characters are wonderful, real people, believable. Sometimes I think of Moody or Dean from his third book, and I wonder what case they are working on or if they are in danger." Samantha leaned in toward Maggie, completely forgetting the audience. "I'm sure other people feel the same way. I get lost in his language, in the way he plots out a story, and the moment when it all makes sense."

"Have you read his new one?" Maggie glowed. "I think it's one of his best."

"I haven't had time to finish it," Samantha said honestly. "We've been doing a lot of traveling, but Steven doesn't disappoint. His writer's voice is so clear, so strong, and so Steven." Her voice trailed off in clear appreciation of his work, but it was obvious he had captured her heart as well.

"Will there be more books in the series?" Jay asked Steven.

"What? Oh, yes, next one will hopefully be out in August." He pulled Samantha's hand back, resting it in his lap. His thumb rubbed deliberate circles across her palm.

"And you're from Charleston, Samantha?" Jay asked. "Are you staying in Baltimore for a while?"

Before Samantha could answer, Steven interrupted. "She's staying in Baltimore, because I'm not letting her get away."

She heard the emotion in his voice, and her heart swelled with love as she redirected the focus. "Steven has introduced me to your beautiful city, and I really like it here."

The interview finally ended, and when they cut to commercial break, Steven guided her back stage, passed Jenny without a word, and into an empty dressing room. He pressed her against the wall, filling the empty spaces between their bodies and kissing her with heat and hunger. Barely able to breathe, he dropped his lips to her throat.

"You are amazing," he panted. "You are full of damn surprises."

"Me?" She pushed against his chest. "When did you decide to call me out there?"

Steven had to laugh and pressed his forehead to hers. "I didn't actually decide. My mouth invited you before my brain kicked in."

"I was terrified, and Jenny nearly threw me out on the stage. Don't you ever…"

He covered her mouth with another kiss till he felt her hands on his shoulders winding around his neck. "I love you, Sam."

"I love you, too, but I am never going anywhere with you again." She brushed her palm across his cheek. Life with him definitely took twists and turns. She'd have to get better at holding on.

Jenny was waiting for them when they returned. She glared at Steven. "She wasn't prepped. Do you know how wrong that could have gone?"

"Admit it, Jen," he said, pulling Samantha closer. "She did great. She's a damn natural."

Jenny swallowed her smile. "Cinderella got lucky today and so did you, Prince Charming."

♥♥

Chapter Thirty-Two

Steven worked feverishly the next day. His ideas were coming quickly as his fingers flew across the keyboard. Periodically, his thoughts circled back to the beautiful woman sharing his life now and could prove to be a huge distraction. To her credit, she understood his need for privacy and had only interrupted him once to leave him a lunch tray. When he needed a break, he found her in the kitchen with crumpled papers on the floor and other pages scattered on the table. She looked angry or upset as he grabbed coffee and offered her a cup.

"Writing?" he asked, watching her stab at the paper with her pen.

She looked around at the mess on the floor. "Does this look like writing? Maybe a sad attempt for someone without talent."

Steven sensed her frustration and was all too familiar with those moments when he couldn't make the story coincide with his vision. "Talk it through, Sam. What are you trying to do?"

"Main character, Tim, is a lawyer. His client and the woman he loves, Sarah, is indicted on a murder charge, but I can't figure out how to write the courtroom scenes. I can't describe the jail or the procedures in court. I did the research online, but I feel like I'm copying it instead of writing a story." She let out her breath in exasperation as she reached for yet another cup of coffee.

"You need to be in a courtroom, Sam. See it for yourself, take some notes, experience it. Grab a jacket; we're going to the county building to do some research. There are always open courtrooms where visitors are allowed."

"But you have work to do," Samantha protested.

"So, do you. Stop arguing and grab a jacket." He walked her to the car and opened her door. "By the way, you know paper and pencil is an archaic way to write. New invention, the computer."

"Thanks for the tip," she frowned, "but I like paper and pencil, at least, initially. I don't like being tired down to a computer. When I have something, then I move to word processing."

Steven started the car and drove to the downtown Baltimore area in the heart of the government sector. Police, court, and general offices were housed over several city blocks. More than once Samantha noticed Steven texting, but she didn't ask. She had her notebook open and was making notes as to the layout of the buildings. Emptying their pockets, they passed through security and took the elevator to the fourth floor. Several courtrooms were open. The first was an arraignment where a defendant was being charged with a B&E, breaking and entering. Samantha made note of terminology and the arrangement of the courtroom. The second courtroom had a trial in progress. Steven and Samantha slipped into the back row and watched the two attorneys argue before the judge. When the prosecutor sat down, the tall handsome thirtyish defense lawyer stood and confidently made his way around the table. With notepad in hand, he questioned the witness efficiently and intensely. He was her main character, Tim, in her novel. He was the character she was trying to create. She watched his every movement from his courtroom manner, to the way he addressed the court, and to the way he leaned in to speak to his client. By the time they returned to the street, Samantha had regained her enthusiasm and perspective.

"Walk with me, Sam. The police station is right next door. Ernesto wants us to stop in."

Samantha looked at Steven warily. She wasn't sure she wanted to be around her soon to be brother-in-law in the station. "What does he need?" she asked.

"Not him, you." He pulled her through the door before she could ask any more questions, and Erno was waiting for them in the lobby.

He smiled with the cat that ate the canary look that aroused Samantha's suspicions. "Tell me you aren't going to arrest me again," she warned.

"No, not today, but Steven explained your writing block, and I think I can help. We do tours of the station for high school kids. Most of them are in alternative education programs but not always. We work with teachers who think they have kids that are headed for trouble. We try to show them where bad choices lead."

"Like a scared straight program?" Samantha asked.

"Exactly. I thought I could show you what I show them."

Steven nodded his encouragement so Samantha reluctantly agreed.

"When we bring someone in, we process them through here." He led her through a door into a small room with camera equipment, computers, and cabinets. Erno pulled out drawers where they kept fingerprinting ink and papers and showed her the computer images. He showed her how mug shots were taken. "We can hold someone for forty-eight hours till we can get a judge. That creates overcrowding, because this jail wasn't built for permanent residents. It's basically a holding tank for jail or court." Erno led her through another door to another small room. "If we can get a judge to do a video arraignment, we set it up in here with the defense attorney and the suspect. The judge can be at any remote location." He led them passed several small offices where attorneys could have privacy with their clients or where deals were sometimes made. "Through this door," Erno continued, "is the real courtroom that connects to the main building you just came from."

Samantha quickly jotted down notes—structure, procedures, details to make her writing more vivid. She caught the look that passed between the two brothers.

"What comes next isn't pretty, Sam. Steven thinks it is necessary for you to see, but it's up to you. The corridor up ahead goes right through the holding tank with the prisoners. Men of all ages and in all conditions. Drunk, hung over, strung out on drugs, arrogant, obnoxious, you name it. It isn't pretty, and you'll get their attention walking through."

"Do I really need to do this, Steven?" she asked, knowing what his answer would be.

"You said you felt like you were copying the research. There's no substitute for the real thing, Sam. We're both with you, and nobody can hurt you."

"You, little brother, need to be calm, too. They will be incredibly disrespectful, but there's no law against that," Erno warned.

Steven shrugged as Samantha agreed. "Let's get it over with."

The seven or eight cells that were visible lined the wall on the left, and Erno walked to that side of Samantha. Steven flanked her on the right. Erno had warned her against making eye contact with anyone; that would only set them off more. At first the cells were relatively quiet with just the voices of specific conversations, but then the first of the prisoners spotted Samantha. They whistled and hooted and eventually became crude. One man grabbed his crotch and asked if she wanted some. Samantha's senses were finely tuned to not only the sound but the smells of sweat, of food, and vomit. She was surprised how old some of the men were, aged rapidly by substance abuse and how young others were, barely eighteen. She noticed one young man leaning against the wall in the corner, holding his stomach, a sickening shade of green. No doubt detoxing from some drug that was ruining his life. The short walk had taken minutes, but long enough to change the course of someone's life or give vitality and reality to someone's writing.

"You all right, Sam?" Steven searched her eyes with concern.

"Yes, I'm fine. Where are the women?" Samantha asked.

"Separate corridor in the other direction," Erno responded. "I had hoped to take you there instead, but they had an emergency today. Called an ambulance in just before you got here. Truthfully, it wouldn't have been much better."

Samantha took over the kitchen again when they returned home. Steven silently checked on her from time to time. She seemed to be getting more done, and fewer pieces of paper were discarded on the floor. He quietly made them a light dinner and ate at the counter as she continued to work well into the evening. Finally, he kissed the back of her neck and went to bed. Hours later feeling capable and wired, Samantha slipped into bed and tried to relax. Her mind tried to calm her caffeine agitated body, but she longed for the man who had the power to change her world. She gently stroked the muscles down his back and slid over to reach the back of his neck and shoulders. When her hand splayed across his ass cheek, he growled softly against the pillow. "What are you doing, *Cara?"*

"If you have to ask, I must be doing it wrong," she purred against his cheek. He turned slightly to capture her lips as she dove into his mouth taking what she wanted, giving all she had. He rolled further, pulling her entire body between his legs and her breasts against his warm ripped chest. She brushed his jaw with her lips, loving the feel of a day's stubble rough on her skin. Her awareness of his masculinity, his power, aroused her till she wanted more. He started to flip her to her back, but she stopped him by pulling herself up and over his hips. He moved farther up the pillows so he could see his goddess in all of her beauty, straddling him and caressing his heat with her core.

"Samantha," he said, trying to hold the pressure building in him. "I want the cowgirl in the bar who rode the bull."

She straightened her back, shook out her hair, and shot him her most dazzling smile. "Hang on, cowboy." Her body dropped; her breasts brushing his chest. Then in one stunning motion he watched and felt her rising and slamming down on his core. He wanted to close his eyes and feel the heat pounding through his veins, but he couldn't take his eyes off her hair, her breasts, and couldn't let go of the handles of her hips. She moaned as she hit her release just as he did and crashed on his chest in an exhausted sigh.

With tenderness, he stroked her back and kissed her temple and slid her in the curve of his arm. She was asleep almost instantly, leaving him alone with his thoughts. Thoughts that rocked him into a quiet sleep eventually. He needed to order furniture and turn the spare room into her space, and he needed to convince her to wear his ring. He pulled her closer and slept till his phone alarm jolted him awake.

"Come on, Sam. Wake up. You're coming with me."

"Where? It's too early," Samantha whined.

"College classes start early—University of Baltimore. Hustle, babe. I don't want to be late."

Samantha closed her eyes till she heard the shower. She guessed Steven was probably doing some kind of workshop, but she wasn't so sure she wanted or needed to go. She laid out a nice pair of pants and sweater then barged into the bathroom.

"Why am I going with you, Steven? Is this a workshop?" she asked.

"Friend of mine is a professor in the English department. She teaches creative writing to freshmen, and it's challenging especially before or after a holiday. I usually take her classes at some point during the semester as a guest speaker. I do it as a favor, trying to motivate her students." Steven dried off as Samantha stepped into the shower.

"Why am I going?" she asked.

He startled her when he yanked open the door. "I want you to come, and I'd like Grace to meet you. Don't you want to come?"

"It's not that. I just don't want any more surprises." She tipped her head under the water and let it run down her back.

"What could I possibly do?"

What couldn't he do? He patted her playfully and returned to the bedroom to dress. Samantha admired him as always as he finished dressing in dark slacks and a light cashmere sweater. Those college girls would definitely have trouble concentrating. Maybe it was a good thing she was going.

The University of Baltimore was only a mile from the heart of downtown Baltimore. Spread over several city blocks, it provided a convenient location for students to live and study, but also shop, eat, and visit area attractions like museums, art galleries, and recreational activities. Public transportation was easily accessible, though students often got around with bicycles or by walking. Samantha loved the look of the campus, a mix of old and new, and Grace Matera was gracious and formidable. Her petite statue and bright blue eyes defied disobedience. She had high expectations and a career that span three decades. She teased that her gray hair had come early in her career in middle school and high school. As she got older and less patient and with two post degrees under her belt, she moved to college freshmen. Some days she felt like she was back in middle school, but it was obvious how much her students not only respected her but genuinely liked her. Steven stood in front of her class of thirty students and easily talked about himself and took their questions. Samantha sat in the back wondering if he ever thought of teaching. He did it effortlessly, and the students listened attentively. Twenty minutes in he had them pick a partner in close proximity and, without any discussion, they were to jot down physical characteristics of the person. It was mostly quiet except when Nikki punched her partner, Jason, and corrected her weight.

"You have to be careful with that one," Steven told Jason sympathetically. "Now, ask your partner to tell you three qualities they possess."

Samantha watched and realized it was a good thing there was an even number of students till Cassie walked in considerably late. She was wearing black leggings and a multicolored tunic top. Her light brown hair with red and purple streaks was braided down her back. She wore a lip ring and a collection of silver bangle bracelets and rings. And the tattooed angel with the broken wing on her arm completed the picture. She broke the quiet when she made her entrance. Grace directed her to the back of the room, and Samantha waved her over to an empty seat near her.

"What are we doing?" she asked, suddenly realizing Steven was in the front. "Oh, my God. I forgot Corso was coming today."

"He's giving them directions for a writing assignment," Samantha answered. "You need a partner. I guess we can be partners."

Cassie pulled out her notebook and shrugged, and quickly and quietly Samantha caught her up. Steven met her eyes with a questioning look, but she only smiled and shook her head.

"Now," Steven continued, "ask your partner three questions to learn something significant about them. Key word is significant. You're going to be writing about your partner as a fictional character so think outside the box. Don't waste your questions on trivial things that will bore your readers."

Cassie looked at her subject carefully. She had already decided Samantha was pretty, educated, and uptight while Samantha had labeled Cassie unconventional, edgy, and smart, maybe too smart. "Me first," Cassie took over. Samantha had a feeling it was what she did best. "I'm not going to waste my question asking you if there is a man in your life. The way you look if there isn't, there should be. So, I'm going to assume there is. When you are with him, how does he make you feel in three words?"

Samantha sat back, avoiding looking over at Steven. Other than Grace he hadn't introduced her to the class, though they had seen them talking before Cassie arrived. "Unique, cherished, sexy."

Cassie grinned. "Cool. I'd ask you more about him, but there are other things I want to know. If money, education, or your own personal fears weren't an issue, what would you be doing with your life?"

Samantha heard the young man next to them ask what his partner did for a living. Cassie was a lot more interesting, and she wondered if she could put her attitude on paper. "I'd be taking risks everyday like skydiving, scuba diving, and maybe climbing Mt. Everest."

"I like you," Cassie said openly and without embarrassment. "I thought you seemed pretty straight laced. Last question, what's more important to you, love or sex?"

Samantha laughed. She was young. "Why do I have to choose, Cassie? Why can't I have both?"

Steven called time. "Now, forget about your partner and write. Create a character and the beginning of a plot. Don't worry about polish; you are writing to get down your ideas."

Cassie's hand flew across the page. Her mind already had the book written. She was quick, creative, and genuine, and

Samantha liked her. She wondered if other people saw her for the free spirit she was, or if they tried to stifle her and fit her into a mold. Several students read or talked about the start of their stories, and the enthusiasm and laughter were not what Samantha remembered from her school days. Toward the end of the session, Steven read from his new book to a silent awe-struck group of freshmen. Even Cassie closed her eyes, and let his voice calm her disorganized soul. As their time ended, several students shook Steven's hand as they exited the classroom. "Would you like to meet Steven?" Samantha asked Cassie.

"I couldn't," she said, suddenly quivering and lacking confidence. Steven had that effect on people especially women who didn't know him.

"Of course, you can," Samantha said, squeezing her hand. "Steven." He caught her eye and joined them, draping his arm around her shoulder.

"Him?" Cassie's eyes widened.

Samantha nodded. "Steven, this is Cassie, and I think she has potential."

His dark eyes softened as he took her hand. "It's nice to meet you, Cassie. Keep writing, and see if you can develop that talent."

She gaped at him with terror. "I will," she mumbled, handing her story to Samantha. "You keep this."

"You terrified her," Samantha laughed as Cassie ducked out the door.

"She had the same look as you when we first met on the plane," Steven added. "I'm not that scary, am I?"

But Samantha was distracted. She was reading Cassie's story, written in just a few minutes off the cuff, and it was beautiful, articulate, amusing, and spot on clever. She read aloud for Steven and Grace.

She sighed as every muscle in her body ached in joyful remembrance of the time they shared—skydiving, plunging to earth, then plunging into the warmth of his body, his arms that night. She wanted him and a life as unique and exciting as he. She stretched and smiled lazily as she thought of their plans to visit the local zoo. Animalistic behavior might make for a creative night."

"She's one of my most gifted students," Grace agreed, "but she is different. She's often late for class or daydreaming. I don't know if she is just young."

Samantha wrote words of encouragement at the bottom of the page and promised to check back with her at the end of the semester. She also included her email. Grace thanked them for coming and hugged Steven thoroughly. "You are still my most successful and talented student," she beamed.

"You taught me more about writing than anyone, Grace, and that's why I'm happy to do this for you."

Chapter Thirty-Three

Steven stared at his computer keyboard. This book, the next in the series, was coming easily, almost too easily. He had awakened with ideas demanding his attention so he covered Samantha with a quilt before coming down. He made coffee and had written for hours, but he was on thin ice. He had never pursued the attraction between his protagonist and his partner, but Boone, a character from a previous novel, needed a resurrection. He was one of Steven's favorite characters, demanding, intense, crude, and critical, but he met his match in his inexperienced first year partner. Steven would never admit it, but he didn't have the confidence to pursue love full throttle with Boone, but it might freshen his work and open up another audience for his novels. And he had Samantha to thank for that. He didn't think, at this point, he could even write what he felt for her, but he could start with Boone. He could get him passed the one-night stands, make him long for something more permanent, and feel the connection all humanity craved. He was still a mystery, crime writer, but a small amount of love might be a different twist. Who could predict where his writing would go from there?

Steven's phone lit up with a text from Jenny. **Need to discuss your schedule. Call me.**

He groaned loudly. She bitched at him to write, panicked when it got close to deadline, but she wouldn't leave him alone to do it. He called her with an irritated edge she picked up on immediately.

"Get up on the wrong side of the bed, honey?" she asked.

"Trying to write so we both make money, Jen. What do you need?"

"December is going to be a busy month for you. We have to harvest the Christmas shoppers looking for the perfect gift, your book. I've got you signing in two department stores where we have distribution of your books, an interview with a morning talk show host just before Christmas, a meeting to finalize the deal on the movie rights to *Summer Heat,* and several *Coffee with Corso* events. Keep up your writing blog and your web page, too, honey."

"Damn it, Jen, it is also the holidays. I have personal things to do. When the hell am I supposed to write?" Samantha, coming down the stairs, heard the yelling from his office. She grabbed coffee and two muffins and entered cautiously.

"You're a genius, Steven. You always manage to juggle things. If the problem is Cinderella, solve it."

"The problem is not Samantha," He said angrily. "I told you back in San Diego weeks ago, I need a break. You can't keep piling all this on me and expect me to make deadline."

"These are commitments," Jenny said tersely, "but you are clear till next week. I guess this weekend is your break."

"I want more."

"And I want a Lamborghini, but we don't always get what we want. You pay me to manage your career and that is what I am doing."

"More like managing my life."

"Enjoy your break. I'll send your schedule."

Steven tossed his phone aside. "I can't keep up this pace, and she just doesn't get it."

Samantha peeled the paper off her muffin. "What about going to the cabin? Isn't that on your list of things to do?"

She was right; that always revived him. "Go pack a few things, and we'll leave in an hour. Neither of us is writing, because we're making this a vacation. I'll show you why I love the cabin so much."

Samantha leaned back in her seat watching the landscape change as Steven drove northwest away from Baltimore. Cities became small towns, flatland became hilly and more wooded, and temperatures cooled a noticeable ten or fifteen degrees. Approaching from a long dirt road, it was hard to see the cabin that sat over the hill. Steven stopped as the road ended in front of a small clear lake. From the cabin's upstairs balcony, the view would take in the woods and the lake for miles. Samantha immediately saw the possibilities, though she hesitated to say anything to Steven. Somethings just wouldn't work out, but… He was taking her hand and guiding her down the path away from the lake into the woods. "I can walk in here for hours. If you listen carefully, you can hear birds and small creatures. Even just the trees and leaves rustling gets me thinking and creating." Wrapping his arm around her for comfort and support, he moved carefully around the overgrown vegetation. "When there is a little snow, it is especially pretty or in the spring, the flowers bloom early in yellows, pinks, and purples. It is one of my favorite places."

Samantha loved this corner of the world immediately. "You said family has been here."

"My brothers have used it on occasion. We actually had Ernesto's bachelor party here before he married Angelina. We managed to fuck that up, too." He laughed at the memory of his brothers so drunk.

"Tell me," Samantha said. "What did you do?"

He sighed happily, pulling her closer. "Salvatore and I planned this party here with lots of beer and booze and about 25 guys. No women. Angelina threatened to kill me if I brought in strippers. So, we played cards on the back deck and as the evening progressed, and we drank enough to fill the lake, I made this stupid bet with Ernesto."

"What did you bet?" He shook his head. "Come on, Steven. You can't leave me hanging. What did you bet?"

He turned purple as he admitted they bet on who could push the other off a log lodged in the center of the lake. They undressed to their underwear and nearly drowned swimming out to it. Then neither could stand on it long enough to knock the other off. "We were idiots," he conceded. "We woke up in the morning on the shore, though neither of us remembers swimming back. The house stunk of beer and tobacco for weeks, and Ernesto was a little late for his wedding. I don't think Angelina has ever forgiven me for that."

"You two are definitely trouble," Samantha said, sliding her hand in his.

"Come on. I want to show you the cabin." He walked through the tallest of trees to the front porch with a traditional glider. The inside was small and cozy. A big fireplace on one wall with lots of rugs and pillows and an oversized couch. No television or cable. Steven liked the solitude. As rustic as the house looked, the kitchen had been remodeled and was fairly modern. Newer appliances and granite countertops reminded Samantha how much this room was Steven's, too. How much of a chef he was. Upstairs one large bedroom with an exceptionally large bed that faced the balcony that faced the lake. The view was breathtaking. A tiny cubical of a bathroom sat off the main room. Her initial thought came back more insistent, but she knew it wouldn't work.

Lastly, Steven took her back downstairs passed the master bathroom to the outdoor deck with barbeque and picnic tables.

"I love it," she smiled, sitting down at a table. "All of it. Maybe."

"What, honey? Something has been on your mind since we got here." Steven sat behind her and leaned her against him.

"It's such a pretty place for a lot of things," she said slowly. "Picnics, camping, maybe even a wedding." She turned to meet his eyes.

"You want to get married here?" Steven asked.

"It would be stunning," Samantha's voice trembled. "Where you first brought me by the lake and in the woods in the spring with the flowers. It would be perfect."

"Then we'll do it," Steven said, turning her around. "If this is what you want, Sam, it will be here."

She touched his cheek gently. "We can't. You have a big family and add mine to it, and this would never work. A small group like your party is all it can handle, though you do have that great kitchen. Still, we couldn't expect people to travel here, though everyone is probably going to have to travel somewhere. But it was only a thought; that and the honeymoon could be right here, too," Samantha sighed. "No place to dance."

Steven listened to the wispiness of her soft voice. He had never heard her actually want something and argue so hard to give it up. She was always giving in to what others wanted.

It wouldn't be impossible, but she was right, the entire family wouldn't fit here.

Steven made dinner that night and lit a fire in the fireplace. They spent two days exploring the woods in long walks, sitting by the water with a bonfire, or making love in front of the fire or in the big bed. The time soothed his spirit and refreshed his soul. "Sam," he said, pulling her into his arms. "I think you should take off the plastic and put on my ring. We know each other a lot better now, don't we?"

Samantha nodded. "Soon, I promise." She saw the disappointment in his eyes and felt a little guilty. "I'm just waiting for the right time. Besides, I have more questions."

"My turn," he interrupted, his eyes dark and shadowed. "Is there something else, Sam? Some other reason you don't want an official engagement?"

"No, nothing I haven't told you." She wrapped her arms around his waist. "Your energy scares me sometimes, but not away. I'm just trying to see how our lives fit together. Over the next few weeks we'll live together and see who has to give." She smiled at him reassuringly.

"You'd tell me if it was something else?" he asked.

"I love you, Steven, and when I marry you, it will be forever. Understand? Now, to my question, do you hunt or fish up here?"

He stared at her a good long minute before tugging her toward the cabin. "Fish sometimes, and hunted only once. I'm usually writing when I'm here."

"What kind of kid were you?" she asked. "Would I have liked you?"

He laughed. "Liked? Maybe, but I had a crazy older brother who I worshipped and followed right into hell and back. Tested my parents constantly. Salvatore was more obedient, but he was five years younger. I got along well with everybody, had lots of friends, and teachers who loved me, but I was a handful. My mother always says I'll pay someday when I have kids."

"Great," Samantha moaned.

"What kind of kid were you?" Steven tossed back. He put the suitcases in the trunk and locked up the cabin.

"Just what you'd expect. I tried to please everyone, my folks, teachers, and friends, but I went through this clumsy streak."

Steven snickered. "Went through? When did it end? I saw evidence of it on the plane when we first met."

She shot him a sideways glare. "I'm not clumsy now. I just get nervous, and strange things happen. Anyway, when you're a young girl and awkward, it can be embarrassing."

Steven started the car and raised the dust on the road. He sensed a story. "What was the most embarrassing thing that ever happened to you?"

"I'll never tell." Her answer came back too quickly, and Steven guessed it was painful and humiliating, and, of course, he wanted to know what it was.

"Out with it, Westerly. I've told you everything you've asked and sharing was your idea."

She squirmed in her seat. "All right, but don't laugh. I still have nightmares about it." She exhaled a deep breath. "We had this end of the year talent show when I was in the fifth grade. I was ten and had taken dance for years. I practiced like crazy, and there were rehearsals on the stage. Everything went well till the night of the performance. I spun and twirled and got lost in the music like only a young girl could. Ok, the lights were dim, and I should have been watching more carefully." She covered her face with her hands.

Steven had a feeling. "What happened?"

"I danced right off the stage, and don't you dare laugh."

Too late, Steven roared; his deep thunderous laughter filled the car.

"It's even worse, because the band kids were all sitting in front of the stage on folding chairs. I sailed right off the stage and landed in the middle of kids, instruments, band stands, and chairs."

"My God, did you get hurt?" Steven asked.

"Bruises, but mostly my pride. I bolted for the door and ran all the way home. If I'd have broken something, I probably wouldn't have noticed. The kids called me Weirdo Westerly after that."

"I'm sorry," Steven said, still trying to hide a smile. "If I'd had been there, I would have beaten them up for you."

"Thanks. Public humiliation. I have a long history. More than just molesting strange men on planes." She finally smiled, reaching for his hand. "You know my parents and yours are so different, Steven. How are we going to raise our kids?"

"That's easy. With lots of love, Sam, by example, and with a firm hand. Kids need boundaries, and parents who enforce the rules."

"So, they don't turn out wild or awkward?" Samantha whispered.

"I would have liked you," Steven said, nodding. "In fact, I would have been proud my girl could fly through the air and bowl over a whole section of kids. We would have fit together even then."

♥♥

Chapter Thirty-Four

Samantha settled into an unusual writing routine, writing in the evening and well into the night while Steven's creative juices flowed in the early morning hours. Jenny kept him busy through the month especially with her *Coffee with Corso* events hosted at neighborhood coffee shops that capitalized on the holiday shoppers' traffic. Steven grumbled, but he seemed relaxed and energized after the weekend in the woods. On the ride back from Baltimore, he had made a mental promise to drop the issue of the engagement ring. He loved Samantha, and he was sure she loved him. Their life was good—beyond good. They were happy, complimented each other, and with work and the holidays, they were too busy to think. So, even if patience wasn't his finest quality, he would give her the time and space to decide when she was willing to make it official. Of course, in the usual Corso way, he executed a totally underhanded attack to diminish her argument that they needed to know each other better. He asked his mother to send him several of the family albums, and while some of the cute pictures embarrassed him, he saw Samantha soften, saw her consider what their children would look like, and pushed her, he hoped, toward wearing his ring.

Gina began spending more time at the Corso home as well. She and Samantha got along well, more like sisters, and she secretly taught her some of her mother's favorite recipes.

"What are we making today?" Samantha asked eagerly.

"An Italian fig cookie—*a cuccidati*," Gina answered, glancing at her busy little ones playing nearby, "but tell me about you and my brother."

Samantha beat the batter for the dough harder. "I'm here. No secret we're together. What do you mean?"

"Don't play with me," Gina grinned. "I have the Corso lack of patience. Did he ask you to marry him, yet?" Samantha didn't answer. The dough clung to the beater, and she scrapped the bowl. "He did, didn't he?" Gina feverishly stopped the mixer and closed in on Samantha.

"I didn't say a thing, Gina. Steven will kill me."

"I won't say anything. Well, my brother is smarter than I thought." She pulled the dough onto some plastic wrap and put it in the refrigerator. "We need to grind the figs, raisons, and nuts for the filling. When is the wedding?"

"Gina stop," Samantha laughed. "There's nothing etched in stone…yet."

"Damn, *cuccidati*." Steven, dressed in a casual pair of slacks and a sport coat, kissed Samantha's cheek. "If you can make these, you are a keeper. What, Sis? You are looking at me stranger than usual."

"Nothing, you look happy."

"I am even if I have to go to work, but cookies and Sam. Don't know which I'm looking forward to coming back to more." He grabbed a bottle of water then leaned in and kissed her. "Definitely Sam."

Late that afternoon after Gina left and the cookies were cooling, Samantha fixed a warm meal, showered, and waited for Steven's return. She tried not to worry when he was well past the time she expected him. Maybe things had gone well at the shop, and he was just busy, but by eight she was genuinely worried. She waited still another hour before her fear grew greater than her embarrassment, and she called Jenny. She would have been at the coffee shop and might know if something had happened or if Steven had changed his plans. Jenny answered on the first ring as if she were expecting a call. "I'm sorry to bother you, Jenny," she began, "but Steven hasn't come home yet. I was worried something might have happened to him. Any chance he may have changed his plans after he left the coffee shop?"

Jenny coughed uncomfortably. "I don't know where Steven is."

Samantha caught the usual snipe of Cinderella was missing from the conversation. Was Jenny worried about Steven too? "Jen, please if you know where Steven might be, please tell me. I'm concerned something may have happened to him. I've tried calling him, but it just goes to voice mail."

"I'm sure he's fine, but he did get a phone call just as he was leaving the shop," Jenny offered. "I don't know who it was for sure."

"Who do you think it was?"

Jenny exhaled loudly. Though she still had her reservations about Samantha, she had grown to tolerate her, and she didn't want to get in the middle between her and Steven.

"It might have been Victoria, but I really don't know for sure."

"Isn't Victoria in Chicago?"

"As far as I know, but surely Steven wouldn't go to Chicago without telling you, would he?"

"No, of course not," Samantha said, suddenly ending the call. "Thanks, Jenny."

Samantha kept dinner warm in the oven, hoping against hope Steven would walk in any minute with some kind of reasonable explanation. He couldn't have dropped everything and gone to Chicago without a word. Jenny had to be mistaken. Steven would have called her unless there was something wrong with his phone. She paced the living room, adjusted ornaments on the tree, and watched the clock.

After midnight, she dumped dinner in the trash and went upstairs. Cuddled down in the bedding, she propped her phone in front of her willing it to ring. Where was he? It was nearly two when her phone flashed, and Steven's name streaked across the screen.

"Steven? Where are you?" Samantha could hardly breathe as she struggled to sit up and speak.

"I'm sorry, Sam," Steven said softly. "I should have called. Things just happened so fast."

"What happened?" Samantha's anger flashed. "Where are you?"

"Victoria needed me. I'm in Chicago. I'll explain when I get back."

What was it Samantha heard in his voice? Fear? Dread? Anger? "And when will that be?"

"Today, I hope. Look, Sam, it's complicated. I don't want to explain over the phone. Just trust me. I needed to get here."

Maybe it was desperation. She wanted to understand, but she didn't. "Maybe today or maybe not? Why didn't you call?"

"I have to go, but I'll call you later." The phone went dead, and she threw it across the room. She had seen the pictures on the internet. They had a long-standing relationship, and, of course, he'd be there for her, be there without thought of anyone else. She beat the pillows and tried to sleep, but she was angry and hurt. All he had to do was call and tell her what he felt he needed to do. Leaving without a word proved they had no business contemplating marriage. That isn't what you do to someone you love. She pulled the black box out of the nightstand, unclasped her necklace, and released the engagement ring. Putting it carefully in the box, she brushed at her tears. He should marry Victoria if she was that important to him.

Since sleep seemed out of the question, Samantha tried writing. It was obvious she wouldn't be hearing from Steven soon—never since she didn't know where her phone landed and hadn't bothered to looked to for it. She ambled through the house all day lingering in Steven's study. His scent filled her immediately while his laptop, still open, caught her attention. His screen saver was a picture of the two of them in San Diego. She didn't know who had taken the picture, but they looked happy. Yesterday, they had been, but maybe there was an explanation. Maybe she needed to be patient and understanding, or maybe she should throw one of his decorative vases at his head when he finally came through the door.

"Sam, I'm home," he called out when he finally arrived early evening. She was behind the counter slicing through a sandwich. She thought she should probably put the knife in the sink before he found her, because she wasn't feeling very understanding at the moment. She pressed her palms to the counter to steady herself and met his eyes when he found her. "You must be upset, but I can explain."

She nodded. "I suspect you've had enough time to come up with an explanation." She poured a glass of wine and moved to the table with her dinner.

"Sam," he slid into the seat in front of her, "I got a call from Victoria as I was leaving the coffee shop."

"I understand that much. Jenny picked up on that."

Steven eyed her uncomfortably. He needed to make her understand why he reacted without thinking clearly. "She had taken a bottle of pills, Sam. Apparently, she and Derrick broke up."

"Steven Corso to the rescue," she mocked.

"Sam, don't be like that. This was serious. She could have died, for God's sake." He reached for her hand across the table, but she pulled away.

"You had to fly to her. If she had already taken the pills…?"

"She did," Steven interrupted. "I called a local hospital, and they sent an ambulance. She was already in the hospital when I got there. I made her stay on the phone with me to keep her talking, but the ambulance was there by the time I got to the Baltimore airport."

"And it never occurred to you to call me? I was worried and resorted to calling Jenny," Samantha argued. "You could have called me at any point, when you got to the airport, here or in Chicago, or from the hospital."

"I did call you from the hospital."

"Hours later, not six, ten, or even twelve. It was after two. Even a text to say you were alive, anything?" She trashed her dinner and started to leave the room, but Steven caught her arm.

"I've been calling all day today, but you were paying me back I guess." His eyes held hers defiantly.

"I don't know where the hell my phone is. I haven't seen it since I threw it last night," she said sharply, her breathing heaving hard against her chest.

"Sam," Steven's voice dropped lower, "I really need you to understand right now."

"That's the problem. You need me to understand; you don't need me," Samantha flashed, tears glistening in her eyes.

"Baby, that's not true." Steven closed the gap between them and pulled her to him. "It just happened so fast. I was worried about Victoria."

"And you didn't give me a second thought." She pulled away from him and ran up the stairs. He found her in their bedroom, grabbing a few things.

"What are you doing?"

"I'm taking a few things I'll need. I'll sleep in one of the other bedrooms."

"Sam, don't do that. We can work this out."

"Is Victoria all right?" Samantha asked.

That surprised Steven. "Yes, I called Derrick. He didn't want to break up. Things just went from bad to worse. He and I talked for a while, and he and Vic were talking when I left."

"She's important to you, Steven. I get that. You have a history, and she was in trouble. You default to each other when life isn't going well, but I'm supposed to be important to you, too. I wasn't even an afterthought."

She pushed passed him, and he listened as she slammed the bedroom door.

She had a right to be angry. In her place he would have been, but he hadn't told her everything. He wasn't sure he could, and he wasn't sure it would make things better between them. He noticed the black box on the nightstand, and his heart sank. He knew the ring was back in the box, and he had miscalculated how angry and hurt she would be. He knocked gently on her door while opening it. "Found your phone. Thought you might want it."

She sat in front of the window with her back to him. "You asked me to share your life, but it looks to me like you are already sharing it with Victoria. I don't think there is enough room for both of us. Maybe I should leave."

"Damn it, Samantha," he said, dropping to his knees beside her chair. "I want you. I want you here, and no one else. You have to believe that." He took her hand firmly, unwilling to release her tug. "Look, Vic and I have known each other for years, and nothing even close to what we have has happened between us. When she called, she was confused and angry with Derrick, and maybe with me, too, for not being available like we used to be. Anyway, she laid it on me to fix things. She knows we are together, but she was hurt and wanted to hurt me for being happy so she said she had taken the pills because of me."

"You didn't believe that, did you?"

"No, she lit right up when Derrick came in the room. She's as shitty at relationships as I am, but I couldn't be responsible for something happening to her if I could prevent it. I told her clearly after they pumped her stomach and she rested a little, I wouldn't run for her like this. I wouldn't jeopardize my relationship with you."

Samantha stared at their intertwined hands. "You should have called. I would have hated it, but you should have called."

"I know, but I was frantic that she was going to die, and I didn't know how or what to tell you. I didn't want you to misunderstand, and it was something we needed to talk about face to face."

"Is that it, Steven?" she said softly. "Or did you simply not think of me at all? I'm too selfish to be second."

He cupped her face gently. "You are always first in my life; you are my life. I may have handled this wrong, but I didn't know how to tell you I was going to Chicago to see Vic."

Samantha moved away to the bed. "Same problem, isn't it? We don't know each other well enough. Good-night, Steven."

He squatted down beside the bed and stroked her hair. "I love you, Sam." He kissed her shoulder and returned to his room. Yesterday, they were fine, better than fine. Today, she's in the spare room wondering if they were a mistake. He let out his breath impatiently. He had helped a friend, and it shouldn't be a big deal, but it was. The bed didn't feel right without her in it. He tossed uncomfortably for a while before considering going downstairs but froze when he heard the door opening.

She shuffled silently to her side of the bed and slipped under the covers. He wanted to reach for her, let her know how much he loved her, and hold her till morning, but he was afraid to move. What did it mean that she came willingly to him?

She stretched out on her back, silently letting the minutes pass. “I know you’re not asleep,” she finally whispered. “I came in here to tell you I’m glad Victoria is all right, and I hope she’ll be happy with Derrick, but if she is going to continue to be your friend, she has to be mine, too. I mean, because we’re together. I should have gone with you to Chicago, Steven.” She paused. “And, most importantly, if you are ever going to be considerably late, you should call so I don’t worry. Agreed?” She snaked her hand into his.

“Agreed,” he returned, tightening his grip. “I’ll call I promise.”

“And I promise to always put you first, Steven,” she added.

“I promise to put you first as well.” He could barely make out her face in the darkness, but he focused instead on the feel of her hand, the brush of her nails on his knuckles, and the pressure of her wrist against his. In the silence, he could feel a pulse that throbbed between them and through their hands. She rolled toward him, gripping his forearm with her other hand and resting her head against his shoulder. He tipped her chin and lowered his head, moving as little as possible to brush her lips.

“Good. We’re learning, right?”

Steven rolled to his side, pulling her against him. He needed to hold her, to get lost in the feel of her, tangling their arms and legs, and claiming her. Stroking her cheek, he swept along her jaw to her throat in soft wet nips and tugs. He met the crystal blue pools that glistened even in the dark in that watery shade he still couldn’t define. She belonged to him, and he would never make the mistake of allowing her to think she wasn’t the most important person in his life, because she was and always would be. He pulled her pajama top over her head and caressed her breasts, kneading firmly till they peaked in hard little beads. She twisted her legs with his, attempting to eliminate the space that kept her body from touching his while her hands outlined the contours of his chest in long smooth strokes. He needed more of her, the more still covered in the pajama bottoms. Forcing the waistband down her slender hips, he positioned himself between her legs, but her eyes captured his heart. Pain, reflected in the longing, pain.

"Sam, I'm sorry."

She cupped his face, pulling his lips near hers. "We're passed that. Just love me, Steven." Her kiss—gentle, tentative, probing his response while he pressed with a hunger for her. He found heart and home in their connection and a commitment to only her. He wrapped her in the cocoon of his arms. No one would ever hurt her again especially not him. Her warm breath on his chest filled him as he remembered the night before without her. How much he had missed her last night, and how much he had needed her. She was right. He should have taken her to Chicago with him to deal with Vic together. He smiled when he thought of the cookies on the counter. He was even tempted to drag her down for a midnight snack, but she was warm and settled against him, and he let her sleep. Soon he drifted off too, satisfied that their love was solidly anchored regardless of an occasional gust of wind.

♥♥

Chapter Thirty-Five

Christmas Eve Samantha's parents arrived to spend their holiday in Baltimore. They settled comfortably in one of the spare rooms. Up until the last few days they had been holding out waiting for Steven and Samantha to commit to traveling back to Charleston. Then suddenly Samantha announced they had changed their plans. Steven couldn't imagine why, but if their daughter knew, she wasn't telling. Brother, Salvatore and his family arrived from their home outside of Detroit hours later and occupied another bedroom. Christmas morning Steven was busy in the kitchen layering and baking the lasagna. He also tried his hand at bread making, and the second oven baked several loaves. Gina was bringing the ham, and Angelina and his mother were bringing other side dishes and a feast of cookies. Samantha carefully arranged the table settings; she wanted it to be perfect. She placed fragrant candles and green garland down the center of the table much to Steven's dismay. That's where the food belonged, and everything else was in the way. Samantha patiently explained she wanted the table to be festive and pretty till the food was ready. She circled his waist and hugged him inhaling the intoxicating smell of warm bread, pasta, and man. Pure heaven. When everything was under control, Samantha went upstairs to get dressed. Her first Christmas with Steven had to be perfect and memorable. She said a silent prayer to the universe to just let today unfold as a happy occasion. She slipped the little black dress over her head, quietly humming one of her favorite songs.

Slipping on her black dress, hair and makeup in place

Knowing she could do this, smile on her face.

Salvatore's children's voices carried in joyful anticipation of Santa as they ran down the hallway. Samantha smiled. Someday it would be their children filling this house and creating their legacy. She slipped on her black flats for comfort then went downstairs to help with the meal as the rest of the family arrived. Samantha watched her parents carefully, knowing they would be uncomfortable with the overwhelming displays of affection by Steven's family. She had begun to enjoy their openness and the huge bear hugs freely given with love and affection. Steven's mother found her adding more cookies to the dessert table with platters of cannoli and cream puffs waiting in the refrigerator. Samantha had also bought a sheet cake that she planned on plating after dinner.

"Your parents are lovely," Mrs. Corso told her. "I'm so glad they came."

"I am, too," Samantha agreed, her face hurting from the smile she couldn't wipe away. When everyone came to the table, and all the food was arranged to Steven's liking, Samantha breathe a sigh of relief. No one had questioned why there wasn't an actual head of the table. She had seated the couples around in such a way that the only couple not sitting together was her and Steven. Last to be seated, he looked confused as he sat down directly across the table from her. The food was rich, fragrant, and delicious, and the wine flowed freely around the table. Her eye caught his as she held out her glass, hoping the next drink would calm her nerves. Samantha's hands were shaking as she lifted the sheet cake to take to the kitchen to slice.

"Need a hand, Sam?" Steven asked.

"No," she snapped. "I've got this." Questioning looks passed around the table, but no one moved except Gina.

"I'll give her a hand," she whispered as she patted her brother's shoulder.

Samantha carefully rested the cake on the counter and found the frosting tube that she had hidden from Steven, but Gina, who walked in just then, was going to ruin everything. She needed to get her out of the kitchen. She plated several pieces of cake and gave them to Gina to distribute.

"Black Forest, my favorite," Gina smiled gently. She could see Samantha was wound tight, but she had no idea why. Everything had gone well. What was wrong? With three pieces left to plate, Samantha insisted Gina relax. She would bring out the three remaining pieces. Finally, alone she finished her task, writing with the frosting on one of the squares. It was a little shaky, but the message was clear. She smiled brightly as she returned to the dining room setting one piece in front of Steven, one in front of Ernesto, and one in front of her father.

She took a deep breath and was almost seated when Ernesto announced, “Hey, what does this mean? *She said yes!* Samantha froze; she couldn’t have mixed up the pieces. Damn universe. She marched around the table, her cheeks burning, and yanked the cake away from Ernesto. “Wait. I’ll eat it.”

“No,” Samantha mumbled. “I’m not marrying you.” Her face flushed a deeper pink as she switched Steven’s piece and sank down miserably in her chair.

The entire room was uncharacteristically quiet watching Steven. He read the message on his cake several times before fighting his smile while waiting for her to meet his eyes. When it was clear, she’d prefer to disappear in a cloud of smoke, he reached across the table for her hand. She still wouldn’t look at him till he pressed a kiss to her palm. Her sad eyes tore at his heart, but so like Sam. “Are you ready?”

She nodded, and he scraped the chair across the hard wood floor making his way around the table. He pulled her to her feet and hugged her tightly. “Still my hot mess,” he said, kissing the side of her face. She stared in his dark eyes, embarrassed and drowning in her unbridled emotions. “Where is it?” He unclasped her necklace and slid the ring on her finger. Both families watched without a sound till Steven announced Samantha had agreed to marry him. Forks dropped in a clatter on plates as the families converged on the couple with hugs and best wishes. Samantha’s parents waited patiently for their turn. They were completely overwhelmed watching everyone else and, for a moment, there was an awkward silence till Steven circled Samantha’s mother in a huge hug. Samantha followed by hugging her father. Her mother blushed but smiled calmly at her soon to be son-in-law.

“A toast to my brother for finding the girl of his dreams,” Ernesto announced. They all raised their glasses, and Steven shared his glass with Samantha. She watched as her mother rearranged her seat with her father to sit next to

Steven's mother. Apparently, the two mothers had hit it off and now were going to dive into wedding plans.

"Wait," Steven said, wrapping his arms around Sam's waist, "before everyone gets too deep into wedding plans, Samantha and I have already made a few decisions. To start, this is most of our family here today. Of course, Samantha's brother is missing, and we will call him later, but you are all our closest family. This is the family we want when we get married at the cabin." Samantha spun around to see Steven's smile broaden. "We decided a trellis in the woods near the lake, food prepared and stored in my kitchen, and I'll refinish the deck as a dance floor with music from somewhere. Oh, in the spring, April, when the flowers bloom."

"But, Steven," his mother protested, "you have lots of uncles and aunts and cousins. They will want to celebrate your wedding."

"And Samantha," her mother spoke up, "you have family, too. Are you sure this is what you want?"

"We're sure," Steven continued, "and we're spending a week at the cabin afterwards as a honeymoon. Now, if you would like, Sam and I would be happy to get all dressed up and show up at a reception whenever and for whomever you want to include."

"A reception with all the trimmings?" his mother asked. "Cake, band, food, flowers, pictures, formal dresses and tuxedos? You mean a real wedding reception?"

"Everything," Steven answered. "Whatever we decide for the cabin can, in a lot of ways, be duplicated for the reception."

"Of course," Gina interrupted. "Same band, same photographer."

"Right."

"We have a lot of planning to do and not a lot of time," Mrs. Westerly gasped. "How are we ever going to plan this with you and I and the bride in different cities?" The women retreated to the living room with a mission.

"It will be stunning in the woods," Mrs. Corso's excited voice carried. "Gina, where is your laptop? Hurry, we need to make some decisions."

"Steven, I love you, but are you sure this is what you want?" Samantha questioned.

"I told you whatever you wanted, I would make it happen. I have some ideas about the trellis, but I need to talk to my brothers first, and those women in there will put this wedding together in a flash. If you want any input, you'd better get in there." He laughed softly. "Just remember this is about us. It isn't about one day but a lifetime."

Samantha kissed him warmly that soon escalated to hot. They had to remember family was just in the other room. "I'm sure they have it under control and don't need me. The setting is perfect and so is the groom." She kissed his neck slowly, deliberately as his hands stroked her hair and pulled her tighter.

"Samantha," Maria interrupted, "oh, sorry. You did want a rustic wedding, right? I mean, if it's in the woods, you want that theme, right?"

"I guess," Samantha said, still distracted by Steven's intense look and gentle touch.

"Well, you better get in here before you have woodland creatures as centerpieces."

"God, no," Samantha laughed, moving reluctantly from Steven. "I'm coming. No squirrels or woodchucks on the table." She stopped at the door to look one more time at her ring and then at Steven. Maybe the universe had decided to cut her a break after all, and maybe it wasn't laughing this time. Just maybe Cinderella was going to get her happily ever after.

♥♥

Chapter Thirty-Six

Between Christmas and New Year's Steven and Samantha returned to New York to see the huge tree in Rockefeller Plaza and to pass along their good news to Steven's grandparents. He hoped he could convince them to make an unusual trip to Baltimore in the spring for the wedding. While they didn't travel much anymore, Steven thought his grandparents might consider it in this situation, and it warmed his heart to see them tear up as they hugged them and welcomed Samantha into the family.

Samantha continued to get texts from both moms regarding the menu and the dresses. The food was easy, but everyone had an opinion on what the bride and the groom should wear. Very formal wear was ridiculous, but Samantha wanted their presentation elevated above jeans. Steven weighed in on the comfort and practicality of jeans, though. No. Less formal, but still a wedding. She deferred on details she hated, letting the delegated family member worry about the photographer, the music, even the minister. She wanted complete control over their attire and the setting, though.

Her brother surprised her when he was less than happy with her news. Apparently, he didn't relish the idea of flying to Baltimore just a month before his own wedding. He couldn't afford any more time off with his own honeymoon plans, and both he and his bride were overextended financially. Samantha sympathized and didn't tell him how much she wanted him to come. She politely let him off the hook, told him he'd be missed, and said they'd see him in May. It was hard sometimes not to make comparisons between her family and Steven's. She knew neither Salvatore or Ernesto would let anything prevent them from attending their brother's wedding.

Pete didn't hide his appreciation when she called. His magazine would have exclusive rights to the engagement and wedding photos. He sent one of his photographers on the next flight to gather some of the inside wedding plans and some engagement photos. Those were casual shots around their home, and Samantha was pleased with the jeans and sweater look.

Within a month major decisions had been made, Steven's load lightened, and both were seriously working at their passion. When Steven's first draft was completed, he needed a break to clear his head before he started his editing and revisions. He never left that to anyone; these were his books, and he took pride in the finished product. With more time on his hands, he noticed Samantha doing more reading on her computer and less actual writing.

"Still reading for Pete?" he asked, stepping into her office.

"Just finishing the last novel he sent," she answered.

"I don't want you to neglect your own writing."

Her brow furrowed, and her eyes shifted back to the screen. "I won't."

"You're finding enough time to write?" Steven asked, sitting on the edge of her desk.

"Of course, although the wedding is taking a lot of time."

"Sam, stop. You're making excuses. I see you reading other manuscripts, but I don't see you writing, at least, not in the last couple of weeks. If you've hit a snag."

"More like a wall. I was moving well through the love story, but weaving the murder trial and the evidence lost me. I keep backing up and changing things, but I can't seem to get ahead. Still think I'm a writer?"

"I know you are," Steven said emphatically. "Stop going back and rewriting. Write the whole story first. You won't be satisfied with it, but that's why authors edit and rewrite. It will make more sense to you with the finish copy to work with."

"Maybe, or maybe I need a break."

"No, you haven't earned one. What you need is a change of scenery to energize you. How about a trip to the cabin? I'll drop you off for the weekend," Steven suggested.

"Alone? I don't think so."

"Sam, alone is the whole point. No interruptions. You can relax, walk in the woods or by the lake, and write whatever time of day the urge strikes you. You need this, and I'm taking you."

"Steven, it is one thing to be in the woods with you, but it is a whole different thing to be by myself. I'll write right here as soon as I finish this manuscript." Samantha anticipated what she had heard too many times from Steven.

"Coward, though I'm not sure if you are afraid of the setting, or if you are afraid you still won't be able to write. Doesn't matter, because we are going to find out. No arguments and dress warm. Might even be a little snow up there."

"You are going to miss me," she pouted.

"That's a given, sweetheart, but I'll make the sacrifice."

Two days later Steven took Samantha to the cabin. They stopped for a bag of groceries, and he piled enough wood for the fireplace inside to last her. "I won't call, Sam. Throw your phone in a drawer for a while, and just relax and write." He gave her a big bear hug. "I'll be back on Monday." He walked slowly to the car. "Oh, keep the doors locked especially at night. Sometimes bears can be a nuisance." He bit back a grin as he climbed in the car.

"Steven, wait. There are bears up here? You never mentioned bears. I can't stay here." She caught the twinkle, the teasing in his eyes. "That's not funny, Corso. Serve you right if a bear does eat me." She stomped back to the porch but not before she heard Steven's deep hearty roar.

He almost turned the key in the ignition but instead followed her back to the porch. "You are too easy to mess with, Sam. Come here." He cradled her to him, eyes bright with love and amusement. "No bears around here." He brushed his fingers lightly over her cheek. "I will miss you, *Cara.*"

Samantha watched till Steven was out of sight. She loved the look of freshly fallen snow, not a lot but enough to glisten in the sunlight and to lift her spirits. She bundled up and strolled through the woods, ending up at the landing where Steven and his brothers would erect the trellis, and where they would say their vows. Steven wanted it natural to fit in with the surroundings so they were making it out of tree branches. Tucked between would be the leaves and the flowers that grew in the area. Steven's mother suggested white ribbons threaded through, as well. It would be breathtaking and much more than Samantha envisioned. Their guests would sit on folding chairs facing the trellis with the lake beyond it. She shook her head. She hadn't come here to dwell on the wedding. Writing, could her characters come to a place in the woods like this? She smiled thoughtfully. Not this book, but maybe the next.

She wrote some, but mostly reread that night, stopping periodically to check her facts on the computer. She knew nothing of guns, but that was the murder weapon. She not only needed a genuine weapon, but she had to learn how to fire it. As she did the research, the story became clearer. As she wrote, she carefully planted the seeds of doubt and the inconsistency in the evidence. Why were Sarah's prints on the gun? How was Tim going to prove her innocence with such damaging evidence? She wrote till she lost track of the time. Samantha awoke, lifting her head off the computer. She had never made it to bed, and the fire had gone out during the night. She wrapped her robe tighter around her and stacked more logs in the fireplace. Making coffee and toast she returned to her computer anxious to pick up where she left off. She couldn't believe how much she had written when her stomach grumbled late in the afternoon. Taking her lunch on the porch with a thermos of coffee, she watched the birds and thought about Steven. She missed him. Maybe one short call while she was eating.

"This is a call I shouldn't be getting," he said, answering quickly, "unless a bear has you in its mighty jaws."

"Very funny. I'm doing a lot of writing, and now I'm having lunch. I shouldn't tell you that I miss you, but I do."

"I miss you, too, Sam, but I'm glad you're writing. I knew it would help you."

"Steven, first novels aren't an author's best work, are they? I feel like I need to get this done, but I keep thinking I can write better than this."

"Your writing will improve with each successive book when you have learned more about your art. I know my first book wasn't written nearly as well as my last, but your readers want a real story, Sam, a complete story with dimensional, believable characters, a serious conflict, a developed plot, and, in your case, a happy ending. They will forgive the choppy sentences or a few typos for the greater story."

"I guess, what are you doing?" She ducked back into the warmth of the cabin.

"I was going to call you tonight. When we go to your brother's wedding in May, is it all right with you if we stay a few extra days? Jenny's lining up a few book signings to keep me in front of the public before my unofficial book launch in July," he asked.

"Sure, have you started editing?"

"Playing around with the title; I may change it. And," his voice dropped. "I found a place about forty minutes from San Diego that charters boats for diving. Groups are small, and each person can make several dives in five or six hours. They show you sunken ships, and the marine life is incredible, Sam. Sam? Are you there?"

"I'm here, Steven," she said, clearing her throat.

"We aren't back in the barnyard, are we, Sam? We are going to do this, right?"

"Yes, I want to, but I'll want to practice some more in the pool before then."

"Any time, honey. It's probably all of thirty today," Steven laughed. "Go back to writing. I just wanted to adjust these airline reservations, but I wanted to clear it with you first."

"Steven, maybe you should pick me up tomorrow or come up and stay tomorrow till Monday," Samantha suggested.

"Tempting, but no. This is your writing time. When I pick you up, I intend to make up for the last three days. I love you, Sam."

"I love you, too, Steven." As much as she should get back to her writing, Samantha instead searched the internet for the charter boats featuring scuba diving outside of San Diego. There were several companies in close proximity, but one thing they had in common. They all had pictures of the underwater marine life. This was something she really wanted to do, and she would be sure to practice and be comfortable under the water by May. This she could give him and enjoy herself. At least, he hadn't mentioned skydiving anymore. Jumping out of a plane would never happen, but this looked like fun and a fantasy world. This she would be ready for. She flipped back to the next chapter of her book. She had a long way to go by Monday with her book and with her longing for her painfully dark and handsome fiancé. She grabbed her phone and sent a text. **How about a sleepover tomorrow night? I promise I'll write till you get here.**

He answered quickly. **You're wearing me down. Are you sure you won't need your sleep, because I will keep you awake if I come?**

I'll be waiting for you in front of the fire. Two nights away from you is torture.

Be there by six. Keep writing. And feel free to dress comfortably, casually, or not at all, *Cara*.

I definitely understand, she replied, pocketing her phone and settling down with her next chapter.

♥♥

Chapter Thirty-Seven

Samantha slammed the front door, threw her keys on the table, and muttered all the way to the kitchen. If it weren't for a huge headache, she'd be grabbing a bottle of wine—bottle not glass. "How would you feel about eloping?"

"Dress hunting didn't go well?" Steven asked, following from his study.

"No," she glared, fighting with the aspirin bottle. "My mother is unbelievable. She's not even here, and she is driving me crazy."

"You went with Gina, not your mother," Steven answered, opening the bottle. "Didn't you find anything?"

"I did." She rubbed her forehead. "Several shorter dresses I thought would be pretty and casual enough for the woods, but I sent pictures to mom as I tried them on, and she found fault with all of them. I finally bought the one I liked best, and she'll just have to live with it."

"My girl finally found a backbone. This isn't your mother's wedding."

"I know, but it makes me angry that she may be right. The dress is probably not dressy enough for the reception they are planning. Did you rent a tux for that?"

"This morning with Ernesto. I still can't believe you want me in jeans at the wedding. I am grateful but surprised."

"Not your old, comfortable, beat up jeans. I looked at Jerry's pictures again, and I thought the look was perfect. Nice jeans, button down shirt, rolled up sleeves in the woods, perfect. Much easier for guys. Gina had a good idea, though. I'm just going to buy a longer dress off the rack after the wedding for the reception."

"Still trying to please everyone," Steven pointed out. "What did you buy?"

"I love it," she said, tearing up. "White, simple A-line flowing skirt, bodice covers my breasts with a sweetheart neckline and a sheer top, a little beading at the waist." She sighed. "Pretty, but too casual to suit my mother."

"You'll be beautiful."

"You'll like the shoes best," she grinned wickedly. "I thought of you when I picked them out—strappy T-bar wedged heels."

He pulled her closer. "I do like you in heels."

"I just want you to be pleased. My mother can have what she wants at Ray's wedding."

He saw the light go out in her eyes. "I'm sorry he's not coming, Sam."

"It's all right. We're not like your family. It didn't fit into his schedule, and, in all fairness, they've been in wedding mode for more than a year. I couldn't expect him to just drop everything for me."

"Actually, you could," Steven said stubbornly. "That's what families do." Asshole, he had one sister, and she was getting married. He should be here for her.

"Your family—some families, mine? I guess not. I'm sorry." Samantha suddenly realized Steven had probably been working when she came in. "Did I interrupt your work?"

"I was ready for a break. Jenny called with news. The movie deal is looking good. She's pushing for a two movie deal, and I'm holding out for artistic control. I want the movie to, at least, resemble the book."

"Steven, that's wonderful."

"Maybe—maybe not. If this works out, I'll be spending a lot of time on the west coast. My schedule is crazy enough, and it will get worse. Jenny's already setting dates for the book tour after August, even London before Christmas. We are going to be doing a lot of traveling."

Samantha shrugged. "I might get used to flying, maybe. Besides, I don't always have to go with you."

"Yes, you do. I'm not going to see you every couple of weeks, because I'm working. We'll be married next week, and you go where I go, and I don't want to hear any excuses about your writing. You can write anywhere."

Samantha smiled, shaking her head. "Do you know how bossy you sound right now?"

"My finest quality. Shouldn't come as a surprise to you that I know what I want, and I get it. Got you, didn't I?" He backed her against the counter, lingering over her lips. "And right now, I want you."

"And right now you promised to take me to the cabin. We have a lot to prepare, and fortunately, since we aren't living there, we can do things ahead, but," she pressed closer to him, "raincheck for later?"

"I'm more the 'in the moment' kind of guy. I think I can change your mind, Sam."

"I know you can," she answered, pushing him back, "but you promised, and we need to get things done."

"I want to get things done, too," he said, nuzzling her neck.

"Not those things. Steven, please, help me out here before."

He laughed softly. "Before you give in? All right, but you owe me … again."

In truth, Steven needed to run out to the cabin to check on the work he ordered on the deck soon to be their dance floor, but he knew there were plenty of things she would want done. He just wished that flexible backbone of hers would stiffen up when it came to his family and hers. She was too compliant and that usually meant she was settling. In the end no one got what they wanted especially his beautiful bride. "Tell me again, Sam," he said on the drive to the cabin. "You did want the wedding in the woods?"

"Yes, you know I did."

"And you did want a week honeymoon in the cabin?"

She slid her hand in his. "Yes, why are you asking?"

"Did you want the music and the dancing on the deck?" he continued, ignoring her question.

"Yes, of course."

"Sam, honey, you told me what you wanted, but you would have none of those things if I had left it to you. Are you all right with the caterer?"

"Gina said he is very good, but what does it matter since your family is bringing additional dishes. I'm sure it will be fine."

"And the wedding cake," Steven asked. "My Aunt Francesca is making it. Is that all right, too?"

"Yes, why are you asking? Your mother said your aunt makes beautiful cakes. What are you trying to tell me?"

"Just you never stand up for what you want. You don't want to hurt anyone's feelings so you set aside what you want."

"That's not true. I got the groom of my choice." She tightened her hand in his.

"Maybe that was more my doing, too," Steven pulled up in front of the cabin. "What kind of cake are we having? You didn't ask me so either you decided, or you let someone else decide for you."

"Two layers are traditional white, and two layers are chocolate. Your mother said that was your favorite."

He wanted to throttle her but took a calming breath. "What do you want, Sam?"

"Really? Your aunt is making the cake for the reception, but I'd still like a cake for the wedding. Just two layers separated with upside down wine glasses. I saw it in a magazine once with flowers under the glasses. It was pretty and would fit the rustic cabin theme."

"I don't know if I want to kiss you or shake you. Do you have any idea how you light up and how beautiful you are when you are excited about something? I know a small bakery not far from the house. I'll bet they can make your cake, and you are not going to discuss it with anyone. Understand?"

"Yes, Steven, I understand you want me to be more take charge. So, when I start telling you what to do, you'll be all right with that?"

"Don't forget I have a wonderful backbone, so tread carefully. Now, you're staying at the house the night before, and I'm staying here. Why?"

"Bad luck to see the bride before the wedding, or so I've been told, but you do have to set up the trellis and the chairs with your brothers in the morning and be here for the caterers and the band," Samantha explained, "and since I didn't want a bachelorette party, Gina has decided it will be girls' night to cut loose."

"Do I need to talk to my sister?" Steven groaned. "I don't want a wild party in my house, and my bride hungover the next day."

"Relax, Gina is undoubtedly going to try and rile you, but it's just pizza and non-stop movies, all romantic love stories. You know which one is at the top of my list. By the way, will there be some activities with Ernesto that I need to worry about the night before?"

He laughed, pulling her closer. "I'm sure we'll have a few beers and call it a night."

Samantha organized several tables for the food, chilled white wine and champagne in the refrigerator, and used garlands of wildflowers around flameless candles around the room. The candles, set on timers, would come on as the day drew closer to evening to illuminate the cabin in a warm golden glow. He found Samantha adding more candles to the bedroom and decking the bathroom with pretty soaps and lotions. Satisfied, they returned home.

The morning of the wedding Gina and Mrs. Westerly burst in Samantha's room before dawn. Gina flipped on the shower and laid out several towels as her mother peeled back the covers and pushed her towards the bathroom. "We have breakfast ready. Hurry, Samantha."

What was the rush? Samantha let the hot water beat on her back. She had missed Steven last night, but tonight in just a few hours she would be his wife. The universe would not win today, because she had everything under control. She heard her mother yelling for her to hurry, and the universe wouldn't dare mess with her mother. She cuddled into a robe and slippers and grabbed a light breakfast—toast to settle the butterflies in her stomach and coffee to survive. Angelina and Maria had stayed the night as well and were upstairs getting dressed. Back in her room, she was attacked with attention.

"Sit, Samantha. I am going to do your hair like I did when you were a child. A pretty up do with the sprig of flowers woven through it." She brushed carefully through her thick hair.

"I thought I'd wear it down, Mom." Samantha immediately saw the hurt in her mother's eyes. "Up is fine. Fix it how you think best." Steven's voice banged in her head—coward—no backbone.

Gina guided the dress over her head, and it slipped perfectly over her hips. She sat carefully, putting on her new shoes then sat again for Gina to apply her make-up. "Light, please. I don't like a lot." After she finished, Samantha took a step back and admired her reflection. It wasn't exactly what she would have done, but the final effect was pretty enough. She grabbed her suitcase and packed some casual clothes for the week in the cabin. The photographer showed up about the same time as her father and bombarded them with the before pictures. Then everyone left except Gina who was driving Samantha to the cabin.

Samantha probably should have been paying attention, but it probably wouldn't have mattered. When Steven drove to the cabin, they talked, or she slept and didn't really notice the landscape. Today, she was nervous and tried closing her eyes and breathing deeply till Gina murmured, "Uh-oh."

"What?"

"Steven said stay on Forest Lake Road till it dead ends at the lake. Does this look familiar?" she asked.

Samantha studied the surrounding area. "I don't remember the trees being this thick."

"Do you think if I keep going, we'll reach the lake?"

"I don't know. Maybe, but…what's that noise?"

Gina's car was sputtering and losing speed. "Damn, Mark didn't put gas in the car."

"Gina, you're not running out of gas?"

The car coasted and rolled to a stop on the shoulder. "No, we just ran out of gas."

The universe was still trying to ruin her day. Samantha forced back the tears. "Call Steven."

Gina tried, but the trees were too thick, and she didn't have reception. "Sam, we're on the right road. It can't be that far. We'll have to walk."

A tiny tear trickled down her cheek. "Walk? I'm getting married in fifteen minutes."

"Not if we don't get there. Come on, Sam."

Samantha pushed open her door and walked to the back of the car. Opening the hatch, she searched through her bag for her sneakers. She couldn't walk any distance at a reasonable pace in her heels. She'd carry her dress shoes and change back at the cabin. Gina locked the car that Mark could pick up later and grinned at Sam. "Like the shoes with the dress—very chic."

"Shut up and walk." Samantha watched her phone. Ten minutes, five minutes, they were never going to make it.

"Relax, honey. They can't start without you."

Samantha shot her a wicked glare. She loved her, but right about now she was going to kill her. "Gina, look." The trees opened up to the lake.

"I knew it. You'll only be a couple of minutes late." Gina saw the horror on Samantha's face as she glanced at the lake. "What's wrong, Sam?'

The tears flowed freely down her cheeks, dripping off her chin. She threw up her hands and settled on a rock. "He is going to be so mad."

"Steven? Why, because we're a few minutes late?" Gina asked.

Samantha turned Gina around. "Do you see a cabin?" she demanded.

"No, but Steven said it was off the road."

"It's on a hill, but you can see it from the road. Gina, the cabin is way over there. I can just see the top of it." She brushed angrily at her tears.

"Where? Oh, God, across the lake?"

"That's right, and if you look to the left, see the white ribbons. That's my trellis where Steven is right now."

"How do we get across the lake?"

Samantha just stared at her and cried harder.

"Wait. I have service. I'll try Steven again." She paced as she waited for him to answer. "Steven?"

"Gina, where the hell are you?" he yelled.

"Well, if you stand on the shore, you might be able to see us. We're across the lake. I stayed on the road like you told me. I don't know how this happened."

He should have told her to stay to the right when the road forked. "Did you see a spot where the road split?"

Yes, I stayed on the main road, didn't I?"

"No, Sis, you didn't, but I know where you are. Get back in your car, and take the other road. You're close."

"I can't do that, big brother. I kind of ran out of gas, and we walked to the lake."

"Shit, are you kidding me? How is Samantha?"

"Uh, kind of a wreck. She's crying."

Steven let out his breath impatiently. "I'll be there in ten minutes. Tell her not to worry. We'll just start a little later."

"Sam, Steven's coming. Try to stop crying; your mascara is running." Gina pressed a wad of tissues in her hand. "You'll get married at three instead of two."

Samantha sucked up her tears when she saw Steven approaching her. "I'll deal with you later," he snarled at Gina.

"It wasn't my fault," she insisted as Mark pulled her toward the car.

"Are you mad?" Samantha asked, staring at the lake.

He squatted down before her and tipped her chin. "Wasn't your fault, *Cara,* though I thought you knew how to get to the cabin."

"I guess I wasn't paying attention. It wasn't Gina's fault either."

"I know, but this is a perfect brother/ sister moment that I can use against her for years," he grinned, "and you can't tell her."

"Is everyone else mad?"

"Everyone was worried, but I blamed it on car trouble so the wedding is just going to be a little delayed."

Her eyes glistened with unshed tears. "I look a mess; my hair is falling and my face."

"You look beautiful, and as for your hair, is this what you wanted?" He pulled the pins quickly out of her hair, letting it cascade around her shoulders. "I don't think so."

"My mother is going to kill you."

He pulled his fingers through her hair, loosening the strands. "I'll take my chances. Brush your hair and secure the flowers. As for that face, wash it, and I think we are ready to go. Today, Sam. We are getting married today."

Samantha brightened. "Give me ten minutes when we get back."

"Five. I've waited long enough." He pulled her to her feet. "Dress is pretty, but I don't know about the tennis shoes." She punched his arm and waved her heels.

Once they pulled up to the cabin, Samantha bolted for the door with Gina on her heels. This was not the entrance she hoped for as she looked around at the startled faces.

"Samantha," her mother cried. "I'll have to do your hair all over again."

"No," Samantha said firmly, waiting for the guilt to hit her. "I want it down." She turned at the top of the stairs. "Everyone go except Ernesto and Dad. Gina and I will be down in five minutes." She caught Steven's slow grin and his thumbs up. Grabbing Gina, she pulled her into the bedroom and plopped on the bed.

"Five minutes?" Gina groaned. "My brother is crazy."

"Less." She switched shoes and carefully straightened out her dress. So far so good. She scrubbed her face quickly and sat while Gina brushed her hair and secured the flowers. At the same time Samantha applied fresh mascara, a moisturizer, and a light blush. Lastly, she added the slightest touch of color to her lips. Done. She stared at her reflection as Gina proclaimed her beautiful and ready. They flew down the stairs and hobbled in heels to the clearing where Samantha got her first view of the trellis, the flowers, the white ribbons, and the tiny white lights strung in the trees.

"Ernesto, the lights," she gasped. "Who did the lights?"

"Sorry, honey," he whispered. "I'm sworn to secrecy."

Best man and matron of honor started down the path as the music hummed. Music? Carefully tucked in the landscape were speakers that didn't detract from the natural setting.

"Are you ready, Samantha?" her father asked as the music changed to the bridal march.

Before she could take a step and as her guests were rising for her big moment, her mother broke from her seat in a full run up the path to Samantha.

"Mom," Samantha cried. "What are you doing?" Her mother shoved her phone at her. "Now? Hello."

"Sam, It's Ray. I'm so sorry I'm not there with you. I should be, but I wanted to tell you how much I love you and wish you all the best."

Samantha could see Steven over her mother's shoulder. He threw his hands in the air and stomped back and forth as Ernesto prevented him from running up the aisle as well.

"Ray, thank you, but this isn't a good time. Don't worry. I understand why you didn't come."

"No, you don't, Sam, but you will next month when you come to San Diego."

"Ok, but I have to go now. Steven is waiting."

"Go, honey, and give Steven my best, too. I look forward to meeting him."

Mrs. Westerly took back her phone and returned to her seat. Who was that woman? Her mother who was easily embarrassed and proper, running in heels, and disrupting her wedding. Maybe Steven's mother was rubbing off on her. They had become thick as thieves in recent weeks.

"Are you ready?" Her father chuckled again, tucking her hand in his arm. "Good luck explaining that to Steven." The music restarted, and everyone rose.

"Get me up there quickly before something else happens, Dad."

When they reached the front, her father joined their hands and kissed her cheek. Steven pulled her closer and whispered against her ear. "Everything all right?"

She sighed nervously. "Finally, yes."

He walked her to the minister where she saw up close the beautiful trellis, the flowers, and the serene water behind them. She was completely at peace and happily turned when Steven cleared his throat. He smiled when her cheeks flushed pink as she realized the minister was waiting for her to tune in.

When the ceremony progressed to repeating their vows, Steven interrupted the minister.

"I decided to write my own vows," he said softly, holding Samantha's hands in his against his chest. He took a long deep breath and kissed her knuckles. "You are the most exasperating woman I have ever met, but you are also beautiful, funny, romantic, and soft hearted. You drive me crazy, but you have touched a corner of my soul that is yours forever. I can't imagine waking up without you beside me, or rolling over during the night without you to roll against. You bring me more happiness than I ever thought possible so today before our families, I am pledging my love to you. No one will ever love you as fiercely as I will. I will never let go. I will always cherish and thank God for you, but, most importantly, I will support your dreams, whatever they are, I will help you attain them."

The minister cleared his throat. "Do you have your own vows, Samantha?"

Unprepared she hesitated, but she didn't want to repeat someone else's words. She had a voice and a tightness in her heart. She met his eyes, warm, smiling, and, encouraging. "I love your strength," she began, "even in the touch of your hand or a passionate look. You've changed my life in the last few months; you made it easy to love you, to hold tight to you, to want you, all that you are. I love that you don't live life. You attack it, wrestle it to the ground, and squeeze every bit of energy from it. I will love and cherish you, Steven, but, most importantly, I will be the wife you deserve. I am going to be open to life as you want to live it."

He leaned in closer. "Be careful what you promise, *Cara*."

After exchanging rings, the minister pronounced them husband and wife. Steven encircled her waist with one arm and cradled her neck as his lips found hers. Soft, tender, delicious, lingering a moment too long till they both wanted more. Both arms pulling her closer, he deepened the kiss and totally forgot they were being watched and photographed. When Ernesto finally squeezed his shoulder, he smiled down at her. “San Diego,” he whispered.

“May I present Steven and Samantha Corso.”

Chapter Thirty-Eight

Steven locked the door and turned off the lights. Their guests had finally gone. He could see Samantha in the shadows standing against the counter debating whether she should attempt some clean up. Her mistake was meeting his eyes. Her knees suddenly buckled from the purely intense lustful glance he was giving her. God, she might dissolve right before him. He met her at the stairs and circled her waist. "Been waiting all night to be alone with you." He tasted her lips softly then pressed harder, drawing her against him.

"I don't know why I'm a little nervous," she whispered as he swooped her up in his arms.

"Maybe because tonight is different; the expectation is different. Tonight, you're my wife, Sam." He cradled her firmly as she studied his eyes, inhaled that distinct scent of Steven, and trailed her fingers along the length of his throat to the center of his chest. She kissed along his jaw and nipped at his ear. The man was as gorgeous as ever, and her heart stirred frantically in her chest.

"Close your eyes, *Cara*." A few minutes later he set her down facing the bed and stepped around her. "Beautiful lady, open your eyes." Her candles lit the room in a soft fragrant glow, but nestled around the window and the headboard were the same tiny white lights.

"You did this and in the trees, too, didn't you?" she sighed as he sat on the edge of the bed. "Steven, it's beautiful."

He pulled her slowly to him, sitting her in his lap. Pressing her lips, they parted without coaxing to a deep scorching kiss. "Take the dress off, Steven," she said breathlessly. He undid the three buttons on the sheer top and let it slide off her arms to the floor. The tiny straps slipped effortlessly off her shoulders, exposing her honey smooth skin as he lowered the zipper slowly, more slowly than his body wanted as he followed the gentle slope of her back. She was right. Something felt different—better, permanent. She belonged to him a way no other woman had. He tucked his arm inside the dress and grazed her ribs with his fingertips and held her still against him. She glanced up and offered sweet lips again in a perfect balance of heat, hunger, patience, and love. Trying to slow the need building in him, he scanned her curves, caressing every inch of her, and rediscovering the beauty of her. She had his shirt unbuttoned and was doing her own methodical exploration till she dove into his mouth again in a heated frenzy. Struggling for air, she broke the kiss allowing him to drop his head and feather kisses along the top of her breasts. Then easing her out of the dress, he pressed her down on the bed and secured one hand in his. He kissed her palm, kissed against the pulse beating in her wrist, and made his way up her forearm to the inside of her elbow. She pulled away, cradling his head till his mouth reconnected hungrily on hers. He threaded his fingers through her hair as she pushed off his shirt and tugged at his belt.

He had often wondered how a man committed to being monogamous. With a bevy of beautiful women to choose from, how did one man end up with one woman? Until he met Samantha he didn't understand how one woman could be at the center of his universe, could be the only woman he would ever desire, but as he stared at her eyes and felt her moved her body against him, he knew he would never tire of this woman—would never be satisfied with today when there would be tomorrow. He formally committed his life to her today, but he had been rushing toward this from the moment he had met her on the plane. That insane moment when a frightened woman had found refuge in his shoulder and had inhaled him. His fingertips dragged over her soft breasts, but her nipples beading tightly, quickly demanded his mouth follow. She was so damn responsive and so beautiful adjusting to his touch and his position. He freed them both of any last bits of clothing to connect skin to skin. The naked truth, he would love her forever. She shuddered and moaned as he kissed over the soft skin beneath her breasts then as if her body couldn't lie still any longer, she pushed him to his back. Leaning over him, her hair tickled his cheek, and her breasts skimmed his chest as she found his lips again. He shifted her hip over his, bringing her leg to rest on his. Slowly, her hands moved down his chest and lower squeezing his thighs and stroking his erection. He was losing his ability to stop her as the fire burned out of control in his core, but he wanted to be one with her on their wedding night. He gripped her hands and pushed her back, stroking her hips and the outside of her thighs while finding his position between her legs. She moaned and arched toward him then sighed, and he was lost in her. She was so beautiful and sexy.

"Steven."

He could barely hear her with the blood rushing through his body, demanding he brand her again as his. He couldn't hold back much longer.

"Steven, I love you."

Words that nearly pushed him over the edge. "I love you, too, beautiful." Two bodies with one mind and one purpose fit together as he controlled her pleasure and then his. Two hearts completely connected with the universe in perfect harmony.

Chapter Thirty-Nine

"I liked it better when I had you all to myself at the cabin," Samantha announced, barging into Steven's office.

"The price of success," he answered without looking up. "Besides, we're leaving for your brother's wedding tomorrow, and then I won't be so busy."

"Wrong again," she corrected obviously irritated. "Jenny has you scheduled for several book signings and the appointments with the movie studio. I won't even see you."

"Stop whining, Sam. I will have time for everything including the trip to Mission Bay for diving. I already made reservations." He glanced up and caught her pouting.

"Do you think I'm ready for that?"

"You're ready. We'll make several dives, and I'll take care of you. The company has a good size boat and tours the sunken ships and sea life. You'll love it."

She ran her hand lightly over his desk. "You're neglecting me."

His hands stopped, and he met her gaze. "Was there another woman in my bed last night? I recall being very attentive to your needs."

"That was last night." A deep pink blush heated her cheeks. "You've been locked in this room all day without a thought of me. You even skipped lunch." She sat back on his desk top and rubbed her bare foot against his thigh.

He cradled her foot in his hands and rubbed gently. "I have been thinking about you, and that's why I haven't finished as much as I hoped. When you try to edit, and your mind is somewhere else, you end up rereading the same scene over and over. You understand that."

"I know, I just missed you today. I'll let you get back to work."

He sat up and slid her hips across the glass top till she was in front of him. She had worked up enough courage, stiffened her backbone enough to ask for what she wanted, and he wasn't going to let it go unrewarded. Didn't hurt that it was a turn on that his wife wanted him. "Too late. Come here. There are some benefits to being your own boss."

She straddled his lap and grinned, but before she could react, two things happened; Steven kissed her hot, demanding, and hungry, and her phone rang. "My mother," Samantha groaned. "She must be calling from San Diego."

"Put it on speaker," Steven suggested. His hand glided over her thigh.

"Hi, Mom. How's California?" Samantha and Steven both heard it, the restrained tension in her mother's voice.

"Samantha, when are you arriving tomorrow?"

"I think three. Is everything all right?"

"Yes, I guess so, but I don't know how to handle this."

"Handle what? The wedding?"

"No, your brother's big surprise, and I do mean big." She exhaled loudly. "I can't wait till you get here so I can talk to you."

"About what?" What had her mother this frazzled?

"Don't take this the wrong way, Sam, but I'd really like to talk to Steven's mother. Do you think she would mind if I called her?"

"I think she'd love it," Steven interrupted. "She keeps telling me how much she likes you. If she could help, I know she would."

"It's just she's a mom, too. She would know what I should do. I'm just so torn."

Samantha stared at Steven. "Torn about what? You love Faith, and in a few days she and Ray will be married."

"You forget about the big surprise," her mother said angrily. "Never mind, you'll understand soon enough. I think I will call Lina. Your mother is so smart and level headed."

What had Ray done? Samantha had never heard her mother so upset with her brother.

Hanging up the phone, Steven turned to a sharp knock at the door.

"Expecting someone?" Samantha asked still sitting in his lap.

"Gwen, she does the graphic designs for my covers. I asked her to come by at five and discuss a cover design for your novel."

"God, really," Samantha exclaimed, sliding to her feet.

"But I am getting a raincheck for this, right?" Steven asked.

She growled quietly as they headed for the door.

Gwen was much younger than Samantha expected. She was bright and creative and listened attentively to Samantha's rushed synopsis of her novel. She listed several items important to the novel that might generate interest on the cover. It was a romance, but Samantha was adamant that she didn't want faces on her cover. She wanted her readers to create the characters from her descriptions, not influenced by models on the cover. Gwen suggested maybe a symbol for love or maybe something legal; it was about a murder trial. Maybe even the murder weapon. They bounced around several ideas for hours till Gwen promised to create some mock covers for Samantha to choose from. She'd have them ready by the time they returned from San Diego.

"I haven't finished my novel, Steven. Is it too soon to be designing a cover?"

"Better to have it ready if you can. You obviously know what your story is about."

Steven's phone was the next interruption. "Hi, Mom." He rolled his eyes at Sam.

"Steven, I want to overnight a small package to you. Will you get it before you leave for the airport?" His mother asked breathlessly.

"It probably won't arrive before tomorrow night, Mom. What is it?"

"Something for Rose. I just got off the phone with the poor woman, and I think it will help her. Maybe I can send it to your hotel in California, and you can give it to her."

"What are you sending Samantha's mother?"

"None of your business, *figlio mio*," his mother laughed softly. "Just a little motherly love."

"Samantha is texting the address of our hotel right now." Hanging up the phone, Steven turned to Sam. "Feels like we are in the middle of a shit storm, we know nothing about. Are you sure you want to go to this wedding?"

"Gets more interesting by the minute. I'm going to finish packing, and Steven, thank you for Gwen. I can't wait to see what she comes up with."

"I love Gwen, but sometimes she gets a bit carried away. If you don't like her designs, don't be afraid to tell her to start over, or I will." He stroked her arm. "Finish packing for both of us, and I'll worry about dinner."

"An offer I can't refuse," she said, heading for the stairs.

"That comes later, *Cara.*"

Chapter Forty

Samantha gripped Steven's hand tightly as their plane landed.

"You can breathe now, Miss not so fine," he smiled, patting her hand. He rose to pull down the carry-ons, and Samantha decided two things. She would always hate flying even if it had brought them together, and she would always get that tingling feeling in her stomach when she looked at Steven especially in these tight quarters. As they finally exited the plane, she heard a familiar voice calling her name.

"Ray, I wasn't expecting you to meet our plane," she exclaimed, falling into his arms.

He hugged her tightly. "I'm glad you're here, Sam, but I wanted to talk to you before you saw Faith." Something was wrong; Ray looked tired and worried.

"Sure, Ray, this is Steven, my husband."

For a moment brother and husband stared at one another. If this were a scene from her book, Samantha would have called it male posturing—a standoff, and she wasn't sure why. She held her breath till Steven finally extended his hand, and Ray shook it, but it was too firm, too intense, and it lasted too long. Ray stood straighter and glared defiantly at Steven. "You hurt her, and I'll kick your ass."

"Ray, what the hell?"

"It's all right, Sam," Steven said heatedly. "Your brother didn't get his peace in before our wedding." He turned his attention back to Ray. "I love Samantha, and I'll take good care of her and protect her, and you would have known that if you had come to our wedding. Any other concerns you want to voice?" He tucked Samantha into his side and waited.

Ray shook his head. "No, I just wanted you to know that there were reasons I couldn't make the wedding, but that doesn't mean I don't love my sister. Look, why don't we grab a drink, and I'll start at the beginning."

"I'm sorry," Samantha whispered as they followed Ray to the airport lounge. "I've never seen him behave that way."

"Don't worry about it. I've done worse protecting Gina. I'm glad he isn't the asshole I thought he was."

As they settled at a table, Ray checked his phone for the fourth time in as many minutes.

"Is everything all right?" Samantha asked as the waiter brought the first round of beers.

"I need to tell you something," Ray hesitated.

"Your big surprise?" Samantha pushed, trying to help him spit it out. "Mom said."

"Mom," Ray groaned. "I guess I should just say it. Faith is pregnant."

"Pregnant? God, Ray, that's wonderful. I'm going to have a new.." she waited.

"Nephew. It's a boy." Ray actually smiled like the brother she knew. He looked younger and confident and in control. "We're pretty excited."

"A baby, that's great," Steven added, patting his shoulder. "So, what's the problem?"

Ray visibly deflated. His shoulders sagged, and he downed the last of his beer. "Faith is really pregnant."

Samantha didn't understand. Pregnancy was one of those things a woman either was or wasn't. There was no sort of, kind of, or really pregnant. "When is Faith due?" she asked.

He glanced between them. "Any day now."

"She's nine months pregnant?" Samantha nudged Steven for more beers. "Why didn't you move up the wedding?"

"She didn't have morning sickness. By the time we realized she was pregnant, she was four months along. By then we had the church and the hall. Damn, Faith even had her dress. If we pushed up the wedding, she'd still be showing, and we weren't trying to hide it. We just thought we had more time, because her due date was the middle of next month." He took a long drink from his second beer. "But the doctor said at her last appointment that the baby was bigger, and the estimated date was an error. She was actually five months when we found out. So, he is due this week."

"Wow," Samantha said slowly. "How is Faith?"

"Stressed. I'm worried about her. The wedding was bad enough, but we had to plan for the baby, too. We turned my spare room into a nursery. All she wants is to be married by the time our son arrives, but I can't promise her that. I don't have control here. I even thought maybe we should just get married before a judge or a justice of the peace, just in case we don't make it to the wedding." He looked conspiringly at Steven. "Do you have any idea how crazy pregnant women are? Double the craziness when they are getting married, too."

"So, what is the plan, big brother?"

"We are just doing the rehearsal dinner and hoping we are at our own wedding. Sam, I do need your help with something, though."

"Anything, Ray. What can I do?" She rested her hand on his.

"Faith's cousin, Jill, is her other attendant, but they aren't close. She can't really talk to her or lean on her. Could you try to be there for her? Take care of the wedding details so she can rest. She denies it, but I know she's exhausted, and I know this is going to sound selfish, but we have our whole lives to be parents. Faith has only one day to feel like a bride. Can you help somehow?"

Of course, leave it to me. I'd be happy to help her, and I'm excited. I hope we're still here when the baby arrives."

"If you are staying more than a few days, you probably will be. The other thing is Mom." Ray shook his head. "She didn't flip out as much as I thought she would, but I think she's just in shock. You know how she is about appearances."

"That might be changing," Samantha grinned at Steven. "She has a new friend."

"She did mention her friend gave her some sound advice. Everyone is probably at my house. You need to jump right in now."

"We've got a car waiting for us. We'll check into our hotel and then come over." Steven paid the tab quickly.

"It's a crazy house," he said quietly. "There's a bar by my house, though, Steven."

"The guys may have to hide till the wedding."

Samantha's head was whirling. Her brother was about to have two major life experiences. He had always been the level headed one. The grounded big brother who broke school records in track and joined the military in his senior year to serve his country. The last thing she would ever call him was impulsive, but maybe Faith had changed him a little. She was a couple of years younger and more adventurous than Ray, but they had been together for nearly four years. There had to be more than chemistry, and now they were having a baby.

"Where are you?" Steven asked as he set the GPS for Ray's house.

"A baby, my brother is having a baby. I know you've been through this with your brothers and sister, but I'm still in shock."

"Which makes me think your mother must be a wreck," Steven laughed. "Did you grab the package from my mother?"

"Got it. There. That's Ray's house," Samantha pointed.

Faith struggled to get up when Samantha entered the living room. Damn, Ray wasn't kidding. She was huge. Could she be carrying more than one baby?

"Surprise," Faith said weakly, pointing to her belly.

"It's a wonderful surprise, honey. Don't worry about a thing. I will check on all those last minute annoying details while you relax."

"I just want this baby to wait till after the ceremony. I don't even care that much about the reception."

"Are you feeling all right?" Samantha asked. What little she knew about giving birth didn't add up to much at this stage of Faith's pregnancy.

"I feel like a beached whale. I am so ready to have this baby, but," she said hurriedly, "not for a couple of days. I feel so bad for Ray. Imagine me walking down the aisle."

Samantha was touched by the love so evident between Ray and Faith. "Ray loves you and this baby so much, and you will be a beautiful bride. You are gorgeous, Faith."

She blushed and turned her head. "I bought this mermaid dress first. It was so pretty with pearls and fit like a glove but that wouldn't work now so I returned it and bought a nice gown with a wide, very wide skirt. Someday my little boy is going to know what he cost his mother." She smiled with genuine affection for the child still snug inside her.

"Let's make a list of what I should do," Samantha suggested. "Steven is busy with the studio tomorrow so I can get a lot done."

As Faith's list grew, Samantha said a silent prayer of thanks for both of their mothers who had handled all the details she didn't have to think about. She would do that for Faith, and she would find a spa that catered to pregnant women to pamper and relax her and make her feel like a special bride.

In the morning Steven was downright grumpy as he left for the studio. She hoped the director and producer were used to dealing with protective artistic writers. She'd catch up to him later, but for now she had things to do. She met with the caterers and tweaked the menu. Apparently, Faith had second thoughts on the shrimp cocktail and wanted to eliminate it from the menu. She sweet talked the owner into adding an appetizer to dilute the alcohol consumption before the meal was served. She checked on the flowers and their placement at the church and at the hall. Less pinks was Faith's directive, more vibrant reds. The bar was well stocked with champagne for the first toast, and the bartender assured her he watched for guests who had passed their limit of safety. She dropped off the gifts Faith had made for their guests and arranged with the limo service to arrive for Faith a half hour earlier. Sam wasn't sure why, but she was learning quickly not to argue with the very pregnant bride. Lastly, she gave a head count to the restaurant for the rehearsal dinner the next day. By the time Steven returned, she was exhausted, and his mood had gotten even gloomier.

"Didn't go well?" she asked as he pulled her into his arms.

"I guess it went all right," he said irritably. "It's my book, and I know there have to be changes to create a movie, but it's my baby, and every change pisses me off. I tried to focus on what didn't need to be changed, but I'm not sure this is going to work."

"I don't have to tell you to stand your ground, Steven. Your books are well read. People will notice and won't forgive huge deviations from the written word, but the movie people won't get that. I assume that is why you insisted on artistic input."

He brushed her hair aside and sank into her shoulder. "You get it. Have I said I love you today?"

"Never tire of hearing it. Let's go to the beach. Maybe that little cove where we hid last time we were here. We both need some air and some sunshine," Samantha suggested.

"Wedding under control?" Steven asked.

"Took care of Faith's list till she throws ten more things at me tomorrow, but I don't mind. Mom's really into being a grandmother all of a sudden. I guess your mother sent her a book on the joys of grandchildren. So, my chores kept me out of most of the craziness. I found a place that is sending a woman to give Faith the spa treatment at home tomorrow, massage, facial, nails, hair, the works. It'll make her feel pretty and, I hope, calmer."

"Wonder woman," Steven smiled, kissing the sensitive area behind her ear. "Now it's our time. Let's get some dinner and check out that beach. I have another day at the studio tomorrow."

"You are coming with me to the rehearsal dinner tomorrow, right?"

"Am I invited? I'm not in the wedding party."

"I'm in charge," Samantha said firmly, "and you're invited."

"Don't let this in charge thing go to your head," Steven laughed.

"You did want me to be more forceful, didn't you? I believe you suggested I get a backbone." She hugged him tighter.

He slid his hand down her back. "This backbone feels pretty damn good to me."

"Dinner and a swim first. We both need to relax. Then we'll come back here and see if we can find something we both want to do."

"Or see if I can convince you to do what I want to do."

"Shouldn't take much convincing." Good food, a late night swim, and a night of lovemaking left Samantha relaxed and happy. She slept well—too well and awoke just as Steven was about to leave for the studio.

"Don't know what's on your agenda, but I have to run. I'll meet you back here before the dinner?" He handed her coffee and leaned in for a kiss.

She nodded, watched him leave, grabbed her notebook, and started a new page.

> Pick up dress for the wedding; hope it fits.
> Check in with Faith.
> Lunch with mom. That will be a disaster.
> Pick up Steven's suit from the hotel cleaning service.
> Buy a gift for the baby (maybe with mom after lunch)

Samantha stared for a moment at her list. Easy enough except for the baby gift. Ray said Faith didn't want a shower till after the baby arrived, but they had created a nursery. What did they have, and what did they need? She'd have to see Faith and ask her before seeing her mother. God, she hoped her mother wasn't in crazy mode.

Pleased with herself for accomplishing most of her tasks, Samantha met her mother at a small coffee shop not far from her hotel. The streets were congested with the business lunch crowd, but Samantha found a table for two near the back. She dug the tomatoes out of her salad and set them aside.

"Have you noticed," her mother whispered in a menacing tone, "that Faith has dropped?"

"Dropped what?" Samantha asked, savoring her grilled chicken slices.

Her mother glared till Samantha felt the tension and looked up. "The baby has dropped. She isn't carrying as high. I didn't expect Ray to notice, but you're a woman, Samantha."

"A woman who has never had a baby. What does it mean when the baby drops?"

"The last couple of weeks the baby drops in the birth canal in preparation for birth. Do you understand what I am saying?" Her voice got tighter and higher, and she stabbed viciously at her baked potato.

"It means," Samantha said calmly, "that Faith is going to have a baby. Everyone knows this, Mom. Ray said she could go into labor at any time."

Mrs. Westerly set down her fork and looked around to make sure no one was listening. "And what happens if she doesn't make it to the wedding?"

"Then she has a baby, and their guests will have a party to attend." Samantha saw the terror in her mother's eyes. "Look, the wedding is tomorrow. Hopefully, this baby will hang on one more day. Otherwise, we'll figure out something. Did you read your book, Grandma?"

Misty eyed, she softened. "I am too young to be a grandmother, but I'm looking forward to holding a little one again. A boy, my God."

"Faith gave me a list of some things they'll need right away. Do you want to go shopping after lunch?"

Mrs. Westerly nodded. "Lina said everything will work out fine. Families take care of one another. Do you believe that, Sam?"

"I believe Steven's mother. Let's go shopping."

Samantha and her mother spent all afternoon in the baby department of the nearest chain store. One of the higher end stores, baby items tended to be pricey, but convenient location won out over cost. They checked out the convertible car seat stroller and went through piles of baby clothes. They were so tiny; it was hard to imagine a human this small. She took all their purchases back to her hotel room to wrap till either the baby arrived, or they headed back to Baltimore. Steven was already back when she arrived and yelling into the phone.

"Just tell me what it says, Jen. I want to know what my options are, because I don't like what I am hearing."

Samantha dropped her purchases and headed to the bedroom to change. She laid out her black dress and heels, a light wrap, and her jewelry case. It was getting late, and she needed to get ready, but she was catching bits and pieces of Steven's conversation, and it didn't sound good. She was pushing off her jeans when he came in the bedroom.

"Perfect. Just what I need. A smart sexy wife to make me forget what a horrible day this has been." He closed in hard on her lips till she breathlessly pushed him back.

"Steven."

"Shh, I'm not asking, Sam. I want you." He pushed the shirt off her shoulders and trailed a finger lightly over the tops of her breast. "You are amazing. You could make me forget my name." He sat down on the bed, pulling her across his lap.

"Steven," Samantha bit her lip. "You've forgotten the rehearsal dinner."

"Fuck it. You're not the bride. You'll be a little late." He unsnapped her bra and cupped her breast in his palm.

"I have to check."

"Damn it, Sam. You have checked and double checked since we got here." He saw the indecision in her eyes, and it pissed him off. He needed her now. "Fine," he said, pushing her up. "Enjoy yourself. I'm not going. I'd be shitty company."

Samantha exhaled as he left the room. She grabbed her shirt and followed him to the terrace. "What happened?"

"They want to change the setting. Put the story in New York instead of Los Angeles."

Samantha knelt beside Steven's chair. "But so much of the story is by or on the ocean. That won't work in New York." She followed his eyes to her open shirt and back to her lips.

"They'll tweak the story a bit to make it work," he snapped. "I told them those weren't minor changes. They are rewriting my book, and I won't let them put my name on it."

"You talked to Jenny. What are your options?" She slid her hands over his chest and felt his heartbeat.

"These meetings are preliminary for me and the studio. Either one of us can pull out till the final screenplay is done. I can't see this happening." He pressed one of her hands harder to his chest.

"Does it matter?"

He met her eyes. "Not really, maybe another time, another deal, if this doesn't work out."

"I see." She straddled his lap.

"Sam, don't. If you're leaving, just go."

"I want you to come with me, but I can see how upset you are. Maybe a little alone time with your smart sexy wife is the prescription." She lingered gently against his lips.

"You'll be late," he warned.

"Probably, but it'll be worth it." She pushed off her shirt and guided his hand to her breast. "Besides, Steven comes first."

He exhaled in defeat. "Samantha comes first. Get dressed, and we'll go."

She wiggled slowly in his lap. "Exactly, and that's why you are finishing what you just started."

Tightly wadding her hair in his hand, he leaned in and kissed her hard, demanding, tangling his tongue with hers. "You're cold," he said, wrapping his body around her, "and on display for all of San Diego."

"Mm, the caption will read, The New Woman in Your Life."

"No, the caption will read, The Only Woman in My Life." Hands securely under her ass, he carried her to the bedroom while she held on, nibbling and biting his throat and shoulder. Gliding his hands down her thighs, she released her legs and melded against him.

"There's something about San Diego."

"Don't write off Baltimore, New York, or Charleston, honey. We're perfect anywhere."

His kisses led him over her breasts, down her sweet center, to the inside of her thighs. Feeling the pressure building and her knees weakening, Samantha leaned on Steven and pulled tensely on his hair. He groaned as he gripped her hips and swung her around on the bed. Rolling her to her stomach, he let his weight down, chest to her back. Hot skin to hot skin, sweaty flesh to sweaty flesh, hands linked in tangled fingers, legs entwined. His solid need pressed against her back, but not for long as he made another long pass of discovery down her back. He was torturing her, but too close to the need would push one of both of them over the edge, and he wanted time with his wife to release his own frustrations and to bring her to an explosive end. She struggled against his body, trying to reach him till he stretched back to suck her needy lips, to kiss her with his entire body, and to listen to her whimpers.

"Steven, now," she cried. "I want you now."

How could he deny her anything least of all, himself? She owned him, belonged to him, and he loved her. He braced himself against her, watching her eyes, and willing his body to wait. Sliding into her, she exhaled and waited as he moved slowly in the moment. He returned to her breasts, tight and wanting his touch as his body picked up a stronger rhythm till he felt her stiffen, heard her cry out, and felt the tension break within him. He closed his eyes against the shudders and collapsed on her. When he could finally lift his head, he brushed back her hair and met her smiling, twinkling eyes.

"Definitely worth it," she mumbled, kissing one last time against his neck. "But we need to get going. Can't linger here, though it is tempting."

By the time Samantha and Steven reached the restaurant, dinner was served, and several people had finished. "Sorry we're late," Samantha said, a hot flush heating her cheeks. "Steven was delayed at the studio." Might as well blame it on him. It was, after all, his fault. She felt his hand rub gently the small of her back, and an unexpected tingle of heat passed through her. She slipped him a knowing glance as she turned her attention to Ray.

"Faith is beat. We're going to call it a night soon."

"What do I do tomorrow?" Samantha asked as a waiter brought her a plate of food. "Meet at your house? Pictures?"

Faith shook her head. She looked beautiful, but the whole event was taking its toll. "No, meet at the church a little earlier than two in case I need a little help. No pictures before. Just a few after we are married. No fuss."

Samantha smiled sympathetically. Faith just wanted it over so she could deal with having a baby.

"Oh, Samantha, thank you for the beauty treatment today. It was perfect. I almost fell asleep during the massage."

"Every bride deserves a little pampering," Samantha squeezed her hand. "Are you leaving after the reception tomorrow?"

"We had honeymoon plans in Hawaii, but we cancelled about a month ago. If Faith feels like it, we might drive up the coast for a couple of days," Ray answered.

"I feel like sleeping, honey. I'm sorry, Ray. Can we go?"

"Of course, I just need to take care of the tab."

Steven made his way around the table. "Take care of Faith. Samantha and I have the tab, wedding present."

Samantha wasn't the only one that looked surprised. She avoided looking at her mother, though who looked angry. After Ray and Faith left as did the other guests, Steven went in search of the waiter to pay the check, leaving Samantha alone with her parents.

"Where were you?" her mother hissed.

"I told you. Steven got back later than expected, and he had to get ready." She couldn't look at her mother as the heat radiated up her neck again. Her father chuckled and patted her hand.

"If we make it through tomorrow, it will be a miracle," her mother declared. "Do you think you can make it to the church on time?"

Steven walked up just in time to hear his mother-in-law's comment, and he couldn't resist. "I guess that will depend on whether your daughter can keep her hands off me."

Samantha spit the mouthful of wine she was about to swallow. Her mother stared at Steven with her mouth open, and her father laughed so hard he almost fell out of his seat.

"I can't believe you said that," Samantha said later at the hotel. "Did you see my mother's face?"

"Honey, everyone at that table knew why we were late. You don't have a poker face, and you're a shitty liar," Steven grinned.

"You didn't have to confirm it."

"Sometimes your mother just needs to back off. We are married. No need for apologies. Maybe I should make you late tomorrow, too."

"Not happening. I have a feeling Faith is going to need everybody to get through that long day tomorrow. I hope she can relax and enjoy her reception once the ceremony is over."

"Come here. Do you know what tomorrow is?"

Samantha stopped to think as she crawled in beside him. "Oh, we've been married a month tomorrow. I've been so busy."

"I know, and that's why I arranged for champagne and a light meal to be delivered here at midnight. Didn't think Faith would last that long so think we'll be clear to leave?"

"We will. We'll just leave for our own celebration. Thank you." She cuddled against him and felt him sigh. Tomorrow would be a long memorable day.

Steven ordered room service before Samantha awoke. Between his soft whisperings in her ear and the smell of bacon and eggs, she was up. The muffins were soft and slightly sweet like a breakfast dessert. Steven laughed. "I love to watch you eat. You always eat like it's your last meal."

"Is that a compliment?" she asked quirking an eyebrow. "Good food is relaxing and satisfying just like good sex."

He choked and grabbed his water.

Steven dropped Samantha at the door of the church. "I'll park and find a seat. Take care of whatever bridesmaids do."

Samantha found the bride standing in front of a full-length mirror in a side room off the foyer. Her hair was beautifully done up with tiny sparkles. The dress was everywhere on the floor. Samantha took a step back. What was Faith doing? She was down on one knee, and her face was scrunched. Oh, God, she couldn't be. "Faith, are you all right?"

She nodded, but the tight straight line of her lips and the terror in her eyes said otherwise. After a moment, she exhaled and gripped Samantha's arm. "Up, please." Struggling to her feet she smoothed out the lines of the massive tulle shirt and smiled serenely. "Baby has his own schedule."

"Faith, are you in labor? Should we go to the hospital?"

"First babies take a long time," she answered calmly. "I am going to get married first."

"How long have you been having contractions?" No offense, but Faith had never had a baby. She couldn't know any more than Samantha when it came to child birth.

"Since about four this morning? I have plenty of time. I've been timing them, and they're still thirty minutes apart."

Four this morning. Two this afternoon. How long was a long time? Faith had been in labor, at least, ten hours. "Does Ray know?" Surely her brother would whisk her off to the hospital.

"No," she gripped Samantha's arm angrily, "and you are not going to tell him. Luckily, I stayed with my parents last night—the whole bad luck before the wedding thing. So, he doesn't know, or he would have had me at the hospital hours ago."

"Faith, maybe you should be at the hospital," Sam said gently.

"Don't. You've been wonderful, Sam, but you should have knocked before you came in. Now, you have to keep my secret. I will be married before this baby comes. I will be Faith Westerly on baby Westerly's birth certificate. Please help me."

Samantha looked at her desperately. She was a mom, and her baby wasn't even born yet. "You'll tell Ray after the service, promise?"

"Yes, I promise."

"All right, what can I do?"

"Just get this thing started on time. Catholic mass is an hour. I can last that long, but I don't want to waste a minute."

Samantha nodded. "I'll get everyone in position now, and, damn, we will start on time." She flew out of the room then hesitated. What did she need to do first, and was she doing the right thing not telling Ray? She promised she wouldn't alert

Ray, but she hadn't promised anything regarding Steven. She ran down the center aisle and slid in next to him in the third row.

"Hey, beautiful. Everything all right?"

"No," Samantha's face flushed. "Faith is in labor, and she won't tell Ray. She wants to be married first. I promised, Steven. What do I do?"

Steven squeezed her hand. "Then I guess you better get them married."

"Yes, we need to get started on time."

"Better start with the piano guy. He doesn't seem too anxious to get started."

Samantha watched the organist sip his coffee and talk to several of the guests. "We'll see about that." She stormed away as Steven laughed.

"Go get him, Tiger." God, he loved that woman on a mission.

"We are starting on time," she interrupted the young man with the annoying stare and relaxed posture. He obviously didn't care.

"What's your hurry?" he asked. "A minute more, a minute less."

Samantha's fists tightened. "I am going to walk to the back of the church and get in line, and I better hear music when I get there."

He had the nerve to say, "Or else what?"

She turned slowly, willing herself to calm down and not strike him. "Or else I will forget to leave you an envelope before I leave the church."

"Got you. Don't be so huffy. This is a happy occasion, and I'm ready to go when you are." She might still hit him and wipe that stupid grin off his face. She looked at her phone and hurried to the back, grabbing Jill along the way. "Get in line. We're starting."

"Damn, who died and made you the boss?"

"Not who died, but who is going to die if she doesn't get her scrawny ass in line." Ok, maybe a little over the top, but Sam's nerves were stretched thin. The music started on time, and when Samantha saw Faith on her father's arm, she started down the aisle. She probably wasn't smiling, but she was focused and took her place on the left. She caught Steven's mischievous smile. Someday she would share the humor of this but not today. Jill was coming down the aisle next. What the hell was wrong with the girl? Couldn't she walk any faster? She stole a glance at Ray who was blissfully unaware that his life was about to change big time. Faith was radiant and walked slowly but steadily down the aisle. Half way to the front her steps slowed till she stopped, fighting to smile through gritted teeth. God, she was having another contraction. That couldn't possibly be half an hour. Samantha shifted from one foot to the other and held her breath till Faith finally reached Ray, looking calm and relaxed again. Catholic masses were beautiful but, depending on the priest, could also be long. He welcomed family and friends and began the service. Both mothers rose to light the individual candles representing their son and daughter. Samantha watched Faith carefully. If she was in any discomfort, she was hiding it well. When they rose, though to repeat their vows, Faith turned away. Ray looked alarmed as Samantha pulled a tissue from her pocket and knelt beside Faith. "You all right to go on?" she whispered.

Faith took the tissue and smiled. "Yes, thank you."

Samantha slipped back to her seat. That one, she was sure, wasn't thirty minutes since the last. She decided to pray. God would understand that they only needed a few minutes, and they would be married. She'd go to the hospital and have the baby. Just a few minutes. They got through the vows, and the priest pronounced them husband and wife. Thank God. As Ray kissed his new wife, Samantha heard a moan and noticed several people in the first few rows snicker. Idiots, couldn't they recognize pain from passion?

After the new couple lit the unity candle, and as the priest gave his final blessing. Samantha heard a different sound like water running. Faith paled and sank on the bench. Ray held her eyes as Samantha slipped closer. "My water broke."

What the hell was wrong with the universe? "Dress is big," she whispered to Faith. "Don't worry. I'll get the limo waiting to take you to the hospital." Her brother looked panicked, but Samantha patted his arm. "Here is where you start taking care of your wife and child." His shoulders broadened as he helped Faith to her feet. The music started, and Samantha ran down the aisle. She grabbed the photographer and ordered him to stay put. Then she ordered the limo driver back in his car now. Faith was nearly doubled over as they reached the back of the church, but Samantha stopped Ray. When Faith could smile, she had the photographer take the one and only picture they would have of their wedding day. Then Ray tucked his wife in the car. "Steven and I will take care of your guests. Keep me updated."

"Sam, thank you." Tears welled up in his eyes as he hugged her tightly.

As they pulled away, Steven took her elbow. "Well, Miss in charge for the night, you need to give these people some direction."

Samantha climbed up the steps of the church so she could be seen. "Family and friends. Thank you for coming today. Ray and Faith are about to bring their child into the world, but they want you to go to the reception, eat well, dance, and keep them in your thoughts and prayers. We'll let you know when something happens. And if you need anything, Steven and I will be glad to help you."

The crowd disbursed, leaving Samantha with her parents. "Are you coming to the hall?"

Her mother grinned. "Surprisingly, you seem to have everything under control. I want to be there when my grandson is born."

Alone with Steven, Samantha sat on the step and leaned against him. What an insane day.

"Somebody could use a drink," he said softly. "Happy first month anniversary."

She sank into his kiss and said a silent prayer of thanks for him. Together they were one, and she drew her strength from him.

At the hall things were under control. She put the rush on dinner since the bride and the groom weren't there to greet their guests. The first glass of wine went down quickly and smoothly, but the second waited till dinner. Well into the evening the band played for their guests till Samantha's face paled, and she hugged Steven in a massive grip. The tears glistened in her eyes as he pushed her toward the microphone. She waved the band to stop playing. "Ray and Faith welcomed a seven-pound baby boy into the world ten minutes ago, Benjamin Samuel Westerly." She was crying as their guests applauded.

Steven, her rock, her lover, and her husband, wrapped himself around her and kissed at her tears. "Do you want to go see him?"

She nodded, and he handed her the keys to the rental. "I'll catch a cab in a little while when it clears out. You go ahead."

Samantha found her brother in the hall outside his wife's hospital door. She rested her hand on his shoulder and squatted down in front of him. "Everyone leave?"

"Mom and Dad and Faith's parents will be back tomorrow. Faith is sleeping."

"You need some rest, too, Daddy," she grinned.

"He's perfect, Sam. I love him and Faith so much I can't breathe."

"Can I see him?"

Ray took her in Faith's room where she lay cradling their new son. "He was hungry," Faith whispered as the baby snuggled in her arms. He was so tiny, fuzzy light hair on his head, and sleeping contently.

"Sam."

"Don't say a word, Faith. It all worked out, and everyone sent their love and best wishes."

"We want you and Steven to be his godparents." Samantha couldn't hold off the tears. Faith convinced Ray to go home and get some sleep then dozed after giving Benjamin to Samantha. She sat in the recliner staring at the helpless infant that insisted on make this his day, too. He was beautiful, and Aunt Samantha hugged her nephew protectively to her chest. She was overwhelmed with love.

"Ran into Ray. He said come in." Steven stopped as he took in the sight of his wife cradling the baby to her. She was a natural, adjusting her position with ease and holding him securely without waking him. "You are a beautiful picture sitting there."

"Steven," she said softly, "I want one. I'd take this one, but I don't think Ray and Faith will give him to me."

He brushed a tear from her cheek. "Then we'll just have to make one of our own."

"When?"

"I thought you wanted to write."

"I did. I'm nearly finished with my book, and it will need some editing, but Jenny wants it out in the fall, and now I want this—our baby with your hair."

"And your gorgeous eyes."

"And your courage and strength."

He let out a slow breath. "I still have a lot of commitments this year, and I want you traveling with me. How about the first of next year? If you get pregnant right away, I'll have Jenny taper down my schedule so I can be home with you."

"Ok, as long as we are going to make one, maybe a couple, or three. Do you want to hold him?"

"Too little, big hands, don't want to hurt him." But Samantha wasn't listening. She set Benjamin in the crook of Steven's arm. The baby opened his eyes and stared at both of them. He cuddled in tight and slipped back to sleep.

"I want one," Samantha repeated, "but this one is our godchild."

Twenty minutes to midnight Steven reminded Samantha of their anniversary celebration. She carefully tucked the baby in his bassinet and left with him. She was in the bedroom changing when she heard the knock at the door. Steven was pouring champagne when she joined him, and they toasted the first month of their marriage. It had been an incredible day, and the universe promised so much more.

♥♥

Chapter Forty-One

"I'm surprised you aren't at the studio this morning," Samantha said as Steven drove up the coast.

"Jenny's handling it for now. She has more patience, and she's already changed their minds on the setting. She wants it to work out, and she'll let me know when I should meet with them again."

"We're leaving tomorrow, though."

"We'll be back, babe, for the christening next month. I can meet with the studio then. Besides, we're scuba diving today. Time for some real fun." He glanced at her, hoping she could muster a little enthusiasm. He had seen it. The sadness every time she picked up little Benjamin. They lived too far apart, and he would grow quickly. Maybe his tight family was what she wanted in her own family, but it was hard to overcome miles of distance.

"Why are we going so early?" Samantha asked. "Didn't you say the reservations were for this afternoon?"

"I thought we should get some practice time in on the beach before we go. I'm going to rent the gear and give you some time in the water to get used to it."

Samantha laughed. "Afraid I'm going to embarrass myself or you?"

"No, of course not, but the suit is tight, and the tank has some weight. And, most importantly, breathing through a regulator is different. I want you to experience it in a safe setting before we are out in the middle of the bay. For this trip, we'll do the shallower dives. Basically, see the plant and animal life. We'll save the ship wrecks till you have more experience."

"You're making this complicated, Steven."

"You'll thank me later. I don't want you freaking out in the water for things we can iron out before we go. There are plenty of other things to frighten you."

"Sounds promising. We'll be together; that's the only reason I'm not freaking out now." In the end Samantha conceded, Steven had been right. The wet suit hugged her body, and it was awkward to walk in fins. The googles were fine, but it took a little time for her to grasp the rhythm of her breathing within the regulator. The tank did feel weighty, but less so once they were in the water.

"You'll need to move your legs to keep moving, and you will feel it. You'll be tired by the end of the day, but it will be worth it."

"What do I do if the fish come up to me?"

"It's their turf, hon. You'll probably feel comfortable swimming around or through schools of small fish, but some of the larger fish are impressive and can be dangerous. Generally, they will leave you alone if you stay out of their way. We could see sea lions or dolphins."

Samantha exhaled. "Maybe."

"Don't go coward on me, Sam. Life experience number two."

"What was life experience number one?"

He smiled. "You had dinner with me right here in San Diego."

"Oh, I see. You mean the note you wrote in my book. You know I will never do the third one, right?"

"Technically, you haven't done the second one. Come on." He grabbed her gear and a duffel bag with towels and warm dry clothing.

The forty-foot boat, The Journey, had five couples on this trip. The crew catered to the passengers with hot tea and coffee, a multitude of stories, and expert advice for the novice and more experienced diver. Unfortunately, they were obligated to give instructions in case of an underwater emergency, just the kind of information Samantha didn't want to hear. Finally, the boat slowed to a stop and anchored. Steven helped her into her gear, adjusting her googles. He helped her onto the ladder to lower herself into the water. She fought the nerves. It was easier to walk out to the deeper water than just drop into it, but this was diving. Lowering himself into the water, Steven caught her eyes. "Breathe," he instructed, placing his own piece in his mouth. He checked her tank again then pulled her away from the boat. He held her hand and descended slowly, swimming out then down. She kicked frantically at first till Steven's hand on her thigh warned her to conserve her energy. She would wear herself out. At a reasonable depth, Steven leveled off and just propelled her forward. The sea life was amazing; rock formations and colorful plant life. Tiny creatures burrowing into and under the rocks. He watched as she moved a tentative hand toward a flower. It was an entirely different world beneath the surface of the water, and even though Steven was an experienced diver, he felt like he was seeing it for the first time through her eyes. He marveled at her lack of life experiences but sighed gratefully that she was willing to try and to trust him. As they swam, a school of small bass surrounded them and swam through them. Samantha glided along totally captivated and unafraid until a large Bluefin quickly filled her sight. She darted toward Steven who carefully guided her away from the impressive tuna. He pointed to a sea turtle, and she followed it slowly behind, holding tightly to his hand. He continued to guide her till he thought they needed a break, and he started the ascent to the surface. When he could see the bottom of the boat, he pulled her above the water and removed his regulator. "You all right, Sam?"

She treaded water and waved. Guiding her up the ladder of the boat, she collapsed on a bench shivering. He took a sweatshirt from the duffel and unzipped her wet suit. He moved the suit off her shoulders and replaced it with the shirt. One of the crew handed her hot, strong coffee. Steven did the same for himself and huddled against her.

"It was amazing, Steven. The vibrant colors and so close to the animal life."

He kissed her temple. "You did well for your first dive. Tired?"

"A little, but I want to go again. Steven, look." Not far from the boat two dolphins swam in a loop, clearing the water completely and landing with a splash. She was happy and that was all he wanted from this day.

On their second dive Steven descended a bit farther. He watched her for any sign of distress. At one point she adjusted her mouthpiece, but she seemed all right till she leaned forward holding her head. Steven moved right in front of her, trying to see her eyes. She was squinting like she had a headache, not uncommon with the change in pressure. He stroked her throat encouraging her to swallow. After a moment, she nodded and gave him the thumbs up sign. When he brought her back to the surface and the boat again, she was visibly tired. She'd never be able to do the third dive of the day. When the boat moved an hour later to Shipwreck Alley, Samantha encouraged Steven to go with another diver, another buddy. There was no reason why he should miss that part of the trip. While Steven dove, Samantha showered in the on-board facilities. A hot shower was just what she needed to get the chill out. Dark clouds were rolling in as she returned to the deck threatening the remainder of the day, but the rain held off till all the divers were back in the boat. Freshly showered as he climbed off the boat, Steven was more relaxed than Sam had seen him in a while.

"You did well. I'm proud of you, Sam." He cupped her chin and kissed her.

"It was fun," she agreed. Walking through the lot, Samantha's voice was barely a whisper, "*Ti amo*, Steven."

Steven's hand tightened around hers; an imperceptible smile that was more apparent in his eyes. "*Ti amo anch'io*. Who's been teaching you Italian, Cara?"

"Gina," she smiled, "Not a lot."

"What else has my crazy sister taught you?" He backed her against the side of the car and stroked his fingertips along her jaw.

"Just a few swear words. She calls them stress relievers, and the kids don't know what mommy is saying." She pressed her hand against his heart.

"Say it again, Sam."

"*Ti amo*, Steven."

"I love you, too," he said, mingling his breath with hers. "*Sempre*. Always." ♥♥

Epilogue

(3 Months Later)

She sat wedged against him, visibly trembling and clutching his hand. He needed to distract her and take her mind off the present. “Sam, Jenny says the advance sale of your book is looking very promising.”

“Uh, yes.”

“Jenny wants you to start introducing your novel at my signings in September before yours officially releases in October.” She nodded. “Baby, relax, I promise I won’t let anything happen to you.”

Samantha turned away and gazed at the couple seated beside her. They seemed relaxed and happy—giddy as the plane gained altitude. “I can’t do this, Steven. I know, I said I’d try, but.” Her voice trailed off as the tears choked her.

Steven wrapped his arms around her shoulders. “Look at me, Sam. We are diving in tandem—together. I’m attached to you from behind and wrapped around you. We went through the hours of instruction. For one minute you fly, arms extended and chin up. Then we pull the cord, and we glide for seven or eight minutes. It’s ten minutes out of your whole life. I can’t believe you are going to be a coward now when we’ve come this far.”

Samantha shook her head. “I will never complain about being on a plane again; inside a big metal bird, not falling from how many feet up?”

“13,000,” the instructor interrupted. “And I think we are ready.”

Samantha tensed as the other couple stood. Once attached they moved to the edge of the open door. Grinning like two fools, they stretched out their arms. Samantha covered her eyes. She couldn't watch them take that first step into the clouds. One of them screamed, and then they were gone.

"Ready, Mr. Corso?" the instructor asked.

"That's us, Sam." He pulled her up as she fought for control. She would not cry nor would she scream like a frightened child. She promised on their wedding day to be open to life experiences, and this was what he wanted. She heard several clicks and refused to process what he was doing. The instructor moved closer, checking the harness and readjusting the straps. He nodded to Steven who took her hands and extended her arms. "Just like that. Raise your chin." He let out his breath. "Keep your eyes open, or this is all for nothing. Ready?" He wrapped his arm around her as he negotiated her towards the door. "Breathe, Sam. I can't feel you breathing."

"Steven." She could hardly get the word out. "I can't. No, please, I can't."

"It's ok, baby, look."

Her toes hung over the edge of the opening like on a diving board, and all she could see were the clouds, soft, billowy, nothingness. Cool air filled her lungs and stayed trapped; she couldn't exhale. She sank back against him, afraid she was going to pass out.

"Sam, are we going to do this?" he asked.

She bit her lip and shook her head violently. "No."

Steven exhaled and took a step back, pulling her back in. He thought she was ready. He thought she could overcome her fear and enjoy this. She trusted him, and he thought that was enough, but he couldn't push her any farther. He wrapped his arms tighter around here. "Calm, down. It's all right. Maybe another time. Not today." He was about to step back again when he felt resistance.

She stood a little straighter and held firm. "Don't let go of my hands, Steven. Please, don't let go." Her voice cracked, and her hands tightened in his. For love, she could do this for love of Steven.

"I've got you, Sam, always."

"OH GOD, OH GOD," she screamed as she fell forward out of the plane, her eyes closed, and her jaw clenched shut. Steven held firmly to her hands and extended her arms. For a second she felt suspended, almost like she wasn't moving at all.

"Open your eyes," Steven screamed against her cheek. "Look, Sam, and smile for the camera."

She forced her eyes open, but she wasn't smiling. She was immersed in clouds and flying through them. She was spinning and tumbling and pressed hard against Steven's body. She was aware of him, wanted to grab hold of him, and see his eyes, but for the moment all she could do was absorb his courage and try to let go of her fear. Hand over hers over the cord, they pulled. The chute jerked them straight up, and they glided faster toward earth. Terror aside, Samantha watched as the colors around her became more apparent and more vivid as their landing strip rose from the ground to meet them. When they seemed to be descending too quickly, Samantha leaned back against Steven's solid support till his feet hit the ground. Samantha's should have, too, but she stumbled, knocking him off balance and backwards. He fell on his back with Samantha on top of him and the chute covering them both.

"Unhook, unhook, now, now," she cried frantically.

"Sam, honey, we're down. Relax, you're fine," Steven said as he unhooked the clamps.

She rolled over onto his chest, kissing his face till she met his lips and sank into his heat. He brushed back her hair gently. "If I knew you'd respond like that, I'd have made you jump months ago."

She pressed her lips to his, hot and passionate. If she loved this man with this much fierceness, she was going to have to hold on tight for the ride of her life. "I love you, Steven, but, understand, I am never doing that again."

He rolled her on her back, kissing the breath out of her and lingering just a moment to soak up the richness of her blue eyes. "That's all right. There are still challenges four and five."

"More challenges," Samantha groaned. What else could he possibly want to experience?

"I think you are ready for cliff diving," Steven grinned, tucking a curl behind her ear.

"Height and water?" Samantha said with disgust. "Steven, I will never."

"Or." He couldn't hide the love. "we could work on making a baby. What do you think, *Cara*?"

Samantha tightened her arms around his neck. She would never, never let go. "I think," she answered, lost in his eyes, "a baby would be an amazing challenge."

♥♥

Other standalone novels

by

Tea DeLuca

A Grip On His Heart

Danny's Sister

Cue Stick

Paige's Heart

Tangled Hearts

Lies, Love & Loyalty

Keeping Hailey

Married To A Cowboy

Samantha's book available now on Amazon.com

A Grip On His Heart

Tim McKenzie, attorney, divorced, and hates surprises! He's in for several shockers.

He didn't expect to meet the girl of his dreams on a usual Friday night's journey to a one night stand. He didn't expect her to be wanted by the Charleston police for murdering her husband and her fingerprints on the murder weapon—a gun she claims she's never touched. And he didn't expect her father, a powerful pricey attorney, to be the prosecution's star witness, because he believes his daughter is guilty. Tim's life just got very complicated.

Sarah, pretty with mesmerizing green eyes, is well on her way to becoming thoroughly drunk when she meets Tim. He's good looking, charming, and willing to hold her and chase the demons away for the night, but she's not into long term relationships, because her life is over as soon as the police find her. She needs her lawyer and her lover to prove her innocence.

It is first a love story; Tim and Sarah discover an immediate connection and, eventually, love as they navigate through life's storms—a bitchy ex-wife, an obnoxious lying former boyfriend, a brother with a pregnant girlfriend, and ultimately Sarah's murder trial. The trial challenges Tim to account for the subtle inconsistencies in the evidence and to dig into the past of the deceased. Through all the distractions, Tim researches leads and tracks down the evidence that he hopes will convince the jury to acquit Sarah. The trial becomes Tim's obsession---to save Sarah, for the love of Sarah. ♥♥

Danny's Sister

Tea DeLuca

Rebecca and Sam's love story available on Amazon.com.

He's military.
Career
Army Ranger
Capable
Bad-ass strong
Hot as hell
And
Alone
Sam's never found a woman willing to marry him and the Army.

She's living in a military town.
Pretty enough
Bright
Stubborn
And
Fiercely independent
Becca hasn't found the right guy, yet.

Can these two find love and untangle the painful family secrets hidden in the past and threatening the future?
This is Becca and Sam's love story, because you never know when love will find you. ♥♥

Follow me

www.facebook.com/teadeluca

www.amazon.com/author/teadeluca

Goodreads

Bookbub

Made in the USA
Monee, IL
23 January 2023